"You have two weeks, Valerie,"

Jonas said. "Two weeks to come to terms with yourself and face the facts of life."

But she didn't want to face the facts of life; they hurt. She didn't want to face the reality of this hard man glaring at her. She wanted to be left alone.

Jerking away from him, she took off at a run. She didn't know where she was going, but she had to get away.

She didn't get very far. "There's only one place left to run, Val," Jonas grated as he pulled her around to face him. "To me."

Dear Reader,

Last month we started telling you about a special tie-in between Silhouette Classics and Silhouette Special Edition. This month we can't resist bringing it to your attention once again. Several years ago Joan Hohl published a Special Edition called *Thorne's Way*, and it went on to become a collectors' item, the sort of book readers go to any lengths to find. In July, also in Special Edition, Joan will publish the much-requested sequel to that book, *Thorne's Wife*. But what of *Thorne's Way*? What of all the readers who have heard so much about this book but have never been able to find it? Here is where Silhouette Classics enters the picture, because this month—and only this month—we're reissuing *Thorne's Way* in a collectors' edition all its own. If you missed this book the first time around—or if your copy is falling apart because it's been read so often—this is your chance to see what all the excitement has been about. We guarantee that after you read *Thorne's Way* you, too, will be eagerly awaiting July and the publication of *Thorne's Wife*.

Of course, Silhouette Classics brings you two books each month, and this month is no exception. Heather Graham Pozzessere has won awards, ridden high on bestseller lists and elicited piles of fan mail. Now we bring you *Night Moves*, her first Silhouette Intimate Moments and a book that immediately established her as one of the line's top authors. Read it and you'll see why.

That's it for now but, as always, you can count on Silhouette Classics to keep bringing you your favorite authors over and over again.

Leslie J. Wainger
Senior Editor

Joan Hohl
Thorne's Way

Silhouette Classics

Published by Silhouette Books New York

America's Publisher of Contemporary Romance

SILHOUETTE BOOKS
300 East 42nd St., New York, N.Y. 10017

Silhouette Classics edition published April 1989

Silhouette Special Edition edition published October 1982

ISBN 0-373-04636-7

Books by Joan Hohl

Silhouette Special Edition

Thorne's Way #54
Forever Spring #444

Silhouette Intimate Moments

Moments Harsh, Moments Gentle #35

Silhouette Romance

A Taste for Rich Things #334
Someone Waiting #358
The Scent of Lilacs #376

Silhouette Desire

A Much Needed Holiday #247
*Texas Gold #294
*California Copper #312
*Nevada Silver #330
Lady Ice #354
One Tough Hombre #372
Falcon's Flight #390
The Gentleman Insists #475

Silhouette Summer Sizzler

"Grand Illusion"

*Desire trilogy

JOAN HOHL,

a Gemini and an inveterate daydreamer, says she always has her head in the clouds. An avid reader all her life, she discovered romances about ten years ago. "And as soon as I read one," she confesses, "I was hooked." Now an extremely prolific author, she is thrilled to be getting paid for doing exactly what she loves best.

Chapter One

The shrill whine of the engines increased in volume as the executive jet charged down the runway. With an arrogant-looking lift to its pointed nose, the plane soared into the deep blue of the late afternoon sky.

Unfastening the confining seat belt, Valerie shifted into a more comfortable position in the overstuffed chair. Her hand idly smoothing the velour-covered arm of the chair, she let her eyes roam over the plane's fantastic interior.

Except for the fact that she *knew* she was thousands of feet above the ground, she could have been sitting in a small, plush living room. The carpet beneath her feet was deep pile, the color of antique gold. Near the rear of the compartment was a gleaming walnut cabinet that opened into a well-stocked bar. The seven other chairs in the compartment were exactly like the one she sat on, overstuffed loungers in varying shades of brown.

A brief smile tugged the corners of her mouth as her eyes rested on the woman sitting on one of those chairs. At the moment the swivel chair was turned to the side and all Valerie could see was her friend's profile and the curly cap of her light brown hair. Her head was bent over a small stack of papers on her lap and when her full, red lips moved Valerie heard the soft murmur of her voice, although her words did not register. A much deeper, though equally soft voice came in reply and Valerie's eyes sought the source of that voice.

The man sitting opposite the curly-haired woman spoke again in that low, soft voice, but as before, the actual content of his words did not reach Valerie. His head was bent also as he studied a paper held in his long-fingered hand. She could see only his profile, not his complete face. But then, she did not have to see his full face. The look of him had been imprinted on her mind at first sight. Glancing away, Valerie closed her eyes and let her mind wander back to that first meeting less than an hour ago.

They had arrived at the airport, she and Janet, flustered and out of breath and five minutes early. The dark blue Mercedes limo had glided smoothly to a stop exactly on time. Before the car's engine could be shut off, the door to the back seat was flung open and a dark masculine figure became visible. There was a moment's hesitation, as if the man had paused to say something to the other occupant of the back seat, and then he purposefully exited the car.

The first thing that struck Valerie was the fact that the hair at his temples was almost the exact silver-gray color of his suit. That observation fled, replaced by a series of others as the man straightened to his full height of over six feet.

From the distance that separated them, Valerie's immediate impression was that he was in his late forties or early fifties. But that impression was contradicted by his athletic physique. His face was lean and dark. The cheeks were high, the jaw and chin thrustingly firm, the nose long and hawkish. His thin, compressed lips were a slashing, straight line in his face. The overall picture was of harsh lines and smooth planes and—when he got close enough for her to see his cold blue-gray eyes—rock hard determination. Oddly at variance with the dark-skinned, hard image, his head was covered with a thick, silky-looking crop of wavy ash-blond hair, gone silver gray at the sides.

He had not paused as he'd drawn near the two women, but had merely nodded curtly and continued in his long-legged stride toward the gleaming white jet poised on the tarmac, awaiting his convenience.

Pushing the button that lowered her chair into a reclining position, Valerie adjusted her body to fit the contour of the seat. A hint of sharpness in the low, male tone scattered her wandering thoughts. Lifting her eyelids fractionally she centered her violet eyes on the man before her.

With studied indifference she noted how the material of his pants stretched tautly over the long, hard thigh that crossed his left leg. Through her lashes she examined with detachment the broad, long-fingered hand as it was raised to rake through ash-blond waves.

Valerie knew now that her first impression had been erroneous. There had been no contradiction between age and body. It was obvious from the supple way he moved that the man was in his prime—probably not more than forty or forty-one.

Had Valerie been impressionable, or looking for a man, she might have reached the decision that this particular male was the most exciting and interesting-looking specimen she'd ever encountered. And had she done so, she would have been joining a long line of women who had reached the same conclusion. But as she was neither impressionable nor interested, she could sum up her opinion of him in one word—formidable.

Despite her yawning indifference Valerie could imagine the impact he had on most people. For a fleeting moment even her detachment had been pierced when, just before they boarded the plane, a sleek-looking Porsche came to a tire-screeching stop alongside the Mercedes and an elegantly dressed woman jumped out to run, very inelegantly, toward the plane, calling, "Darling, wait!"

A grimace of extreme annoyance had twisted his mouth and Valerie had, surprisingly, felt a flash of anger when he'd turned his back and entered the plane with a coldly ordered "Get rid of her" to the uniformed steward.

Stunned by his callousness, Valerie had stared at the empty portal in disbelief until her companion had nudged her forward, advising tersely: "Go inside unless you want to witness the histrionics. This one's an actress and I can just imagine the performance she'll put on for Parker in her attempt to get on the plane to him."

Parker, of course, being the luckless steward.

Valerie had entered the plane just as the woman had begun her pleading, and not really wanting to feel *anything,* let alone compassion, she sighed with relief when, after she had stepped into the small plush compartment, the door was closed behind her, shutting off all outside noises.

Her amazement on entering the compartment had wiped all thoughts of the elegant woman from Valerie's mind. Standing transfixed, she had gazed around, bemused. She had been on private planes before. One had even been jet propelled, but never had she seen anything like the luxury displayed before her now. The abrupt movement of the man as he came to stand in front of her broke her rapt concentration on the lavish appointments of the plane's interior. Her eyes focused on the large hand extended to her at the same time his cool, deep voice reached her ears.

"I gather you are Valerie Jordan?"

Stiffening at his clipped, insolent tone, Valerie nodded shortly and answered with a frigid, "Yes."

A tiny, icy shiver went tiptoeing down her spine at the way his eyes narrowed on her face.

"Jonas Thorne," he snapped curtly, barely touching her fingers before dropping his hand. "Your employer."

The emphasis he'd placed on his last statement left little doubt in Valerie's mind that her coldness annoyed him. What, she asked herself, had he expected? A genuflection? A torrent of gushing thanks for being granted the privilege of her new position? Straightening to her full five feet three inches, she stared into his cold, blue-gray eyes unflinchingly.

"You *do* want the job, Miss Jordan?" The iciness of his tone sent another chilling tingle down her spine. There was a definite warning woven into that simple question. Even in her indifference Valerie did not miss the message within that warning, and she knew, without a doubt, that he would dump her back onto the tarmac without hesitation if her answer did not please him.

"Yes, sir."

Valerie felt no shame in her meekly voiced reply. She was indifferent, not stupid. And to be rejected by him now, through her own perverseness, would be sheer stupidity. She did not like him, but that was unimportant. She did not have to like him. If she found herself, now, standing on the tarmac watching as his plane became a black dot on the horizon, she would be not only without employment, but without a place to live or funds to fall back on, in a country that was not her own. Only a fool was that indifferent.

Apparently her answer suited him, for he turned away with a curtly ordered, "You had better sit down and buckle up. We will be taking off shortly."

Now, studying his harsh profile through the inky screen of her long black lashes, Valerie had the uncomfortable feeling that she'd allowed herself to be pushed in the wrong direction. Shifting her gaze, she studied the curly-headed ball of energy who had done the pushing.

As if she could feel Valerie's brooding perusal, Janet Peterson glanced up. The gentle smile that touched Janet's lips fleetingly told Valerie that her friend thought she was asleep. Valerie made no move to correct Janet's impression. She knew Janet was concerned about her health—both physical and mental—so she allowed the older woman the satisfaction of believing that she was enjoying the sleep of contentment.

"She's obviously sleeping." The conclusion came from Jonas Thorne in an unconcerned, emotionless tone. Then the tone took on a sardonic inflection as he added, bitingly, "You surprise me, Janet. I had no idea you had latent maternal instincts."

Although she remained still, a startlingly strong curl of anger flashed through Valerie's mind. How dare he attack Janet like that? Janet had done nothing the whole previous week but sing his praises, and here *he* sat slinging verbal abuse at her. The soft chuckle with which Janet received his insult added shock to Valerie's anger.

"I suppose the instinct is in every woman. It's just buried deeper in some than in others." Janet replied calmly. "Valerie has inspired protective feelings in me from the first day I met her seven years ago." Janet paused, then her voice took on a pleading quality that touched Valerie's unwilling conscience. "I promise you won't be sorry about this, Jonas."

"We'll see," came the disbelieving retort.

His tone left little doubt in Valerie's mind that he firmly believed he *would* be sorry. It was at that moment that Valerie decided to prove him wrong. The decision made, she lowered her lids entirely and allowed her thoughts to drift back over the events that had led to her present unenviable position.

Etienne.

Just thinking his name caused pain. Swallowing a moan, Valerie let an image of him form in her mind. At five feet nine inches, he had been only six inches taller than she, and yet she had looked up to him as to a god. Etienne, with his Gallic darkness of skin, hair, and eyes, and the classic, aesthetically beautiful face.

Was it possible it was only a little over a year since she had glanced up from her typewriter on hearing someone enter the office, to encounter his dark eyes fastened on her? Even now she could feel the thrill that had twisted pleasurably in her midsection. He had literally stolen her breath and heart with that one warm, caressing glance.

Valerie had known, without conceit, that she was very good at her job as private secretary to the manager of the Paris office of J. T. Electronics. Yet, caught by Etienne's warm-eyed glance, she had sounded like an inarticulate, inexperienced fledgling.

"Can I—uh, may I help you, sir?" she'd stuttered, a warm stain flushing her creamy cheeks.

"Yes, you may, *mignon.*"

The smile he had bestowed on her had scattered her senses. His charmingly accented voice melted her spine. "You may help me enormously by saying you'll have dinner with me this evening."

That had been the beginning. She had said "yes," of course. In her awe of him she could not have refused him anything. She had gone out with him every night for a week and by the end of that week she was hopelessly in love.

Etienne was everything she had ever dreamed of and never hoped to find. Intelligent, urbane and charming —he was all these. But what captured Valerie's heart was the deep streak of tenderness he was unafraid of displaying. He proposed to her six weeks after their first meeting. She had accepted at once, unable to believe her good fortune. But the most amazing thing of all was Etienne's fervently confessed adoration of her.

Valerie had been in France for six years, having requested a transfer to the Paris office of J. T. Electronics soon after her twentieth birthday. Young and eager to taste life, she had availed herself of every opportunity to meet new people and see as much as possible of the country.

Small, delicately boned and wafer thin, she realized without vanity that she was not unattractive. What Valerie had never seen in her mirrored image was the elusively haunting beauty of her small, heart-shaped face, a quality that instilled envy in most women, and the urge to protect in all men. She knew, of course, that her pale-skinned face, large violet eyes, and long, wavy black hair were appealing to men. But she innocently had no idea of exactly how appealing she was. And the fact that she was, so obviously, innocent tripled her appeal. And so, in the years she'd spent in Paris before she met Etienne, Valerie had had no lack of male companionship.

Valerie was not a prude. She was, in a word, fastidious, and she had remained innocent for one reason only. She simply could not engage in indiscriminate sex, and, until Etienne, she had not been aroused enough, either physically or emotionally, to take the final step into full womanhood.

For months she was gloriously happy. It had been early February when they met, and as spring came to breathe new life into Paris, Valerie blossomed in the warmth of Etienne's love. Declaring he could not possibly endure a long engagement, he set the wedding day for the end of May.

Breathless and starry-eyed, Valerie had blinked back tears of happiness as Etienne slipped an exquisitely beautiful ruby-stoned engagement ring on her small finger. She had not been able to keep the tears from rolling down her cheeks when he lifted his handsome head and declared reverently that he would love her forever.

For Valerie and Etienne, forever was to be a very short time.

Blissfully unaware of what the future held, Valerie delighted in the spring weeks they spent together. The weekend after he'd proposed Etienne drove her to his parents' home some miles outside of Paris. The French countryside was bursting with new life, as were the parklike grounds that enclosed the very old, very lovely chateau that was her beloved's birthplace.

Madame and Monsieur DeBron greeted Valerie like a long-lost daughter, and Etienne's older brother Jean-Paul teased her from the beginning as outrageously as he would have teased a much loved younger sister.

In a state of rosy-hued euphoria, Valerie soared on cloud nine as Etienne introduced her to his friends and favorite places. Never had she enjoyed the sights and sounds of Paris more. Never had she thrilled so deeply to its history and antiquities.

Although Etienne had whispered lovingly that he wished to wait until the wedding night to savor the fullness of their love, in a moment of overwhelming passion, he broke his own self-imposed time limit.

They had had a rare evening alone together and after a leisurely dinner had returned to Valerie's tiny apartment for a good-night drink. For a half hour or so they relaxed on her low sofa with good brandy and quiet conversation. It was the first time in weeks that they had been alone together in the evening, as their many friends had feted them nightly with dinners and pre-wedding parties.

"Do you know, I have missed you very much?" Etienne had said as he placed his empty glass on her small coffee table.

"Missed me?" Valerie had laughed. "But, darling, we've been together every evening."

"Yes, together, but not alone." A rueful smile curved his perfectly formed lips. "And, on bringing you home I have had to be satisfied with a quick good-night kiss." His lips turned up into an enticing smile and he held his arms out to her. "Come, let me hold you a moment before I must leave."

Valerie didn't need further coaxing. She had been longing for the feel of his arms and the touch of his lips on hers.

Etienne's kiss began as a tender exploration, but, as Valerie parted her lips with a sigh, she heard him groan and then his kiss deepened with hunger.

"Oh, my precious life," he'd groaned in husky English as he dropped tiny kisses over her face. "These last weeks have been torment for me, being so close to you yet unable to hold you, touch you, kiss you properly."

They were the last words he'd said to her in English that night. As each successive kiss became more urgent with desire, he whispered age-old words of love, made excitingly new to Valerie, in his own tongue.

Not once had it even occurred to Valerie to try to stop him. When he had lifted her into his arms and carried her into the bedroom she had curled her arms around his neck and murmured, "Yes, yes," against his heated skin.

Caressing the silkiness of her body with reverent sweetness, Etienne had tenderly prepared her for their lovemaking. Very, very gently he led her into the knowledge of physical pleasures. Inside the safety of his lightly stroking hands and his whispered words of adoration, Valerie had felt not one moment of fear. When it was over, and she lay within the glow of his love, and the circle of his arms, Valerie's heart was filled to overflowing with happiness and contentment.

Six days later, after yet another prewedding party, that happiness was shattered. Her world came crashing about her head as a drunken driver sent his vehicle skidding across a rain-wet road to crash head-on into Etienne's car.

Telling herself there had to be some sort of mistake, Valerie had rushed to the hospital where Etienne was being treated. Some seven hours later Valerie stood staring at the still, pale face of the man on the bed and felt hope trickle out of her like sands from an hourglass.

Reality seemed to recede as she glanced around in a desperate effort to maintain some point of contact with the real world. But there was no reality for her in the people around her—Etienne's parents, his brother, the doctor in charge of the case—or in the room itself, or even in the knowledge that the room was in a small private hospital several miles outside Paris. Indeed, even the magical word *Paris*, which she had learned to love during the last six years of her life, held no concrete reality.

No, for Valerie, at six-fifteen on a stormy May morning, the only reality existed in that still pale man lying on the sterile-looking bed. Recognizing in that man the lover she'd laughed and danced with only ten hours earlier was a task she was finding next to impossible.

In her imagination the form on the bed changed. For fleeting seconds he became again the smilingly gallant man who had toasted her, his fiancée, such a short time before. After the toast he had lifted her fingers to his lips and murmured, "The next two weeks will seem interminable, my love."

In a purely reflex action Valerie now clutched at that same hand, resting limply on the covers. The contrast between the hand she now held and the vitally warm one that had enclosed hers the night before caused bitter gall to rise chokingly in her throat.

Vitally alive! The descriptive phrase repeated itself painfully in her mind, and she sent up a silent, agonizing plea. Dear God, please, please let Etienne live.

With the unvoiced prayer came the realization she'd managed to block out of her consciousness till now. Etienne DeBron, her fiancé, her love, her entire life, was very likely going to die. And with that realization came rage. A rage that filled the void created by dissolving hope. A rage that clouded her vision and made her hands shake. A rage that finally settled on the unscathed man who had caused the unbelievable anguish of the previous hours.

Damn that drunken fool, she thought furiously. Damn him to hell! The curse brought an image of the small, skinny farmer, and an echo of his whining voice.

"Mon Dieu!" He'd invoked the Lord as his witness. "I didn't see his car," he'd sobbed brokenly. "The rain was lashing against the windscreen so heavily, I could hardly see anything through it."

And even less through your drunken haze, Valerie now accused the farmer silently. For although he was reasonably sober by the time they'd reached the hospital, the man had been very intoxicated when the gendarmes arrived at the scene of the accident.

He had been out with friends, the farmer had nervously explained, celebrating the birth of his long-awaited first child. Perhaps he had imbibed a little too freely, he'd admitted grudgingly. But, he'd qualified in a belligerent tone, the weather was more at fault for his car's crashing into Etienne's than he was himself.

The sheer outrageousness of his claim had stunned

an already deeply shocked Valerie, and it was not until this moment, hours later, that the farmer's sniveling excuses fully registered. The man was actually blaming Etienne's injuries on God! Without a twinge of guilt, Valerie silently repeated her curse: Damn him to hell.

The faint movement of the fingers in her clasped hand drew Valerie's attention back to the bed—and the face of her love.

"Je t'aime, Valerie."

Whispered through colorless lips that barely moved, the vow, though faint, touched every ear in the hushed room.

"I love *you,* Etienne."

From a throat dry with fear, Valerie repeated the pledge softly, hoarsely.

A mere hint of a smile feathered over the pale lips, and cold fingers pressed hers weakly in an attempted caress.

Valerie's hand tightened convulsively around his fingers as if willing her strength into him.

The very stillness of the air in the room gave her warning; and then it happened. From deep in his throat came the final exhalation of life.

"Etienne?"

Softly, almost timidly, Valerie called to the still form on the bed.

"Etienne!"

Valerie's tone had sharpened into a demand that defied the truth. Violet eyes, wide with growing horror, searched the white, waxy-looking face for a reason to defy that truth. There was only stillness. A stillness that made her blood run cold.

The white-coated figure of the doctor bent over the still form. Short, blunt fingers moved a stethoscope over the exposed chest, then the doctor straightened, head moving side to side.

From the other side of the bed came the harsh sound of weeping from both Etienne's parents. The strong arm of his brother slid over her shoulders, his hand grasping her upper arm firmly.

"Etienne, no—please, no!"

The hand on her arm tightened at her anguished cry and the arm turned her in, against his chest, forcing her eyes from the ashen face. Strong fingers pried loose her grip on the lifeless hand.

"Valerie, he can no longer hear you," Jean-Paul coaxed in his enchantingly accented voice. "Come away, *petite,* he is lost to us."

Valerie lifted her tear-streaked face to gaze pleadingly into his dark eyes, so like Etienne's, bright now with his own unshed tears.

"Can't I stay with him, Jean-Paul?" she begged softly. "Please, he'll be all alone."

"He is not alone, *mignon.*" Jean-Paul's lips moved in a faint, sympathetic smile. "Come." Turning her firmly, he walked to the door, giving her no choice but to go with him. "Etienne would not want you to stay."

Moving like a sleepwalker, Valerie had allowed herself to be led to the door. She'd turned to gaze once more on the beautiful features of the man who was to have become her husband in two weeks' time.

The flame of joyous animation that had burned so brightly inside Valerie had been extinguished with Etienne's last breath. From the moment Jean-Paul led her from that hushed hospital room, Valerie had slipped into a numbed shock. In a blessedly frozen state, she had been able to receive the condolences of friends and co-workers and had stood mutely in the small cemetery while the shell that had contained the essence of Etienne was interred in the family vault.

It was after she was alone in her apartment, having declined Jean-Paul's pleas that she stay with his parents for awhile, that the shock wore off and the real pain began. In an agony of remorseless grief, Valerie sank from despondency into a deep depression that even her closest friends could not break through.

The one person who might have been able to reach her was unaware of her withdrawn state. Jean-Paul, with a gentle understanding so like his brother's, had respected her request for solitude after the funeral. He had called her at least once a week to ask if there was anything he could do for her. But her answer had always been the same: There was nothing she needed.

Then, three months after Etienne's death, Jean-Paul's company had sent him to New York City. He had stopped to see her before leaving Paris, and again she had assured him there was nothing she needed. He had left with obvious reluctance, his dark, compassionate eyes shadowed with concern.

"Don't worry about me, Jean-Paul," Valerie sighed when he hesitated at her door. "Go and enjoy yourself. You'll love New York."

"Petite," Jean-Paul had murmured. "I cannot help but worry about you. You are—" he had paused, his voice cracking with an emotion Valerie was beyond noticing. "You are special to me," he had finished lamely.

"I will be fine, and I will be here when you return," Valerie promised, sending him on his way. She had been neither.

As the weeks slipped into months, she grew more

withdrawn from the people around her. Her work suffered and she didn't care. In fact, she was totally unaware that her boss was frantically covering up for her. Nothing touched her, nothing moved her, and she would have shrugged indifferently had someone told her that her superior's sympathetic efforts had failed, and management was all too aware of her slipshod work.

The Paris weather was unusually harsh that winter, and for the first time in her working life, Valerie was constantly absent from the office. *That* also did not go unnoticed at the home office of J. T. Electronics.

Holed up in her tiny apartment, Valerie could not have cared less about anything. Too disinterested to prepare proper meals, yet continually hungry as a result of emotional emptiness, she ate constantly—all the wrong kinds of foods.

By the time winter was on the wane her hair had lost its gleaming sheen, her complexion was no longer translucently glowing, and she was fifteen pounds heavier. She didn't care.

This, then, was the state of Valerie's existence on a blustery day one week before she found herself taking off in a luxurious private plane. She had once again not gone to the office.

To begin with she had overslept. Then, after glancing out the rain-spattered window, she had shrugged and, after calling the office to inform them she would not be in, she had gone back to bed.

She had been sitting on the sofa, her fingers tracing then retracing, the embossed design on the upholstery, when a sharp, imperative knock on her door broke her fixed stare. For a moment she had considered ignoring the caller—whoever it was—then, with a shrug, she walked listlessly to the door, and swung it open. She stood staring in disbelief at Janet Peterson.

"My God, Val!" Janet cried in astonishment the moment she was inside. "What have you done to yourself?"

Valerie's unconcerned shrug told Janet more than any defensive explanation would have. Janet had come to Paris for one purpose, and as she studied Valerie's appearance that purpose hardened. She didn't bother mincing words.

"I've come to get you, Val," she announced flatly. "I'm taking you home."

"Why?" Valerie asked dully.

"Why? Why!" Janet exclaimed. Grabbing Valerie's arm, she pulled her into the bedroom, not stopping until they stood before the dressing table mirror. "You can look at that reflection and ask me why?" Lifting her hand she caught at the limp, dull pony tail Valerie had secured with a rubber band. "Look at this rat's nest. When was the last time it saw the busy end of a brush?" Her hand moving swiftly, she caught Valerie's chin, turning her head so they faced each other. "Your skin is the color of wet cement," Janet declared brusquely. "And you are literally bursting out of your clothes. What have you been living on? A steady diet of gooey pastries?"

"Pretty much so, yes," Valerie admitted tiredly. "What difference does it make, anyway?"

"I'll tell you what difference," Janet snapped. "The difference between vital, glowing health, and this—" her hand moved to indicate Valerie's figure, *"mess* you've become."

Valerie had enough pride—or sense—left to wince.

Taking her reaction as a hopeful sign, Janet forged ahead.

"I knew things weren't good with you, but I had no idea they were this bad. Come back into the living room, Val, and prepare yourself for a much needed lecture."

And lecture she did. For over a solid hour Janet expounded on the fruitlessness of Valerie's withdrawal from the human race. With biting logic, she pointed out the futility and utter waste of becoming a recluse at the age of twenty-seven. On and on she talked, driving her truths home relentlessly.

Valerie had not wanted to listen, had, in fact, tried to shut the sound of Janet's voice out completely. It was impossible. Janet had not reached the executive position she held with J. T. Electronics by being ineffectual. She was smart, and she was quick, and, as the saying goes, she could think on her feet. She brought every one of those talents into play in her bid to save Valerie from herself.

"You've been relieved of duties at the office starting now," Janet tacked on at the end of her lecture. "That means we have what's left of the afternoon and six full days to whip you into shape."

"Relieved of duties?" Valerie had repeated in confusion. "Whip me into shape? What for? Janet, I don't know what you're talking about." A twinge of alarm pierced her indifference. Even when one no longer cared about living, the rent had to be paid. "Janet, are you telling me I've been fired?"

"No, I'm telling you you've been relieved of duty in the Paris office." Janet hesitated, then went on with deadly seriousness. "Val, I want you to listen very carefully to what I have to say. We've been friends almost since the first day you started working for the company—right?"

Her attention fully caught by Janet's tone, Valerie nodded her agreement.

"Well, honey, I'm afraid I may have risked my career for you on the way over here. If I've miscalculated in my belief in you, and you let me down, I just might find myself in line at the unemployment office by the end of next week."

"But why? How?" Valerie shook her head in an effort to comprehend what Janet was getting at. "Janet, I don't understand."

"No, there's no way you possibly could." Janet sighed. "I'd better start at the very beginning." She paused to glance meaningfully at the postage-stamp-sized kitchen. "How about a cup of coffee while I talk?" she suggested.

"Yes, of course." Valerie had the grace to be embarrassed that she hadn't made the suggestion herself. "I'm sorry, Janet."

Janet waited until Valerie had placed the tray of coffee things on the table in front of the sofa. Cradling a cup in her hands, she launched into her explanation.

"I've been worrying about you ever since—" she hesitated, then reworded, "for some time now. I could tell from your short, infrequent notes to me—and from various other sources—that you were more than normally despondent. The last two months I've been wracking my brains thinking of how I could help you."

"But, Janet, I neither asked nor expected—" That was as far as Valerie got before Janet cut her off.

"I'm more than aware of that," Janet scolded gently. "But I was determined to help you whether you asked for it or not. Anyway, the solution came very unexpectedly last week when Jonas's secretary suddenly skipped town with a married man." She grimaced. "Needless to say, he was furious."

"Mr. Thorne?" Valerie inserted.

"None other." Janet smiled grimly. "His behavior was somewhat like that of a lion with a thorn in his paw." Janet smiled. "A tiny play on words there."

"Very tiny," Valerie agreed.

"Anyway." Janet shrugged. "She couldn't have picked a worse time if she tried. Besides being in the middle of several contract negotiations, Jonas had finalized appointments for a long-planned trip to Paris. He refused to even think about changing his plans and commandeered his assistant's secretary. Then the agencies were requested to come up with a paragon to fill the desk chair in his outer office."

She stopped speaking long enough to swallow the last of her coffee and refill her cup before continuing her story.

"When a replacement had not been found by yesterday, I badgered Jonas into letting me come over here with him. I sang your praises all during the flight. Finally, in a desperate bid to get him to agree to take you back with him as his new secretary, I said I'd give him my resignation if you weren't as good at your job as I claimed you were." Janet drew a deep breath, then added quietly, "He agreed to give you a chance—if you can be ready to quit Paris permanently in a week's time."

Janet neglected to tell Valerie the exact words Jonas had used: "You are walking a very fine line here, Janet. I've had numerous reports on this 'exceptional secretary,' and in my estimation she has turned her back on life. And I have no time for quitters."

Janet's appalled shock upon laying eyes on Valerie was two-fold. She was, as a friend, sincerely concerned about Val. But she was also suddenly concerned about losing her own job.

In the main, it was this possibility that brought about Valerie's decision to go home. That, and the realization that within weeks spring would be coming to France. And suddenly Valerie knew she could not bear to be in Paris in the springtime without Etienne.

Chapter Two

$\mathcal{A}$ soft smile curved Valerie's vulnerable lips as she shifted slightly in the upholstered seat. Behind the barrier of her closed lids, she was unaware of the sharp blue-gray gaze that pondered that soft smile.

The smile was for Janet, and it was prompted by a rush of memories. Valerie had been a frightened, lonely nineteen-year-old when she'd entered the offices of J. T. Electronics for the first time. She had been frightened because it was her first job after leaving the security of business school. She had been lonely simply because she had so suddenly found herself alone.

Her father's death, after a lengthy illness, had not been the cause of her loneliness. There had been sadness, of course. A sadness touched by guilt because, near the end, Valerie had found herself praying for his release from pain. No, it was not her father's death, but the shock of her mother's remarriage, less than three months later, that had brought on her feeling of loneliness. The man was an Australian businessman on vacation in the States. He was, Valerie admitted to herself, charming and good-looking. He was also eight years younger than her beautiful mother. Shock followed shock, the final one coming with her mother's announcement that she was leaving for Australia with her new husband just one short week after her wedding.

Stunned, Valerie had stood by mutely while her mother disposed of her home, furniture, and all the collected belongings that she had shared with Valerie's father.

"Please try to understand," Celia Jordan—now Finny—had pleaded to an unresponsive Valerie. "Edwin must be back in Australia by the end of next week, and he wants me with him. Valerie, he's willing to have you with us. Please come." It was not the first time her mother had made this impassioned request. Valerie's answer had been the same every time.

"No."

She had been filled with bitterness and resentment at what she had considered her mother's disloyalty to her father's memory. In her bitterness she had punished her mother by remaining adamant in her refusal to go with her.

Valerie had moved in with her grandparents, and, with an insolence foreign to her nature, refused to accept any financial aid from her mother. Within two weeks after her mother's tearful departure, Valerie had dropped out of business school and had secured a position in the typing pool at J. T. Electronics.

And so it was that a scared, lonely, very young, but unrepentant Valerie walked through the wide doors of the steel and glass edifice that was the home office of J. T. Electronics—and found there a friend. It was Janet Peterson who had, eventually, brought about the reconciliation between Valerie and her mother.

From the day of their first meeting, which happened to be the second day of Valerie's employment, Janet took Valerie under her wing. The friendship that developed between them surprised everyone, for they were complete opposites.

Janet was a walking advertisement for women's lib. She didn't talk about it. She didn't bore or annoy people about it. She lived it. Yet, despite her rapid rise to an executive position in the firm, she had retained her femininity.

On the other hand, Valerie, at nineteen, had no real personal ambitions. She was a good worker. She was an accurate typist who had the potential of becoming an excellent secretary. But, at that point in her young life, her main concern was collecting her paycheck twice a month. Never would she have believed that one day she would be offered the position of personal secretary to the owner of the company. In fact, she had never so much as set eyes on the man who was her employer.

Valerie was soft, inside and out. Her eyes were soft. Her voice was soft. Her skin was soft. And her attitude to life had been to take the path of least resistance. Until her father's illness had dampened her exuberance she had thought of life as a joyous adventure. Why not enjoy it to the full? His death, and the events that followed it, had wrought a change in her personality. Her gaiety had been overshadowed by resentment, her contentment with life had been poisoned by bitterness. Janet had been instrumental in helping her break these emotional chains.

Ten years her senior, Janet had become many things to Valerie. Besides being her best friend she was surrogate mother, mentor, and at times, the insistent echo of her own conscience.

Two months after meeting Janet, Valerie sat down and composed a letter of apology to her mother. Her mother had reciprocated, with great emotion, by return mail. The mending of the rift lifted a weight off Valerie's shoulders. Free of the encumbrance, her laughing, soft-hearted nature surfaced once more.

During the months that followed, Valerie enjoyed herself enormously. She formed many new friendships in the office and was much sought after by her masculine colleagues for dates. Thus, when her grandmother informed her that when her grandfather retired at the end of the year they would like to follow the sun to Florida, she was able to accept the news philosophically. She would miss them, she assured her grandmother, but she could appreciate their desire to spend their retirement years in the sunshine.

Jonas Thorne had had his office complex erected on the outskirts of Philadelphia and for several weeks Valerie scoured the area for a small apartment. Although Janet had offered her her own extra bedroom, Valerie had declined, with thanks, claiming the urge to taste independence.

Meanwhile her grandparents had begun implementing their plans, and were scheduled to depart Pennsylvania in six weeks' time. Beginning to feel a bit desperate, Valerie had put a deposit on a tiny apartment on the third floor of a rather rundown building in an area she had previously avoided.

That was her situation on entering the office a few days later and discovering a new notice to all departments, posted on the bulletin board. The notice informed all employees of the fact that J. T. Electronics would be opening business offices in Paris in the spring, and it contained a list of positions available to employees interested in working out of the country. The one prerequisite was that the applicant had to speak, read, and write French.

For Valerie, the notice had seemed like the answer to her prayers. Her French was not only good, it was excellent. She had learned the language from her paternal grandfather, a Parisian whose family had left France just before the second World War.

Valerie had been the only woman to apply, and after a brief interview with the personnel manager, she had been given the position of front desk receptionist in the new office. She had left the States nine weeks after her grandparents' departure for Florida. During the weeks between her grandparents' move and her own, she had stayed with Janet.

Now, seven years later, another man's death had brought Janet to her rescue again.

Lifting her eyelids, Valerie studied her friend with admiration. Asleep Janet looked anything but the dynamic executive. The riot of curls that framed her face softened its contours, usually set in determination. The dark lashes that fanned her cheeks were long and full. And her mouth, in repose, had the soft, appealing curves of a young girl's.

But those lips had not been soft a week ago. Her mouth set grimly, her eyes sharply assessing, Janet had circled Valerie while she made a visual examination of her person.

"Good, God, Val, you do look a mess," Janet had scolded gently. "I can see we are going to have a very busy week." Reaching out, she lifted Valerie's loose over-blouse to reveal the unsnapped waistband of her jeans.

"How much weight have you gained?" she'd asked flatly.

"I don't know." Valerie had shrugged. "Does it matter?"

"If all your clothes fit like these jeans—yes," Janet answered sharply. "Do they?"

"Well—everything I've worn lately has felt a little snug," Valerie admitted.

"And what size is everything you've worn lately?" Janet demanded.

"Threes, mostly."

"I think you have graduated to a five," Janet decreed. "We are going shopping first thing tomorrow morning."

The following morning had been the start of a six-day marathon.

In the dressing room of an elegant shop, stripped to newly purchased lacy panties and bra, Valerie submitted to Janet's smiling survey of her figure. "Well, the *jeune-fille* look is gone." Janet's smile had deepened as her eyes met Valerie's in the mirror. "But, *cherie,* the mature woman, as they used to say where I come from—" her smile stretched into a grin, "ain't half bad."

The evidence before Valerie's eyes confirmed Janet's observation. The young girl look was definitely gone. The diet of quick-to-put-together meals, heavy on starch, that she'd been existing on for months, had filled out her formerly sylphlike figure.

"It's a good thing I came when I did," Janet had stated, her eyes following Valerie's over the appealing shape reflected in the mirror. "Another few weeks of French bread sandwiches and pastry, and your figure would have been too voluptuous."

Perusing her new figure with detachment, Valerie had to agree with Janet's judgment. Her breasts, though not very large, were full, and owed none of their height to the lacy scrap of material covering them.

Her waist, though no longer a twenty-inch span, was still narrow. And, although her hips had flared to a mature roundness, her stomach was still flat, while her slim, shapely legs gave a false illusion of length. Yes, she concurred indifferently, her more mature look was not half bad.

The shopping binge that Janet had initiated all but wiped out Valerie's bank balance. Then, added to the total for clothes, there was the cost of several hair treatments, facials, and a manicure. When Valerie took a final reckoning, she was astounded. She had the French equivalent of exactly seventy-two dollars and nine cents left.

"Don't worry about it," Janet had advised with a careless wave of her slim hand. "I'll talk to Jonas. I'm sure he'll be willing to give you an advance until you get squared away."

Now, having met Jonas Thorne at last, Valerie decided she wanted no advance from him. As a matter of fact, she wanted nothing from the man. Certainly not the position of private secretary that Janet had talked him into giving her.

Moving her head fractionally, she let her narrowed gaze hone in on the object of her unsettling thoughts. He appeared to be asleep, yet even in repose, his face had lost none of its hardness. Valerie shivered with a chill that feathered down her spine. What a frightening specimen he was! And what satisfaction it would give her to be able to tell him exactly what he could do with his job.

But she wouldn't tell him, and she knew it. She was not concerned for herself; she could always find a job elsewhere. She *was* concerned for Janet, though. Valerie felt certain that if she in anyway aroused his displeasure, Jonas Thorne would ruthlessly put an end to Janet's career.

Antagonism, hot and strong, surged through Valerie's mind. The intensity of the emotion shocked her, and Valerie closed her eyes completely to shut out his harsh visage. Never before in her life had she reacted to anyone so strongly—or so adversely. But then, she had never encountered anyone quite so coldly unemotional before, either. Jonas Thorne was so, so—inhuman— the unkind appellation jumped into her mind.

The idea of working with him, day after day, five days every week, was an unpalatable one. She would very likely suffer a severe case of frostbite before the first week was over! The mildly humorous thought was almost as shocking to Valerie as her earlier antagonistic feelings had been.

With a sigh of acceptance, she faced the fact that Janet had talked her into a trap. She had no other choice; she had to work for him. At least, she temporized, until Janet's job was secure again. No, she corrected herself grimly, remembering his disbelieving "We'll see." She didn't just have to work for him; she had to *excel* for him.

Even after being in his presence for only a few minutes, it hardly seemed possible to Valerie that this could be the same man Janet had raved about all week. It had seemed that everything Janet said was prefaced by: "Jonas is" or "Jonas does" or "Jonas doesn't"; her friend had gone on and on with Jonas and more Jonas. Valerie had been convinced she was to meet and work for some sort of paragon. What she had met was a statue that just happened to walk, talk, and breathe. One had to assume, she supposed, that somewhere inside that marblelike casing a heart beat with regularity and blood flowed.

Valerie moved restlessly, more uncomfortable with her thoughts than with the padded contour of the chair. She had a prickly feeling, as though a limb had gone numb from being in an awkward position. Only with Valerie the sensation was mental. Her mind had been, figuratively, asleep for months, and its sudden arousal was as unpleasant a sensation as the renewed flow of blood to a numbed arm or leg.

Sighing, Valerie wished fervently that Janet had stayed at home and left her alone in her cocoon of misery. *That* thought made her more restless still. Before Janet's arrival the numbness had been so complete she had been unaware of it. Now, as reality took on new meaning for her, Valerie writhed with the prickly sensation of self-awareness.

And now, unsavory as the thought was, she faced the realization that she had been harboring an unconscious death wish. From the moment that dry, dreadful-sounding rattle whispered through Etienne's pale lips, she had ceased living in any normal sense of the word.

It was unhealthy. It was self-destructive. Janet, with her forceful personality and her rational arguments, had dragged her out of the shadows of self-immolation, and into the sunlight of self-interest.

Valerie was restless, and uncomfortable, and prickly in the mind. But, for the first time in a very long time, she was alive. Not fully, not wholly alive; that would come slowly at first, and then with shattering swiftness.

But it was a beginning, and she was every bit as scared as she had been at age nineteen. The only difference was that this time it didn't show. She was feel-

ing again, but more important, she was thinking
again. And that thinking led to the conclusion that, unless she protected herself, this man could hurt her. She
wasn't quite sure how he could do it—possibly through
Janet—but she felt sure that he could. And she had
been hurt enough.

Standing on American soil after a seven-year ab-
sence, Valerie felt a fluttering in her stomach. She was
home! Suddenly she was very glad Janet had forced this
move on her. Blinking against the hot sting of tears
brought rushing to her eyes by a welter of emotions, the
uppermost being plain old-fashioned patriotism, Valerie hurried across the tarmac in the wake of Jonas
Thorne's long strides. Their destination was a long,
gleaming, silver-gray Cadillac limousine, which was
waiting for them off to the side of the single-building
airport.

Valerie, already tired from the trip, was experiencing
a mild feeling of disorientation. They had left France
late in the afternoon and had been served a very early
dinner—due, Valerie had learned, to Jonas Thorne's
having skipped lunch—and now, at a small airport
some miles outside of Philadelphia, it was not yet
dinnertime. Valerie knew her disorientation was
caused by the flight through time zones. But knowing
why she felt strange didn't help much. The fact that
Jonas Thorne seemed totally unaffected by the flight
added a layer of irritation to her feelings of strangeness.

"Is he always like this?" Valerie asked Janet softly,
hoping against hope that she had analyzed him incorrectly.

"Like what?"

Janet's tone, combined with her look of confusion, was all the answer Valerie needed.

"Never mind," she sighed.

"But, Val, what—" Janet began.

"Janet!" Jonas Thorne snapped impatiently. "You have the entire weekend to gossip with Miss Jordan. Whereas I have an appointment in exactly," his arm shot out and he sent a swift glance to the face of the large, round gold watch on his wrist, "thirty-seven minutes. Will you close your mouth and get in the car?" His lips curved into a sardonic twist before he added, "Please."

Detestable man! Valerie had to bite her lip to keep her opinion of him silent. Casting a quick, compassionate glance at Janet, her eyes widened in surprise. Not a hint of indignation or hurt was revealed on Janet's face.

"Sorry," Janet murmured, a small apologetic smile touching her lips as she increased her pace toward the big car. "Hello, Lyle," she said softly to the driver, who had jumped out of the front seat to open the back door.

"Miss Peterson," the small, wiry man murmured as Jonas Thorne strode around the car to the front passenger's door. "Good flight?"

"Yes, very smooth." Janet hesitated, then said quickly, "Lyle, this is Valerie Jordan, Jonas's new secretary." On the last word she bent and stepped into the car.

"How do you do, Miss Jordan?" Lyle smiled broadly as he turned his gaze directly at her.

Valerie took an instant liking to the man. Not much taller than she, he had a very ordinary face and an extraordinarily sweet smile. Although she judged him to be about her own age, he had the look of a man who had experienced much of life, and his compact body had a tough, tempered look. Now, spontaneously returning his smile, she replied, "Fine, thank you, Lyle—?" She lifted her eyebrows in question.

"Magesjski." Lyle's smile deepened.

"Pleasantries over?" Jonas Thorne asked, his tone hard.

Valerie felt a flash of hot anger, followed by baffled surprise. As had Janet a moment before, Lyle smiled apologetically. Yet, strangely, the eyes Lyle turned to his employer held a glint of laughter.

"Yes, sir."

More strange still, and totally incomprehensible to Valerie, the blue-gray gaze that caught and momentarily held Lyle's reflected that laughter. On the point of entering the back seat, Valerie stopped cold.

"My luggage!" she blurted.

"Val, don't worry—" Janet began from the far corner of the seat.

"Parker will bring it with him." Jonas Thorne's impatient tone cut across Janet's soothing voice. "Your cases will be quite safe with him, Miss Jordan." After folding his long frame into the front seat he twisted around and pinned Valerie—positioned half-in, half-out of the car—with a cold stare.

"In or out, Miss Jordan?" he drawled. "My time has now been cut to thirty-two minutes."

Clamping her lips together, Valerie slid onto the back seat. Sitting stiffly erect, she returned his stare until he deliberately turned his head to the front in a dismissive gesture.

The pink tinge of embarrassment heating her cheeks,

Valerie sat glaring at the back of Thorne's head. A light pressure on her arm drew her attention, first to Janet's hand, then to her eyes. Her lips pursed, Janet shook her head while tilting it at Jonas Thorne. At Valerie's frown she gave a shrug, as if to say, "Don't let it bother you."

The drive from the airport to the J. T. Electronics building was made in silence and completed in twenty-five minutes, most of it along a new by-pass road constructed during Valerie's sojourn in France.

"Seven minutes to spare, Jonas." Lyle grinned as he brought the limo to a stop at a private side entrance to the building.

"I'm impressed," Jonas Thorne drawled dryly, flinging his door open and stepping out of the car. "Drop Janet and Miss Jordan off and then come back here," he ordered, already moving toward the private entrance.

Janet sighed as Lyle set the car in motion again. Smiling ruefully, she slid slim fingers through her close-cropped curls.

"If he was in such a hurry," she said, "I'm surprised he didn't have the chopper waiting for him."

"The chopper?" Valerie questioned.

"McAndrew flew to Washington in it this morning," Lyle informed Janet, before adding for Valerie's enlightenment, "The chopper is the company helicopter. We use it mostly for short trips."

"I'm impressed." Valerie imitated Thorne's dry drawl.

The following twenty minutes were interesting ones for Valerie. The changes made in the area during the years she'd been away were startling. Many places were totally unfamiliar to her, because of all the building that had taken place, and the alterations gave her an odd feeling. She had come home and she felt like a stranger; a foreigner in the place where she was born.

Lyle turned off the highway onto a road that led to yet another group of unfamiliar high-rise buildings. He brought the car to a stop at the covered entranceway to the one in the forefront.

"Here you are, Janet—Miss Jordan," he announced as he swung open the back door for them. "Delivered as ordered."

"Thanks, Lyle," Janet murmured when she and Valerie were standing on the pavement. "Now you had better scoot back to Jonas. See you Monday."

Janet introduced Valerie to the security guard stationed inside the heavy glass doors, told him the younger woman would be staying with her for awhile, then led the way to a row of elevators on the other side of the wide carpeted lobby. The elevator stopped at the fifth floor. After traversing a long hall, Janet unlocked a door marked 5B.

Compared to her tiny flat in Paris, Janet's apartment seemed enormous to Valerie. The living room was large, as were the two bedrooms. The bedrooms each had connecting baths, and there was a small powder room off the living room for use by guests. There was also a small dining area and a kitchen equipped with all the latest conveniences.

"This place is absolutely beautiful," Valerie breathed as the tour ended in the kitchen. "I wouldn't begin to guess how much it costs."

"Plenty." Janet grinned, pausing in the act of pouring water into the coffeemaker. "But it's worth every dollar." She shrugged. "I've worked very hard to get where I am. This place is the reward I've given myself."

She glanced around possessively. "Actually, I owe it all to Jonas," she added.

"I don't buy that," Valerie scoffed. "You would have succeeded in any company. I think Mr. Thorne probably owes you."

"Not so." Janet shook her head sharply. "Jonas has been very good to me." She frowned. "Did Jonas bruise your sensitivity in some way, honey?"

"Bruise," Valerie repeated consideringly. "You couldn't have chosen a better word, for I find your Jonas Thorne very abrasive." Her voice took on a grating edge. "I don't like him—at all."

"Oh, Val!"

Janet's worried exclamation made her feelings clear to Valerie.

"Don't worry, Janet," she was quick to promise. "I have no intention of giving him any reason to be dissatisfied. If your job depends on my performance as his personal secretary, you can consider it secure. I promise you I will be a very, very good little girl—no pun intended." She accepted the steaming cup of coffee Janet handed her, sipping at it carefully before giving a little laugh. "I plan to be the best damned secretary he has ever had—bar none."

Janet stared, openmouthed, at the vehemence of Valerie's tone. "Honey, I know Jonas was a little testy once or twice on the flight home," she said when she'd found her voice again. "But I think you'll realize before too long that you've been a little hasty in your evaluation of him."

"And what's your evaluation of him?" Valerie asked with unaccustomed sarcasm. "A diamond in the rough?"

"On the contrary." Janet's sharp tone was accompanied by a shake of her curly-haired head. "I think you'll find him very polished. Oh, he's as hard as the stone you mentioned," she conceded. "He's had to be to get where he is today. He's tough, yes," she went on in a tone that bordered on reverence. "But all the rough edges he started out with are gone. And he is, at times, ruthless. But, personally, I find the combination of a brilliant, tough, ruthless mind in a supremely fit body quite awesome."

Awesome! Now Valerie was the one to stare open-mouthed. And the amazing thing was that Janet had spoken in deadly earnest. Janet's attitude and a flashing memory of the ease with which both Parker and Lyle responded to Thorne's rasping sarcasm convinced Valerie the man had the three of them completely buffaloed. Did he perhaps, she wondered, have all his employees believing he was invincible? Not me, Valerie promised herself.

Apparently she was the only one who saw him as the brute he was. Perhaps she could see him more clearly because she had not been involved with him all along as the others had.

The chime of the doorbell broke the silence that had settled between Valerie and Janet.

"That's probably Parker." Janet sighed in obvious relief as she hurried out of the kitchen. Valerie followed at a more leisurely pace, a smile of welcome curving her lips when Parker glanced at her.

"Good evening, Miss Jordan." Returning her smile, Parker dipped his head respectfully before reaching for the doorknob.

"Would you like a cup of coffee?" Janet asked.

"No, thank you." Parker's tone held regret. "I have to get back to the plane. Jonas is flying to L.A. tonight with several business associates, and I want to have everything squared away before he boards."

"I swear—" Janet smiled ruefully at Valerie when the door closed behind Parker, "ever since Jonas bought that Gulfstream, Parker has cared for it like his own child. And he didn't even buy it new!" She paused, then laughed out loud. "Which isn't too surprising, considering what those babies cost."

"An awful lot?" Valerie queried.

"Millions, I'm told," Janet answered with a grimace.

Millions! Janet had said he'd fought his way up, but Valerie had had no idea she'd meant *that* far up! Her first impression came back to her in a rush; he was a formidable man, indeed.

"Well, he's welcome to it," Valerie observed, picking up her two large suitcases. "Especially tonight." Lugging the cumbersome cases as she trailed Janet to the smaller of the bedrooms, she sighed. "Personally, I'm bushed. I'm glad I don't have to face another flight tonight."

"Me too," Janet agreed heartily. "But I doubt it bothers Jonas one way or the other. He does so much dashing back and forth, I'm beginning to think he's immune to the effects."

Although Janet's tone held bemused admiration, Valerie shivered. The more she heard about him, the more inhuman he seemed. And now the reason for the free time he'd given her before reporting for work was clear. He had not acted out of consideration for her as she'd thought. Not in the least. He simply had no need of her in the office if he was in California.

Valerie lay awake a long time in the strange bed in Janet's guest room, but for the first time in a long time, her sleeplessness was not caused by tormenting memories of Etienne. She was tired, very tired, but her mind was alert forming plans of how to go about becoming the perfect secretary.

Valerie and Janet spent the weekend catching up on each other's experiences of the last six years. In minute detail, Valerie described the orgy of sightseeing she'd indulged in during the years before she met Etienne.

"It all sounds wonderful," Janet sighed at one point. "Especially Greece. I've promised myself that some day I'll take a long vacation in Europe." Her eyes glowed teasingly. "Maybe I'll save it for my honeymoon."

"Are you planning one?" Valerie asked eagerly.

"Isn't everyone?" Janet drawled, then changed the subject.

In between their many conversations, Valerie practiced her typing on Janet's manual machine, and took dictation from her obliging friend.

Janet and Valerie left for the office earlier than Janet's usual time on Monday morning and went directly to the personnel office. After filling out the required forms, Valerie was given a small, plastic-coated identification card and a key to the office she would be working in.

"Charlie McAndrew's secretary handed that key in on Friday afternoon," Janet told her when they left the personnel office. "You remember I told you Jonas had commandeered her?" Valerie nodded, following Janet without question as she started down the familiar hallway. Valerie was finding that the layout of the office came back to her easily, but she had never before had occasion to go up to the executive floor where Jonas Thorne worked.

"She'll be in the office with you today, to help you get acquainted with the routine," Janet went on, turning right into another, shorter hallway. "Charlie's office is just down the hall from Jonas's. His secretary's name is Eileen Skopec, by the way." Janet finished her briefing as they approached a curved, counter-high desk inside a door at the end of the hall.

A tall, burly man of about thirty half sat, half leaned on a high stool behind the desk. From his position he had a clear view of the door and both strokes of the L-shaped hallway. As they walked up to the desk a big smile creased the man's face.

"Good morning, Janet." His smile widened. "You're a little early this morning, aren't you?"

"A little, yes." Janet returned his smile. "Steve, this is Jonas's new secretary, Valerie Jordan—Val, Steve Dunn. He'll be checking you in and out of here every day." Janet nodded at the door. "You'll be using that entrance from now on."

"Welcome to the funny farm, Valerie." Steve grinned broadly.

"Thank you—I think." Valerie smiled uncertainly. "Funny farm?" Her eyebrows went up questioningly.

"Just an expression." Steve laughed. "Even though things can get pretty crazy around here. Especially when the coal-cracker goes on a rampage."

Frowning in confusion, Valerie glanced at Janet, who smiled wryly and explained, "Steve is referring to our employer. He's been on a rampage ever since his secretary left."

"Maybe now that you're here," Steve nodded at Valerie, "Jonas will go back to his normal occasional growl."

Valerie smiled weakly and groaned silently. Good

47

Lord, she thought, walking to the metal door to glance out of the small square of window. It's not enough that I have Janet's job riding on my shoulders, now I find I'm also expected to soothe Thorne's ruffled feathers. She stood staring out the small pane several seconds before she realized this was the entrance where Lyle had dropped Thorne off on Wednesday afternoon. His own private entrance, she mused wryly, and I'm to be allowed the use of it. How lucky can one girl get? A tiny shiver stole along her spine and she turned back to Janet abruptly.

"Where do we go from here?" she asked brightly, in an effort to dispel the chill of apprehension.

"Up." Janet indicated an elevator across the hall. "See you later, Steve." She waved as she walked away.

"Very likely," Steve drawled, before adding, "Nice meeting you, Valerie. Good luck with the cracker."

"It was nice meeting you, Steve," Valerie called back as she followed Janet into the elevator. The boxlike car swept up, then came to a smooth stop. The doors swooshed open to reveal a hallway carpeted in dark green plush. Janet ushered Valerie out with a sweeping of one arm.

"There are only two suites of offices on this floor. Jonas has the larger suite. Charlie has the other." She walked down the hall to a walnut door that was devoid of all marking. "This door is locked every night. You'll have to use your key."

After opening the door, Valerie stood back for Janet to precede her into the office. Following her, Valerie took three steps into the room and stopped in her tracks, her lips parting in surprise.

Whoever had decorated the room had considered both efficiency and comfort. The latest model in electric typewriters rested on the side of a large desk. Within easy reach were a word processor and a copying machine. The floor was carpeted with the same plush that covered the hall. The room's two large windows were draped with a loosely woven material in a rich cream color. Three chairs—one behind the desk, two in front of it—were upholstered in tawny, glove-soft leather. The overall effect was both businesslike and sumptuous.

"This, of course, is the cell you'll be working in." Janet laughed at Valerie's bemused expression. Striding across the room, she threw open a door on the wall nearest the desk. "And this," she nudged Valerie inside the room, "is where the warden works."

Jonas Thorne's office was the epitome of understated elegance. The carpet in this room was *not* the same as in the hall. A chocolate brown color, it was wonderfully, luxuriously thick.

The desk looked huge, even in the large room, and gleamed like satin in the morning light. The wall behind the desk had one enormous window draped in a roughly woven beige fabric. A long couch, covered in white leather, was placed along the wall facing the desk. Two chairs in a misty orange leather fronted the desk and a smaller one in the same color rested beside the desk. Valerie did not have to be told the small chair was the one she'd sit in to take dictation.

"And this," Janet walked to a door in the far wall, "leads to Jonas's bath and dressing room." She grinned at Valerie's lifted eyebrows. "Yes, it's a full bath. He has been known to work through the night, then catch a few hours' sleep on the couch. He keeps a closet full of clothes here. When he has those—" she hesitated, as if searching for words, then shrugged—"all-night sessions, he simply has a shower, puts on fresh clothes, and starts all over again."

"Is he some kind of workaholic?" Valerie asked, peering into the black-and-gold-tiled bathroom.

"Full time," Janet stated.

"Good morning."

"Good morning, Eileen," Janet returned warmly, smiling at the small, plump brunette standing in the doorway between the offices.

After introducing Valerie to Eileen, Janet left the office with a wave of her hand and a promise to come for Valerie at lunchtime.

"Well, I must admit I'm glad to see you," Eileen laughed as Janet swept out.

"Has working for Mr. Thorne been that bad?" Valerie frowned.

"Bad? Not really." Eileen shook her head, leading the way back to the other room. "He's very exact, and he expects his secretary to follow his example—but he's no ogre."

Not very reassuring, Valerie thought, remembering her easygoing boss in Paris. Then she was forced to concentrate as Eileen launched into a detailed explanation of what Thorne expected from his secretary. Time flew by, and, concentrating with every brain cell she possessed, Valerie was unaware of someone's entering the office until, glancing up with a bright smile, Eileen said, "Good morning, Jonas."

Digesting the fact that apparently everyone called him by his given name, Valerie turned from the copying machine as Thorne replied:

"Good morning, Eileen—Miss Jordan."

"Good morning, Mr. Thorne."

As she returned his greeting, Valerie marveled at the

steadiness of her own voice. Her tone had conveyed a cool composure she was far from feeling, for on making eye contact with her employer, an uncomfortably familiar chill ran down the length of her spine.

Within the few seconds he paused before striding to his office, Valerie's eyes took a complete inventory of him. He was, again, suited in gray, a darker shade this time, and his eyes seemed to reflect the color, showing not a hint of blue. His sharply defined features gave his face a coldly forbidding cast that the straight line of his mouth did nothing to dispel. Valerie's estimation of him was exactly as it had been at first sight: he was cold, emotionless, formidable.

Valerie was fully aware that while she assessed him his eyes were flicking coolly over her. As they did, his expression seemed to tighten into implacable hardness. A tiny shiver followed the chill as she felt herself dismissed. At the doorway to his office he paused again to issue a terse order.

"I want one of you in here at once to take dictation."

For several seconds pure, blind panic gripped Valerie, and then she squashed it as Eileen offered softly, "I'll do it. You stay with the machine."

Reaching for the pad and pencil on the desk, Valerie shook her head determinedly, and even managed a brief smile.

"I've got to start sometime; it may as well be now."

Having issued the brave statement she straightened her spine and walked unhesitatingly into Thorne's office.

"Close the door—please."

The harshness of Thorne's order was not relieved in the least by his sardonically tacked-on "please."

Controlling the sudden urge to slam the door shut,

Valerie closed it carefully before walking to the chair beside his huge desk. Seating herself on the edge of the chair, back straight, legs seemingly glued together, she poised the pencil over the pad and glanced up at him with what she hoped was a professionally expectant expression.

Though his own expression was bland, his eyes mocked her little show of secretarial efficiency.

"Are you quite ready?"

"Yes—sir."

The brief flicker in Thorne's eyes at her tiny, but deliberate pause before adding the term of respect sent a small thrill of pleasure coiling through Valerie's midsection. The equally brief flash of amusement that replaced the flicker of annoyance transformed her thrill of pleasure into a disquieting sensation that felt very uncomfortably like *real* respect.

Now Valerie was annoyed—although she succeeded in hiding it. She did not want to feel even a glimmer of respect for this man. This was the monster, Valerie reminded herself harshly, who was prepared to accept Janet's resignation in the event she could not meet his high standards in the execution of her duties.

At this point all other considerations were cut off as Thorne launched into dictation.

By the time his quietly clipped voice came to a halt, Valerie felt like all her nerves had been tied into tight, throbbing knots. Her sole consolation was the somewhat surprising realization that she had kept up with him. As she concentrated on getting out of his office while maintaining at least the frayed remnants of her earlier composure, Valerie sent up a silent prayer of thanks for the urge that had set her to practicing her shorthand with Janet over the weekend.

"How did it go?" Eileen's query came with the closing of the door that connected the two offices.

"The man's a machine," Valerie declared in a tone that held both weariness and hard conviction. "How long was I in there?"

"Exactly two hours and thirty-seven minutes," Eileen laughed, glancing at her watch. "Not too long, really," she murmured. "He's been known to go on a lot longer than that." Her grin turned into a soft, compassionate smile. "The first time is always the hardest. You'll get used to his ways."

"If I survive long enough," Valerie opined softly. "Honestly, Eileen, I feel like I was in there for days." She sighed, then went on, "I'm afraid I'm going to have to evict you from that chair. He wants these," she lifted her steno pad, "typed as soon as possible."

"He always does," Eileen returned quietly, rising and moving away from the desk. Plucking another pad from the desk top she added, "I'll give him his phone messages while you start that."

Valerie had no sooner rolled the first sheet of paper into the typewriter than Eileen came out of Thorne's office again, a small, apologetic smile on her lips.

"I've been ordered back to my own desk," she said in a near whisper. "Apparently Charlie's about ready to tear his hair out." At Valerie's confused, questioning look she explained, "Jonas's assistant, my boss, Charles McAndrew, remember?" Valerie nodded impatiently, which drew a soft laugh from Eileen. "Well, it appears the girl from the typing pool has not handled things to Charlie's satisfaction." She shook her head sadly. "Charlie is—ah—shall I say—*almost* as exacting as Jonas. Poor kid, she is very young. She's an excellent typist, but not qualified to keep up with Charlie."

"I see." Valerie hesitated a moment, then asked flatly, "Is everyone on a first-name basis around here?"

"Just about," Eileen confirmed, heading for the door. "I suppose it's a little—well—unorthodox, but, it is by request." Valerie's frown indicated that she didn't fully comprehend Eileen's meaning and Eileen explained. "Everyone you've heard refer to Jonas or Charlie by their given names has done so because they have been asked to. Charlie, being in absolute awe of Jonas, is the next thing to his reflection—in action and attitude—if not in looks." She paused in the doorway to smile encouragingly. "Within a week you'll very probably be using their first names as unselfconsciously as all the rest of us."

Valerie seriously doubted Eileen's assertion, but she kept her doubts to herself. She was typing away at an incredible pace when Janet called to her from the doorway.

"Are you ready to go for lunch, Val?"

Startled, Valerie looked at Janet blankly a second before her question registered fully. "Why, I don't know," she answered vaguely, darting a glance at her watch. "I'll check with Mr. Thorne."

With fingers that were suddenly, inexplicably shaky, Valerie lifted the receiver and pressed the button that buzzed the phone on Thorne's desk.

"What is it?" he barked impatiently into his receiver.

Valerie fleetingly considered snapping back at him, but then reconsidered and said, very coolly, "I'm going to lunch now, sir."

"All right, Miss Jordan," Jonas replied with much less impatience. Then he rendered Valerie speechless by adding, with an almost human understanding of the morning she'd put in, "Take your time."

Chapter Three

During that first week in the office, Thorne's attitude toward his new secretary was characterized by a bewildering combination of impatience and sensitivity. By late Friday afternoon Valerie couldn't decide if Jonas Thorne was the worst or absolutely the best man she'd ever worked for.

He was, above all, thorough, and he expected the same degree of thoroughness from his secretary. Valerie had never worked so hard in her life. Although she fell into bed early every night silently cursing the man, each successive day of working with him added another layer to the unwanted respect she felt for him.

Even when he was most impatient with her, he was unfailingly polite—tacking on sardonically drawled "thank you"s and "please"s—until Valerie found herself swinging between simple dislike and total loathing of him.

Charlie McAndrew, on the other hand, was thoroughly likable. Of medium height, with pale blue eyes, sandy hair, and an abundance of freckles, Charlie looked anything but the ambitious young executive. At their first meeting, late on the afternoon of her first day in the office, Charlie had insisted she call him by his given name. Until she saw him in action the following day, Valerie had some difficulty seeing Charlie in the role of Jonas's live-wire assistant. Blushingly shy and easygoing, Charlie appeared more the type found at a small corner desk, pouring over bookkeeping ledgers.

Which only proved, Valerie decided wryly near the end of the week, exactly how deceptive appearances could be. In action Charlie was almost, but not quite, as dynamic as his idol.

By quitting time Friday, positive she'd failed both Janet and herself miserably, Valerie prepared to slink out of the office in defeat.

"I'm afraid I owe Janet an apology." Jonas's quiet voice drew Valerie's startled eyes to his. She had not heard him open the connecting office door, and seeing him leaning indolently against the door frame unnerved her. In fact, seeing him in an indolent position *anywhere* would have unnerved her.

"An apology?" Valerie repeated blankly. "What for?"

"You don't know?" The tilt of Jonas's right eyebrow, combined with his dry tone, mocked her show of ignorance. Of course she knew what he was referring to. Hadn't she been deriding herself about it when he'd made his sudden appearance? But how did she go about explaining to him that the sound and sight of him had scattered her thoughts? She had been listening to him, seeing him all day. He'd think she was an idiot, and rightly so, she berated herself. His exasperated sigh told her she'd been quiet too long.

"The—bargain—Janet made with me to secure this position for you," Jonas prompted. "You *were* aware of it?" The words were more a statement than a question.

Valerie was convinced she'd let Janet down, and after a week of exposure to both his cold-eyed observation and the confusing nuances that laced his tone, she was oversensitive to just about everything about him. His chiding remark put an end to the polite facade she had assumed in his presence. Lifting her head, she met his cold stare with equal coldness.

"Yes, sir, I was aware of it," Valerie returned frostily. "You were to have Janet's resignation on demand if I was unable to fulfill your requirements." Valerie's tone went from frosty to icy. "Isn't that correct?"

"Not quite," Jonas clipped acerbically. "*I* made no demands. Janet made the terms of the bargain."

"But you didn't hesitate to accept them," Valerie accused frigidly, even though she had no real proof of her charge.

"Why should I have hesitated?" Jonas's tone betrayed his growing anger. "Janet's been with me a long time; I like and respect her. I simply agreed to her proposition."

"You were prepared to accept her resignation if I fell on my face," Valerie asserted.

"But you did not," Jonas shot back. "So it's a moot point." His glittering steel-gray eyes narrowed on her indignant expression. "Unless you persist in rousing my anger more than you already have. I'd advise you to speak carefully, Miss Jordan, or instead of offering Janet my apology I'll be showing her the way out of this firm. Needless to say, should I do so, she will be following *you.*" He paused to let his warning sink in, then went on, very softly, "Have I made myself clear?"

"Perfectly," Valerie whispered through stiff lips. She was not concerned about her own job, she assured herself unconvincingly. But she could not take any chances with Janet's. Nevertheless she grew weak with relief when the object of her thoughts sailed blithely into the office.

"Are you ready to leave, Val?" Before Valerie could respond, Janet spied Jonas in the doorway. "Oh, hi, Jonas, am I interrupting something?"

"Not at all," Jonas replied smoothly. "As a matter of fact, we were discussing you."

"Me?" Although Janet managed to keep her smile intact, her eyes darted from Jonas to Valerie then back to Jonas.

"Yes, you." Jonas's teasing tone drew Valerie's startled eyes to his face. She had heard at least a half-dozen shadings in his voice during that long week, but never one of affectionate teasing. "I was just telling Miss Jordan that I owe you an apology."

"An apology?" Janet echoed Valerie's earlier words. "What for?"

"For doubting your judgment. You were right. I'm not sorry I let you badger me into bringing Miss Jordan back from Paris."

The smile he bestowed on Janet stole Valerie's breath. It was not until Steve called good night to her and Janet as they left the building that she pulled herself together. What, she wondered, had Janet and Jonas said to each other? Snatches of their conversation skipped in and out of her mind.

"You mean you're really satisfied with her work?" Janet had asked—thereby revealing exactly how concerned she'd been.

"Very satisfied." Jonas's surprising answer had left Valerie so stunned that the content of his subsequent words was lost to her.

Whatever had come over her? The question tormented Valerie as she walked across the parking lot beside Janet. Clearheaded now, Valerie wondered at her odd reaction to the flashing smile that had transformed his face. Good grief, it was the first time she'd ever seen it!

"Val, are you listening?" Janet's exasperated tone put an end to Valerie's bemused thoughts.

"No, I'm sorry, I wasn't." Valerie smiled ruefully. "What did you say?"

"I *said* I'm proud of you." The frown creasing Janet's face smoothed out as she smiled. "Of course, *I* knew you could do it. The thing that worried me was whether *you* knew you could do it."

"I really didn't," Valerie admitted, sliding onto the passenger seat of Janet's car. She fastened her seat belt before adding, "As a matter of fact, I was positive I'd failed. His apology was as much a surprise to me as it was to you."

"He gave no indication that he was satisfied with your work?" Janet asked, placing a cigarette between her lips.

"None."

"Strange." Janet finished lighting her cigarette then turned the key in the ignition. "Usually Jonas is quick to show his approval when he's satisfied."

Thinking wryly that a number of meanings could be put on Janet's statement, Valerie shrugged. "I don't like your Jonas very much, Janet."

"My Jonas!" Janet exclaimed loudly. "He's not *my* Jonas." Bringing the car to a stop in the line of cars waiting to exit the parking lot, she turned a wicked grin on Valerie. "Would that I could call him mine, but I don't think there's a woman alive who can." She gave a mock shiver, and her smile turned dreamy. "God, I've wondered for years what he's like in bed."

Cold, Valerie thought disparagingly. Cold and un-emotional and mechanical. Aloud she said, "I doubt he's anything to get excited about—in bed I mean."

"Really?" They moved forward four car lengths, then stopped again, and Janet gave her an arch look. "I don't doubt it for a minute. There have been one hell of a lot of females chasing him for as long as I've known him. He's got something."

"Money." Valerie sneered. "There are one hell of a lot of females anxious to marry it."

"Won't wash." Janet shook her head emphatically. "The way I hear it, the women were after him long before he had the money."

"Before?" Valerie's eyes widened with surprise. "You mean he wasn't born with the proverbial silver spoon?"

"Jonas? Hell no!" Janet's burst of laughter was cut off by the blast of a horn, alerting Janet to the space growing between her car and the now moving line in front.

Janet was quiet as she concentrated on maneuvering the car off the lot and onto the highway. When they had finally merged into the thick throng of traffic, Janet said abruptly, "I think we should celebrate. There's a bar near here where a lot of people from J. T.'s stop most Fridays for an end-of-the-week drink. Let's stop and join them."

"Oh, I don't know," Valerie hedged. "I'm very tired, Janet." Tired hardly described the way she felt—half dead on her feet came a little closer to the mark.

"But that's exactly why we should stop," Janet argued. "Val, honey, you're tighter than an overwound watch. You need to relax, be with other people. Lord, girl, how long has it been since you've had a night out?"

Valerie went stiff with the memory, and she had to force herself to answer. "There—there was a pre-wedding party—" she moistened her lips—"the night before Etienne—" She couldn't say the words, and, turning her head sharply, she stared out the side window.

"Oh, Val." Janet sighed. "I'm sorry, really sorry about Etienne, but, honey, you have got to pull yourself together. The longer you put off being with others, the harder it will be. I really think we should stop. Okay?"

"I suppose you're right." Valerie didn't suppose anything of the sort. She didn't want to be with other people. What she wanted was to go home and sleep the clock around. But Janet had been more than kind, and so she gave in, grudgingly. "Okay, Janet."

"You don't have to sound like it's a punishment." Janet's laughter fell flat. "You just might enjoy it. They're a good group."

Good group or not, Valerie discounted the possibility of enjoyment. Feeling irritable and tense with the effort to hide it, a sudden thought chilled her and she asked stiffly, "Will Mr. Thorne be there?"

"Jonas! You have got to be kidding." Janet shot her a quick grin before returning her attention to the traffic. "And here it is," she informed her a few minutes later.

Valerie studied the unimpressive two-story frame building as Janet drove the car onto the macadam parking lot that was over half-full of cars. All from J. T.'s? she wondered, eyeing the sign above the bar entrance.

"The Drop Inn Lounge." She read the words aloud. "Cute. Are you sure Mr. Thorne never drops in?"

"Not that I know of." Stepping out of the car Janet tossed her a questioning glance. "Val, are you afraid of Jonas?"

"Seven days a week." The fervent admission surprised Valerie as much as it did Janet. Falling into step beside her friend she went on harshly, "I think he's as tough as a cheap cut of beef."

"Oh, he's tough all right." Janet frowned at her. "Was he—well—unpleasant to you this week?"

"Unpleasant?" Valerie repeated consideringly. "Not exactly unpleasant. He was more . . ." She searched for words. At least a half-dozen unkind ones sprang to mind but she settled for "impatient."

"Oh, well." Janet paused, hand on the knob of the bar door. "That's nothing to get worked up over. Jonas is impatient with everyone. Come on." She pulled the door open. "I'll prove it to you."

The inside of the bar was a surprise after the unimpressive exterior. It was dimly lit, but the hand of an excellent decorator was evident. The stools in front of the long bar were covered in a vibrant red fabric, as were the captain's chairs around the dozen or so tables in the room. The indoor-outdoor carpeting was in a black and red tile pattern that was repeated in the material of the cafe curtains that hung at the four windows. Pewter hurricane lamps burning scented oil were placed in the center of every table. The crowded room buzzed with laughter and conversation, and vibrated with music from a flashing jukebox sitting just inside the door.

From the moment she stepped inside, Janet was hailed from every section of the room. Smiling and waving back, Janet headed toward a large round table in the corner, around which sat five women.

Trailing behind Janet, Valerie returned the greetings of several people she'd met at various times during the week, and ignored the suggestive glances of several men she had not yet met. As they approached the table Valerie identified three of the five women. Searching her mind, she named and placed them. The small, chunky, dark-haired woman of about thirty was Doris Mercer, secretary to one of Thorne's executives— Valerie couldn't remember his department. Next to her was Sharon Templin, a tall, slim young woman who worked in the mail room. The third was Judy Blume, a dark-haired woman of about Valerie's own age who was assistant to the manager of the typing pool.

Janet waited until they were seated at the table before introducing Valerie to the other two women.

"Valerie Jordan." Janet waved a slim hand at her, then at the lovely platinum blonde directly across the table. "Annette Liemiester—she keeps the file room from falling apart."

Valerie smiled and returned Annette's "hi," and then her eyes moved to the tall black woman with the very pretty, but somewhat stern, face.

"Loretta Harris." Janet grinned at the solemn-faced woman. "She's the top-kick in personnel."

The lazy smile that Loretta turned on Valerie completely changed her visage from stern to devilish. "Hi, Valerie." Her voice was husky, her tone teasing. "Sorry I missed you Monday morning. How are things going in the high-rent district?"

"I beg—" bemused by the chameleon-swift change in Loretta, Valerie was uncertain of her meaning, then the light clicked on in her head. "Oh!" She laughed softly. "You mean the executive suite. All right I guess. At least I haven't been given notice to vacate as yet."

"And won't be," Janet inserted firmly. "Jonas himself told me he is satisfied with her work."

"That's encouraging," Loretta drawled. Fixing her beautiful brown eyes on Valerie, she pleaded. "Please, try to *keep* him satisfied. For as long as you do, Legree's whip won't fall on *my* back."

Her plea was met by total confusion from Valerie and derisive comments from her four companions.

"Poor Loretta," Doris cooed.

"Summer's coming and she won't be able to bare her scarred back," Sharon chided.

"Work, work, work." Judy lifted a hand languidly to smother a yawn.

"Tote that barge, lift that bale." Annette fluttered incredibly long lashes.

Lifting her glass, Loretta sat back in her chair, her huge grin revealing white teeth. "Oh, the price one pays for being indispensable," she said pleasantly.

"Loretta's been feeling the lash of Jonas's tongue ever since your predecessor took off," Janet explained, taking pity on Valerie's obvious confusion.

"I just don't understand why it was so hard to find a replacement." Annette's long eyelashes swooped down and she swept the faces around her with eyes that glittered from behind narrowed lids. "I'd jump at the chance to work closely with Jonas—really closely, I mean."

"Mmm," Judy agreed, taking a quick gulp of her drink. "Don't say any more. Just *thinking* about it is enough to give me shivers."

"Personally," Loretta murmured huskily, "I enjoy

imagining what those late nights in the office might be like."

Valerie felt her skin grow warm. Impossible though it was for her to believe, these women were actually drooling over Jonas Thorne! They're putting me on, she decided. Expecting a burst of laughter at any moment, Valerie glanced around the table, a hollow feeling growing inside as she noted the gleam in several pairs of eyes. They're not putting me on! Even Janet wore an expression of flirtatious interest!

The arrival of a waitress at the table broke the spell, and to Valerie's relief, the subject was dropped. Valerie and Janet ordered drinks and another round was requested for the others.

"On me," Janet declared. "Val and I are celebrating the successful conclusion of her week on the hot seat," she went on to explain. "No pun intended."

The tension slowly eased out of Valerie as easy laughter, followed by teasing banter, flowed around her. The conversation revolved around the doings at J. T.'s. Some of the talk concerned serious matters, but most of it was harmless gossip. Valerie, content to simply sit back and listen, was halfway through her second drink when Doris interrupted a rather juicy anecdote that Sharon was relating. Doris was sitting facing the door, and as she glanced in that direction, her eyes widened in shock.

"I don't believe it!" she exclaimed softly.

"Well, Jean insists it's true," Sharon said defensively, casting Doris a look of annoyance.

"Not that," Doris snapped, not even bothering to look at Sharon. She nodded her head toward the bar's entrance. "That."

Valerie's eyes moved along with five other pairs, and then she froze in her seat.

"Is he real or did we conjure him up?" Loretta asked dryly.

"I agree with Doris," Janet murmured. "I don't believe it."

Valerie, however, was uncomfortably aware of how real Jonas Thorne was as he made his way through the room. His progress was slow, as he was stopped every few steps by someone either at the bar or at a table. Before he was even a quarter of the way into the room a drink was handed to him by a young man from the accounting department whom Valerie had met the previous afternoon. Thorne accepted the glass with a sardonically raised eyebrow and a brief shrug.

When it became apparent that his destination was their table, Valerie very deliberately withdrew into a state of mental detachment. Secure inside the shelter of self-induced indifference, she awaited his arrival.

"Ladies."

For the second time in less than two hours, Valerie was witness to Jonas Thorne's smile. Only this time, safe in her fortress of indifference, she coolly observed its effect on her companions. Right before her eyes they seemed to melt before the dazzling warmth of that smile.

"Washing away the bad taste of J. T.'s?" The slight dip of his head indicated the glasses on the table.

Valerie remained silent as the others laughingly denied his words. She wanted very badly to label his tone condescending or patronizing. She wanted to, but she could not. He displayed nothing but warmth and friendliness. His eyes circled the table, resting briefly on each face. Was it her imagination or had his eyes sharpened momentarily when they took in her closed expression?

How had they answered him? What had they said? Although Valerie had heard the breathless, fluttery sound of their voices, she had not absorbed their actual words. Her attention focused intently on Thorne and the manner in which he received this near adulation. Expecting arrogance, Valerie grudgingly admitted that though he obviously enjoyed their overtly sexual reaction to him, he did not bask in it.

"I stopped here in the hope of catching you before you went home, Loretta." The abrupt change in his tone announced business as usual. Though his cool, blue-gray eyes were focused now on Loretta's, no one but a fool would think he had singled her out for any personal reason. Loretta was anything but a fool. Straightening in her chair as if snapping to attention, she became once again the efficient personnel manager.

"There's a problem?" The somewhat stern expression was back in place—her tone matched it exactly.

"No, no problem," Thorne replied easily. "I had a phone call from Maria Cinelli a short time ago."

This seemingly innocuous statement had an electrifying effect on every woman at the table, bar one— Valerie frowned her confusion.

"And?" Loretta prompted respectfully.

"She wants her job back." His answer came without inflection of any kind.

Valerie had the sensation of being pinned to her chair by the sympathetic glances turned to her by her tablemates. Seeking an answer, she lifted her eyes to Thorne. His face revealed none of the concern written clearly across the faces of his employees. The silence seemed to stretch interminably, yet in truth it lasted no longer than a few rapid heartbeats. "Find her some-thing to do."

A soft sigh, issued collectively from six throats, followed the terse order. Shifting her eyes to Loretta, Valerie watched as the woman mentally reviewed avail-able job openings.

"Jonas." Loretta's eyes narrowed in defeat, her tone held an odd pleading note. "I have nothing open for someone of her capabilities."

"I didn't ask you to crown her queen, Loretta." A taunting smile curved his lips. "Only to allow her back at court."

A devilish grin was Loretta's immediate response. "Will do, sir."

"Glad to hear it." His soft drawl banished the taut atmosphere. Doris giggled, and as if it were a signal, Thorne turned to leave, then paused.

"The tab's on me." A wave of his hand indicated their drinks.

"Oh!" Annette fluttered her long lashes at him. "We were planning to have dinner here." She waited pret-tily.

"Then you've lucked out, haven't you?" Once more they were favored with that dazzling smile. "Enjoy your dinner, and the weekend, ladies." His pause was very, very brief. "You too, Miss Jordan."

Chapter Four

*A*rrogant swine!

Valerie silently repeated the epithet for at least the fifthieth time since Thorne had delivered his parting shot.

Damned arrogant swine. Valerie threw her leather shoulder bag onto her bed with the force of suppressed anger.

"Pig, pig, pig." Seeking an outlet for the fury that seethed in her mind, she muttered the words aloud, slowly, vehemently. She had no idea exactly what he'd meant by his taunting, "You too, Miss Jordan." She didn't even know exactly why the taunt had enraged her so. All she knew was that he'd pierced her armor of detachment with one carelessly tossed barb. And having to hide her dislike of him from Janet and the others hadn't helped much.

What a gaggle of simpering idiots! Jerking around, Valerie kicked her shoes in the direction of her closet. What motivates these career women? she asked herself despairingly. All of the women at that table were around Valerie's age or older. Yet none were married. Why? Why hadn't they married, or—in the case of Annette and Judy, who were divorced—remarried? What were their goals? The questions had hammered away at Valerie for hours while she sat, shocked, listening to their comments about Thorne.

Dropping tiredly onto the edge of her bed, she replayed the scene in her mind in an effort to glean something, any small understanding, from it. Loretta had been the first to break the tiny silence that had followed in the wake of Thorne's departure.

"That is one big, sexy man."

"I'll say," Sharon breathed softly. "God, when he smiles like that I have to fight the urge to tear my clothes off."

"Yes, but everyone knows that you're oversexed." Doris laughed. "I know what you mean though. With me the urge is to tear *his* clothes off."

"I get shivery all over just thinking about what he'd look like without his clothes," Judy sighed.

"I live in hope." Annette smiled smugly, her long lashes seeming to tremble as her eyes caressed Thorne's retreating back.

"And you'll very probably die in disappointment," Janet inserted dryly. "I have worked for him almost fifteen years and in all that time he has singled out only one female employee for personal attention."

"And now the witch is back." Doris moaned.

"Unfortunately," Sharon added.

"We haven't heard from Miss Cinelli's replacement." Annette's lovely face was turned in question to Valerie. "What do you say, Valerie?"

She had plenty she dearly longed to say, but the fleeting expression of alarm that passed over Janet's face cautioned her to mind her tongue.

"Nothing." Valerie gazed calmly into Annette's disbelieving eyes. "I'm not interested. Not in him—or any other man."

"Why?" Annette probed. "Are you a man hater?"

Now that Thorne had made it through the room and out the door all their attention focused on her. Valerie, already angry, was not about to subject herself to an inquisition. Getting to her feet, she smiled sweetly at Annette.

"No, I don't hate men. Now, if you'll excuse me, I'd like to freshen up a little."

She had spent ten minutes in the ladies room making believe she was touching up her makeup and brushing her hair; but all the while she had chided herself for the disgust their comments about Thorne provoked in her. You are twenty-seven years old, she silently lectured her reflection. You have seen quite a bit of the world. You are not an innocent; you have experienced a man's body.

She lowered her eyelids, blocking out the pain reflected in the violet eyes in the mirror. When she looked again most of the pain was gone, replaced by a shadowed, haunted look. For all your traveling around, you *are* an innocent, she silently informed that lost little face in the mirror. And the reason their blatantly sexual talk offends you is that it has nothing to do with the beauty you shared with Etienne.

Thinking his name hurt. Jumping to her feet, she scooped up her purse and hurried out the door. The atmosphere at the table had undergone a complete change. The subject under discussion was food and the varying degrees of starvation each woman was suffering from. Not once during the rest of the evening was Thorne's name mentioned. Nor did Valerie's avowed disinterest in men come up again.

Now, hours later, still fighting the last remnants of her anger, Valerie paused in the act of unbuttoning her tailored shirt, a sudden thought belatedly striking home. Rebuttoning her shirt as she went, she left her room and walked into the living room where Janet sat watching the late news on TV.

"You told them about Etienne, didn't you?" Valerie accused the back of Janet's head. The head jerked around to reveal eyes soft with understanding.

"Yes," Janet admitted calmly. "While you were in the ladies' room." A small smile touched her lips.

"Janet—why?" Valerie had to bite her lip against crying aloud.

"Because I didn't want you badgered by a lot of questions," Janet explained in the same calm tone. "Val, they are nice people, really. At one time or another they've all experienced loss or rejection. They won't pry."

"Maybe not," Valerie groaned. "But by noon Monday every employee at J. T.'s will know about Etienne."

"Very likely." Janet lifted her shoulders in resignation. "But, if nothing else, it will keep the wolves at bay—at least for awhile." The smile tugged more forcibly at her lips. "With your looks it won't be for long, but it will give you some breathing space." Her eyebrows arched. "Have any of the self-proclaimed great lovers made an approach yet?"

Valerie sighed wearily. "Yes, several. And their reasons for coming into my office were suspect, now that you mention it."

"Well, there you are." Janet's shoulders lifted again. "Either you put up with their advances, or they know about Etienne and leave you alone for a respectable period."

Valerie sighed again, this time in defeat. "I suppose

so," she muttered, turning to go back to her room. She took two steps then swung back to cry, "Damnit, Janet, why did you have to come after me? I was perfectly all right where I was," she lied.

"You were perfectly miserable, and you know it," Janet returned gently. "Give it time, honey; it will pass." Her voice gentled even more. "And, meanwhile, Val, I suggest you rub the stardust out of your eyes."

Janet's advice kept Valerie awake long after she slid between the sheets of her bed. It didn't take an Einstein to figure out that Janet had been well aware of Valerie's adverse reaction to the sexual remarks made by their table companions. Turning and twisting uncomfortably, Valerie tried to conjure up the purity of Etienne's face, and for the first time, the image was shadowy and unclear. Blind panic filled her mind, and lying still, barely breathing, she pleaded: Don't go, please don't leave me.

During the weekend, Valerie repeatedly asked herself two seemingly unrelated questions: Did she really have stardust in her eyes? And, what difference would it make if she suddenly found herself dispossessed by her predecessor?

It would make a lot of difference, she realized on Monday morning as she dressed for work. All during the drive in, and as she unlocked the office that she now thought of as her own domain, Valerie felt a mixture of anger and despair. Damn this faceless Maria, she thought angrily. Damn this ex-secretary, ex-mistress, ex-whatever, for coming back now.

Standing in front of her desk, Valerie was shocked into immobility by the intensity of her feelings. Staring at her neat desk top, she slowly curled her fingers into tight fists. True, Thorne had ordered Loretta to find another job for his ex-secretary, but, if what they said was true, and Maria was also his ex-bed partner—how long would it be before Maria was back at this desk, and she found herself out hunting for a job?

"Are you posing for my benefit, Miss Jordan? Or are you simply hung-over?"

Valerie's body jerked violently—as if his taunting tongue had been placed against an exposed nerve. Swinging around, she faced him squarely, lost her cool, and blurted, "Do you want me to clean out my desk?"

Nails digging into her palms, she watched the transformation in his face. Amused mockery disappeared to be replaced by a stern, hard look.

"You've decided to leave us?" The very softness of his tone, so at odds with his expression, sent a chill of fear down her spine. "You're going to dash back to Paris—and the past?"

Back to Paris? The past? Valerie shook her head dumbly. What did Paris or the past have to do with Maria Cinelli? Misinterpreting her vague head movement as a negative response, Thorne snapped, "You've found another, better position perhaps?"

"No!" Valerie denied softly. "I didn't mean—"

"If you haven't got another job, and you're not going to leave the country," Thorne interrupted harshly, "would you care to explain just what the hell you do mean?"

The very hardness of his tone added to Valerie's confusion. Why was he so angry? She'd have thought he'd be delighted at having the way so smoothly paved for his girlfriend's return. Why was he attacking her? That thought stiffened her spine with anger. Who did he think he was talking to?

"I *mean* just what I said." Valerie fairly spat the words at him. "Do you want me to clear out?"

"Miss Jordan," he barked exasperatedly, "as I'm never very good at reading minds on Monday morning, would you kindly explain exactly what the hell you are talking about?"

"About Miss Cinelli," Valerie barked back.

"Miss Cinelli," Thorne repeated slowly as he crossed the room to her. "What about Miss Cinelli?" He stopped less than a foot in front of her and Valerie had to tilt her head back to look up at him.

She didn't particularly like what she saw. Up close he gave the appearance of a man very near the end of his patience. Valerie held her ground, hanging on to her composure by sheer willpower. In truth, he scared the breath out of her.

"I thought you'd want her back," she gulped. The narrowing of his eyelids made her add hastily, "As your secretary."

"You heard what I told Loretta, didn't you?" His tone, though very soft, was threatening. Valerie suddenly found it very difficult to swallow.

"Y-Yes."

"Then why are we wasting time on this discussion?"

"I-I," Valerie paused to wet hot, dry lips. "I just thought—"

"Wrong," he interrupted. "You thought wrong. Now, do you *think* we could get on with the electronics business?"

Valerie wanted very badly to back away from him, but even had her pride allowed her to do so, the solid form of her desk mere inches behind her prevented retreat. To make matters still worse, her legs had begun to tremble with nervous weakness and she wanted very badly to sit down. Feeling trapped, she stared up at him mutely. He was the most fierce-looking male she'd ever encountered. After only one week of listening to the chatter in the cafeteria Valerie was well aware of what the female employees on his staff thought of him. There was evidence of respect in abundance, but, first and foremost, the general consensus was that he was handsome, terrifically put together, exciting, and sexy as the very devil—not necessarily in that order.

Gazing up into his face now, Valerie made her own evaluation. Handsome? Hardly. Etienne had been handsome. Thorne's face was too thin, the bones underneath the tautly drawn skin too prominent. There was not a hint of softness or tenderness in his cold eyes or in the long, slightly arched nose that jutted below. The lines formed grooves from either side of his nose to the corners of his thin-lipped mouth spoke of harshness, and his sharply defined, not quite square jaw thrust forward in determination. That he was built well she'd concede. And she had to admit he was exciting— at least as an aggressive businessman. Sexy as the devil?

"Have you reached a verdict?"

Valerie's thoughts splintered like shattered glass at the sardonically drawled question. What in the world was she doing? What must he think?

"I'm sorry." Valerie raked her mind for an explanation of her odd behavior. Nothing presented itself. "Mr. Thorne, I—"

"You didn't particularly like what you saw, did you?"

Startled, she blinked at him, then lowered her eyes. How did one answer a question like that tactfully?

"You have a very strong, determined face," she finally managed. The laughter that erupted from him startled her and her eyes flew again to his face. Looking at him was a mistake. Friday, his smile had stunned her, now his soft laughter had a paralyzing effect. Fleetingly she wondered why, when he could produce such a delightful sound, he laughed so rarely. Abruptly, he turned and walked to the door of his office. Before entering the room he shot her an amused, meaningful look.

"Strong and determined, huh?" The grin that spread across his face could only be described as wicked. "You don't know the half of it, sweetheart."

Groping behind her, Valerie clutched at the desk for support. The doorway was empty now but she could still hear his low chuckle, which unnerved her even more. Making her way around the desk she dropped into her chair, staring blankly at her shaking hands. She hadn't the vaguest idea how long she'd been sitting just staring at nothing, when the phone rang, bringing her to her senses.

With the first call of the day Valerie eased back into her normal routine. By the time she entered Thorne's office to take dictation she'd pulled herself together enough to speak to him in her usual cool tone of voice. His first, distant "Miss Jordan" assured her that he had also reverted to form.

Before drifting off to sleep that night, Valerie replayed the morning's scene over again in her mind in an attempt to make some sense of it. Why, she wondered sleepily, had Thorne's closeness to her, and his taunting jibe, shaken her so ridiculously? It wasn't as if she cared what he thought of her; she didn't. And she was positive he didn't give a damn what she thought about him. So then why had his face seemed to become taut with tension when he'd asked, "Have you reached a verdict?"

Unable to find any plausible answer for his attitude, Valerie sought sleep. She was tired but, for the first time in the last year, she had good reason for her weariness. She had been exceptionally busy all day. The phone had rung incessantly and Thorne had required her presence at several meetings to take notes. Yawning widely she curled up on her side, dismissing all thoughts of the baffling Jonas Thorne.

Midmorning Tuesday, refreshed from a deep, dreamless eight hours of sleep, Valerie shifted her gaze from the keys of her typewriter to the woman who entered her office and felt her breath catch in her throat. The woman was not really beautiful, but she certainly was arresting. Tall in comparison to Valerie, she stood before the desk with the poise instilled by an exclusive finishing school—or a good modeling school—her head tilted slightly as she coolly studied the smaller woman. Her makeup had been applied with an artist's touch to enhance her high cheekbones and full-lipped mouth. Every dark hair on her regally held head was in perfect place, and her brown eyes were filled with disdainful amusement as they finished their perusal of Valerie.

Feeling herself weighed, measured, and found decidingly wanting, Valerie felt annoyance prick her mind. Who was this haughty woman? Careful not to let her annoyance show, Valerie responded with her most professional smile.

"May I help you, Miss—?"

"Cinelli," the woman supplied, not bothering to return the smile. "Maria Cinelli, and I want to see Jonas."

Who cares what you want? Valerie had to bite back the retort. So this was the ex-everything, she sneered to

78

herself. Very impressive, I suppose, except I'm not impressed.

"Of course you do," Valerie purred silkily, and felt rewarded by the tiny frown that fleetingly marred Maria's smooth brow. Allowing a glimmer of her own disdain to sneak into her eyes, Valerie swept the tall, elegant form with a dismissive glance as she pressed the button on the intercom.

"What is it, Miss Jordan?"

Valerie stiffened at the smug, catlike smirk of satisfaction that curved Maria Cinelli's lips at the impatience in Thorne's tone.

"Miss Cinelli is in the office, sir," Valerie answered in a neutral tone. "She would like to see you."

"Well, then, send her in."

"Yes, sir." Wondering what the maximum was for murder in Pennsylvania, Valerie forced herself to face the Cheshire smile on Maria's red lips. "You may go right in, Miss Cinelli."

"Of course I may," Maria taunted. "There was never any doubt of that."

Valerie decided then and there that she hated Maria Cinelli. She may as well wear a sign on her back that reads "for sale—expensive," she thought waspishly, as she watched that slender back glide into Thorne's office.

The door clicked shut with what sounded to Valerie like sharp finality. Turning back to her typewriter, she tried to relieve her frustration by attacking the innocent keys.

One white sheet of paper followed another around the roller, and still the connecting door remained firmly closed. Pounding away, making mistakes at a rate she had not equalled since leaving the Paris office, Valerie tried in vain to keep the questions at bay. Is Maria pleading with him to be taken back, into his life as well as the office? Is she succeeding? What *is* going on in there? Valerie shook her head suddenly, fiercely. The questions were bad enough. But with the last one came a mental picture of the long white couch in Jonas's office. The figures on the couch were tangled in an intimate embrace, and on the face of one, red lips curved in a smile of triumph.

"Oh, blast," Valerie muttered aloud as several keys, all positioned to strike the paper at the same time, stuck tightly together. What was the matter with her? Hadn't he as much as told her her job was secure? As to the other part of the picture, what did she care who he fooled around with? Valerie assured herself she did not care—all the while swallowing against the sick feeling that climbed from her stomach to her throat.

Thirty-odd minutes later, Valerie cast the still closed door a sour look as she left the office to go to lunch. When she returned, the door stood wide open and Thorne's office was empty. As she circled her desk to sit down, a dark scrawl across her dictation pad caught her eye.

I'm leaving for the day. Have Charlie keep my 2:30 appointment.

J. T.

Well, that about says it all, Valerie thought tiredly. Suppressing a sigh, she lifted the receiver to call Charlie McAndrew.

By quitting time Valerie was in a mood so foul that

even Janet could not tease her out of it. That mood had not changed when she reentered the office Wednesday morning. A call from Charlie McAndrew informing her that Jonas had flown to Chicago for the rest of the week did nothing to relieve her irritability. Nor did the news, imparted by Loretta at lunchtime, that Maria had also left town.

Damn Thorne *and* his paramour, Valerie cursed silently through most of Thursday and Friday. The weekend brought thoughts of escape. Perhaps I'll just chuck the whole thing and hunt for another job, she decided late Sunday night, preferably in another city, or another state. Would Thorne give her a decent reference?

"Good morning, Valerie," Thorne greeted her pleasantly as he strolled into her office five minutes after her arrival on Monday morning.

For some obscure reason his casual use of her given name set the spark to her fuse, which had become very short over the weekend.

"Good morning, *sir*," she returned with icy brittleness.

The change in his demeanor was both instant and somewhat frightening.

"Something on your mind?" he asked smoothly. Then added, even more smoothly, "Val?"

"Yes," Valerie snapped, unreasonably angered by his deliberate shortening of her name. "I want to tender my resignation."

"Fine," he snapped back, pivoting around and striding to the connecting door. "Tender it in writing."

His mockery of her terminology affecting her like a slap in the face, Valerie flounced around the desk.

Without bothering to sit down, she snatched the cover off her typewriter, rolled a sheet of paper into it, and with trembling fingers tapped out her resignation.

Still not pausing to consider the rashness of her actions, she stormed into Thorne's office and presented the sheet of paper to him wordlessly. Moving slowly, lazily, Thorne accepted the paper. Then, after barely glancing at the contents, he tore it in half and dropped it into his waste paper basket.

"Now," he said softly. "Suppose you sit down and tell me what in hell this is all about?"

His soft tone didn't fool her for a second. Suddenly all the annoyance drained out of Valerie and she felt utterly tired, and unbelievably stupid. What had he done to earn her disdain, really? The words, "Get rid of her," slithered into her mind, and Valerie realized with a shock that she had, in a way, been trying to punish him for them ever since. But what did they have to do with her, for heaven's sake? Had she designated herself the champion of her entire sex? A swift image of Maria's smirking face brought an equally swift answer to her question—not very likely.

"I'm waiting, Valerie." Jonas's sharp tone nudged her into alertness. But what could she say?

"I—think it would be best if I left your employ," she told him weakly.

"Best for you—or me?"

"For me."

"Why?"

Why? Why? Because the idea of you and Maria together sickens me, that's why. Maria or any other woman. Valerie stiffened visibly as the truth hammered its way through the mental defenses she'd erected.

God! She had to get out of here. But first she had to tell him *something*.

"Advancement," Valerie clutched at the first thought that came to mind.

"Strange." His tone, softly musing this time, was belied by his coldly calculating expression. "You didn't strike me as being a career woman." He paused, his eyes measuring her. "What sort of advancement?"

"W-What do you mean?" Valerie was beginning to feel uncomfortable under his penetrating gaze.

"I mean, what are your goals? Your long-range goals? What do you want out of life?"

"Want?" Valerie repeated confusedly.

"Yes, want," Thorne probed relentlessly. "From life, eventually?"

Where, she wondered, had she lost the thread of this conversation? It was obvious Thorne was no longer talking about her job. Unable to figure out his purpose, Valerie answered truthfully.

"The same as most women want, I guess. A home, some contentment. Children."

"Children!" Thorne repeated in feigned astonishment. "That will be difficult to manage, won't it?"

"Why should it be?" Valerie bristled.

Leaning back in his chair, Thorne ran a lazily assessing glance over her. "Well, a mate is required to produce children. Not a husband, necessarily, but a man." His thin lips curved mockingly. "And the word's around that you're off men."

Hot anger seared through Valerie, the power of it making her shake. Clenching her hands into tight fists she stood up just so she could look down on him.

"There will be a husband." She pushed the words

through her teeth. "I intend *my* children to have legitimacy as well as a father."

"I'm glad to hear it," Thorne applauded. Goaded beyond caring what she said, Valerie went on the attack.

"And what do *you* want from life?"

Thorne didn't bat an eye. "A son," he replied instantly. "An heir to all this." He waved his hand to encompass the building.

"But I thought you already had an heir!" Valerie exclaimed. Janet had told her that though Thorne was now single, he had been married once. Although the union had been short-lived, it had produced a child.

"That's correct, I have." Thorne nodded. "A daughter."

Valerie blinked in surprise. Why had she thought he was different? Because of Janet and a number of other women who had advanced according to their talent and ability? But then, conferring advancement on employees was not quite the same as conferring an entire company on a daughter.

"And a daughter isn't good enough?"

"Don't be stupid," Thorne retorted. "I'd have been proud to have her take over in time, *if* she had been interested. The sad truth is, Valerie, my daughter's interest in this firm is totally centered on her monthly allowance check, nothing more."

"I'm sorry," Valerie murmured, blushing.

"So am I," Thorne returned. He shrugged. "That's the way it goes." He ran his eyes over her again as he slowly stood up. Then, as if coming to a sudden decision, he shocked her speechless by quietly asking, "Would you consider being my son's mother?"

Valerie felt her mouth drop open slightly. She was

powerless to close it. Had she heard him correctly? Apparently she had, for he repeated his question. Beginning to shake her head, she opened her mouth to answer him. He didn't give her the chance.

"I'm not suggesting anything clandestine, Val." His smile twisted strangely. "I also want legitimacy for my child. I'm asking you to marry me."

"But why me?" she blurted out.

"Why not?" Thorne countered.

"We barely know each other, that's why not," Val cried.

"Does anyone ever know anyone else?" Thorne questioned. "You just told me what you want. You know me well enough to be assured I can give it to you. And I assume you are physically capable of giving me what I want." His eyebrows arched, "Right?"

Valerie nodded in automatic response.

"Well, then." He forged ahead before she could voice a protest. "Why not join forces and each supply the other's wants?"

"Because I don't—" She got no further.

"I know you are still hanging on to the memory of a dead love," Thorne stated coldly. "But if you are ever going to achieve your goal you're going to have to let go sometime. For your own sake, I think the sooner you let go, the better."

Valerie was trembling from the cruelty of his advice. Gritting her teeth she began, "Mr. Thorne—"

"Jonas." Again he would not let her speak. Striding around the desk he grasped her arms with his big hands. "You're going to have to face cold, hard reality sometime, Val. I'm giving you the opportunity to face it comfortably, from behind a protective cushioning of wealth." He smiled at her widened eyes. "Yes, Val, I'm a wealthy man, and I'm willing to make you a full partner. All you have to do for it is produce one son."

"You can fill a field with daughters, while hoping for a son." Valerie repeated one of her father's sayings, feeling like an idiot even while she spoke.

"I won't ask you to go that far," Thorne drawled. "If you are wise, Valerie, you'll consider your answer very carefully. You said your plans include a husband. Well, as far as husband material goes, I'm probably the best thing going."

Chapter Five

*Y*ou damned arrogant fool! he silently berated himself.

She was going to say no. And it was his own fault. The best thing going, indeed! Jonas watched the play of emotions on Valerie's face for several long seconds then, when she still did not speak, he released her arms and strode to the window to stare out, his jaw clenched so hard the bones hurt.

God, he wanted her! The sun glaring off the hoods and roofs of the rows of cars parked in the building's rear lot was an assault on the eyes and he narrowed his lids against it. He couldn't remember the last time he'd wanted a woman quite this badly. And she was going to say no. He knew it and the frustration of that knowing clawed at his guts.

He'd never taken time to regret his decisions. He'd never had time for regrets of any kind. But right now, this minute, he was sorry as hell that he'd indulged Janet by bringing Val back with him. I should have left her in Paris, he thought savagely. Left her to wallow in her grief and self-pity.

Sliding his hands into his pants pockets, Jonas massaged his knotted upper thighs with the tips of his fingers. What the hell kind of man had he been, this Etienne, this dead lover of Val's?

Fingertips dug painfully into taut muscles as a picture formed before his eyes, obscuring the sight of lot, cars, and even the brilliant sunlight. In the picture Val lay with her glorious black hair spread out around her head. Her breathtaking violet eyes were softened by love and her white arms and whiter legs encircled the shadowy form of a faceless man. Dead or not, Jonas hated the thought of that faceless man.

"Mr. Thorne?"

The soft, hesitant sound of Val's voice dissolved the mirage. Releasing his breath slowly, silently, Jonas turned to face her. "Yes?" At that moment he was sure he knew exactly what a man facing a firing squad feels.

"Could I have some time?" His fingers dug yet deeper as he watched her wet her lips. Had she done that on purpose?

"How much time?" Jonas cursed himself for his cold tone when he saw her wince.

"Until—tomorrow morning?"

A reprieve, and he hadn't even heard the phone ring when the governor called. Reprieve hell! He felt like he was hanging on a very sharp hook. Why don't you tell her to get out of your life and get it over with? he advised himself mockingly. Because I still want her, that's why.

"Of course," he answered coolly. "Would you like the rest of the day to yourself?" Say yes, please, he pleaded silently, and get out of my sight so I can think straight.

"No." The sun struck glinting blue lights off her hair as she shook her head. "That won't be necessary."

That's easy for you to say. Jonas watched the smooth movement of Val's body as she walked to the door.

Your mind's been numbed by grief and your body's immune to arousal. The door closed with a final-sounding click. I wish I could say the same for my body.

With a grim smile of self-mockery pulling at his lips, Jonas walked to his desk and lowered his long frame into the padded chair. Resting his head against the back of the chair, he lifted one hand to massage his temple. Lord, he was tired, and he didn't like that. He was hardly ever tired, at least not at this time of the morning. And he could never remember being *this* kind of tired.

It seemed there really was a first time for everything. But who needed all these firsts within less than a month? Never before had he had to fight to suppress an almost relentless physical desire for almost three weeks. Yet the opportunity for satisfaction had presented itself in the very lovely form of Maria Cinelli and he had simply not been interested.

Moving his head restlessly, Jonas closed his eyes, fully aware that he was experiencing another first by ignoring the work on his desk. The physical need for that one particular woman has rattled your brain as well as your libido, he told himself dryly.

Why? Why the urgency to possess this particular woman? Eyes still closed, Jonas examined the question clinically. True, she is a very beautiful woman, in a wistful, elusive way. But thousands of women are beautiful, in as many different ways. So why this one? She'd certainly never given him any encouragement. The only side of her he'd seen thus far had been the prickly side.

The grim smile disappeared. Now you're getting close, Thorne. Close hell, he was on top of it, and he knew it. Had known where his convoluted train of thought was heading right along. He knew exactly why, and when.

The ride from Edouard Barres's Paris office to the airport had seemed surprisingly short, and not only because Barres's Mercedes ate up the distance so smoothly. He and Edouard had been involved in business meetings and discussions that whole week and still the ideas and plans flowed like a never-ending river between them. Jonas respected Edouard's knowledge and expertise and he was well aware the respect was reciprocated. Even after the car had pulled to a stop he had paused in the act of alighting to give consideration to Edouard's last remark.

Still pondering the feasibility of Edouard's idea, Jonas had taken very little notice of the two women waiting for him, merely nodding in Janet's direction as he walked to the plane. He had just reached the decision that Barres's idea was very probably worth the time, energy and money that would be required to develop it when the screech of tires broke through his concentration.

About to enter the plane, he had turned to find the source of the racket, and groaned silently. What's-her-name, the rising young whatever of the French film industry, was running toward the plane screaming, "Darling, wait."

Darling? Sudden irritation quickly bloomed into full anger. Damning Edouard for his stupid dinner party, and himself for going in the first place, he stepped by Parker with a tersely ordered, "Get rid of her," knowing full well that Parker would.

Inside the plane, he headed straight for the bourbon. Glass in hand, he started toward his seat, stopping midstride when Janet's fledgling entered the compartment. In the few seconds the door was open, the pleading, somewhat rehearsed, and definitely hysterical sound of the actress's voice reached him and his anger changed to disgust with the female sex in general. They were all leeches! The only difference being that they sucked a man's money as well as his blood.

The blanket condemnation was unfair, and he knew it. Jonas had been around long enough to realize there were every bit as many male leeches in the world as female; maybe more. At that moment, though, he wasn't too concerned with being fair.

Lifting his glass to sip at the bourbon, he studied the young woman who stood, seemingly mesmerized, just inside the doorway.

Beautiful package, he mused. Lovely face. Good figure. Perfect breasts. Big deal. If what Janet had told him about her was true, and he had no reason to doubt Janet's word, she had turned her back on life. Had he come all this way to end up playing nursemaid to a stupid little fool with a death wish? That thought in no way sweetened his disposition.

Why had Maria picked this particular time to do her disappearing act? Jonas fumed. He knew the answer, of course. She was pushing him, turning the rack. At least, *she* thought she was. Jonas suppressed a sigh. He would have thought, after all this time, that she'd know better than to actually put the screws to him.

All the while he was ruminating on Maria's unwise actions, his eyes remained fixed on Valerie Jordan. Now he moved impatiently to her. Was she in a stupor, for God's sake? Biting down on his anger, he extended his hand.

"I gather you are Valerie Jordan?"

"Yes."

Jonas felt his lids narrow in automatic response to the iciness of her tone. For the first time in his life he had to fight the urge to strike a woman. Sure that if he gripped her hand he'd crush it, he briefly brushed her fingers before withdrawing.

"Jonas Thorne." Jonas made his tone insultingly curt. "Your employer." The last was a deliberate nudge. Watching her closely, he felt a tiny flicker of respect at the fearless way she returned his stare. *Was* she fearless, he wondered, or was she past caring about anything? Jonas decided to find out.

"You *do* want the job, Miss Jordan?"

"Yes, sir."

Ahh, better, much better. At least she cared about something. Pivoting away from her, he advised her to sit down and buckle up, and then he dismissed her from his mind; or he tried to.

Her spark of defiance had drawn an answering spark of interest from him. After the plane was airborne, he got down to work with Janet in an attempt to ignore Valerie's presence. Doing so proved not only difficult, but almost impossible. Janet's concern for her friend was obvious, and she repeatedly shot worried glances across the aisle. That was another thing in Valerie's favor. Jonas knew Janet. She was not a woman to expend time and energy on a total washout.

His inability to give his complete concentration to his work stirred fresh anger in Jonas. Not one to evade any issue, he faced the fact that he was much too aware of Valerie's slightest movement. Although Janet thought she was asleep, Jonas knew better. Valerie Jordan was playing possum, studying them through slitted eyelids. This deepened his anger to the point that when Janet assured him he would not be sorry for taking Valerie back to the States, he deliberately drawled a disbelieving, "We'll see."

When he'd finished briefing Janet on the Paris transactions, he tilted his seat back and played his own game of possum while returning her careful regard.

How had he known? What had been the tip off? She certainly had not betrayed herself. To anyone else watching her she would have appeared soundly asleep. Yet, somehow, Jonas knew the moment she decided to prove him wrong about her. And, at that moment, everything alive inside his body responded to that decision. The feeling of sexual excitement that had gone through his body at that moment was one he had not experienced in a very long time—if ever.

A very sobering thought. Not curative, but sobering. Sitting in his chair, behind the enormous desk, eyes closed, a small smile tugged at Jonas's harshly etched lips. I want that woman. After nearly three weeks of continual want, there's no doubt at all. I want that woman more than I've ever wanted anything. And I'm going to have her. With or without her consent.

Lifting his lids lazily, his gleaming eyes focused on the long white couch. You had better come up with the right answer tomorrow morning, my sweet, he advised Valerie silently. Or you just may find yourself on that couch, giving me what I want without benefit of the legal sanctions.

He was still tormenting himself with picturing the scene when his private phone rang.

His lips twisting in self-mockery, he snatched up the receiver and growled, "Thorne."

"Jonas, it's Marge," his ex-mother-in-law said hesitantly. "Am I disturbing you?"

Not nearly as much as my own thoughts, he answered silently. Aloud, he soothed, "Not at all. What's up, Marge?"

That something unusual had happened he was sure. Marge never called him at the office on a mere whim.

"I got a letter from Mary Beth." Marge's voice hummed with excitement.

"And?" Jonas prompted.

"Jonas, she's coming home." Marge sounded ready to explode. "Our baby's coming home."

"When?" Jonas's tone revealed none of the emotions leaping in his body. Their baby. His baby. His Mary Beth.

"She's booked a flight for May fifteenth, the day after school's over. Oh, Jonas, I can hardly wait. She's been away so long."

"Yes, I know," Jonas murmured. Although he knew the date, his eyes shifted to his desk calendar. April sixth. Six weeks. Six weeks and he'd have her home again. How would she react to Valerie? The thought was a revealing one. Pushing it aside temporarily, Jonas addressed the more immediate question. "I'm afraid you have no choice but to wait, Marge. But I have a suggestion on how you could fill the time."

"Do you? What is it?" Marge's eagerness was endearing.

"Why don't you fix up her bedroom? As a matter of fact, go the whole route, redecorate completely."

"May I, Jonas? Really?"

Jonas could practically see the wheels turning in Marge's head. The image amused him and he laughed softly. "Yes, Marge, you really may." Suddenly the laughter was gone and his voice held a hint of rebuke.

"I would have thought, by now, that you wouldn't have to ask."

"Oh, Jonas—"

"Never mind, Marge." Jonas sighed. How many times had they had this same kind of conversation? "Make as many changes as you like. Don't—I repeat—don't consider cost. Remember, it's all for Mary Beth. Send the bills to me here at the office."

"Thank you, Jonas, I—"

"Marge." Jonas cut in on her teary-sounding voice. "Enough, okay? Oh yes, don't plan on me for dinner tonight."

"All right." Marge paused, then murmured timidly, "And—Jonas? I love you, you know."

"Yes, Marge, I do know," Jonas replied huskily.

Jonas sat staring at the phone long minutes after he'd replaced the receiver. What a woman, he mused. Too bad the daughter was so unlike the mother.

That thought was the catapult that flung him into the past.

He was seventeen the first time he saw her. Seventeen and hungry for life, starved for affection, filled with unnamed desires.

It was midsummer and it was hot. It was lunchtime, and he was starving, but, as he was also broke, he faced the empty feeling in his stomach stoically. It was nothing new. He was nearly always hungry and always broke.

A sound—half-sigh, half-groan of relief—hissed through his lips as he entered the small air-conditioned appliance shop. For an ecstatic moment he closed his eyes, savoring the cool air against his sweaty skin. For

95

another moment he gave in to the weariness pulling at him. He'd been up at four and by four-thirty he'd just about finished squeezing the carton of juice oranges for the breakfast trade. The small diner where he'd worked for over a year now as short order cook was not air-conditioned.

Jonas's moment of delight in the sweet coolness came to an abrupt end when someone entered the shop behind him, and a young female voice called, "Daddy, where are you? You've got a customer out here."

Swiveling around, Jonas felt the breath hiss out of him again, only this time not from the cold.

She was young, somewhere around his own age, Jonas guessed, and the most beautiful thing he'd ever laid eyes on. She had sun-kissed gold hair and skin tanned to a golden brown. Bright blue eyes sparkled in a face that belonged on a goddess, and her red mouth pouted prettily at him. As if her face alone were not enough of an assault on his senses, she had a figure that wouldn't quit, with high, pointed breasts that seemed to quiver under his gaze. Suddenly, painfully, all of his vague, unnamed desires were centered on that one female body.

"Hi, can I help you?" She asked sweetly. "I don't know where Daddy is."

"Uh yeah, that is, I don't know." Feeling like a jerk, Jonas felt his face redden. "I saw the sign in the window." At her blank, frowning expression, he stuttered on, "The—the help wanted sign? I—I came in to apply."

"Oh, that." Her red lips parted to reveal small, white teeth. "Sure, you can apply, that is, if I ever find Daddy." She paused to draw a deep breath—an exercise that had Jonas staring in reaction to the thrusting lift of her breasts—then she yelled again, "Daddy?"

"For crying in a bucket, Lynn, I heard you the first time."

Jonas spun to face the rear of the shop and the gruff-voiced man entering it from a back room. Lynn! Her name was Lynn. Beautiful.

"I brought your lunch." Lynn walked to the counter and deposited a brown paper bag Jonas had not even noticed she'd been holding. "And this guy," she tipped her gold head at Jonas, "wants to apply for the job you have open."

"Okay, thanks, honey." Although his tone had altered, the voice was still rough.

Jonas had been aware that he was being scrutinized by sharp blue eyes ever since the medium-sized, stocky man had entered the shop. Dragging his gaze from Lynn, he coolly returned her father's appraisal. The man had closely cropped, curly blond hair, a shade darker than his daughter's, and his face had a ruddy hue that spoke of high blood pressure or too much alcohol, or both. He was overweight, but his shoulders and arms were muscular and hard-looking. The bright blue eyes that returned Jonas's stare were shrewd.

"Okay, honey, I'll take care of him." He shot a quick smile at the girl. "Run along."

"Can I have a dollar, Daddy?" she coaxed. "It's so hot. I want to stop for a coke."

The sweetness of her voice charmed Jonas and had he possessed a buck himself he'd have whipped it out and offered it to her. She obviously had a similar effect on her father, for he dug in his pants pocket and withdrew a bill, handing it to her with a rueful grin.

"A coke costs a dollar now?" he teased.

"No, silly," she teased back. "But I want to treat a friend." As she turned to leave she shot Jonas a mischievious smile.

"Stosh Kowalski."

The rough voice penetrated Jonas's bemusement and he shifted his eyes back to Lynn's father.

"Jonas Thorne, sir," he replied respectfully, stepping closer to grip Stosh's outstretched hand. "I came in to inquire about the help wanted sign in your window." Not a hint of the stuttering boy remained in Jonas's demeanor. Without Lynn's tongue-tying presence he was all business—and all premature man.

"You know anything about electrical appliances or television repair?" Stosh asked, not unkindly.

"No, sir," Jonas answered truthfully. "But I learn fast, and I work hard." Jonas watched as Stosh ran his gaze over his tall, too skinny frame, and felt his hopes sink. He was unaware that though his lanky body appeared weak, his face had strength of purpose and determination indelibly stamped on it.

"You out of school, son?"

"No, sir," Jonas admitted. "I have one more year to go. But," he went on quickly, "I can work full time for the rest of the summer, and after school during the winter. As many hours as you'd want."

"Wouldn't your parents object?"

"I have no parents, sir," Jonas said steadily. "I live in a foster home."

"And your foster parents would have no objections?" Stosh probed gently, his eyes observing the wisp of a cynical smile that fleetingly touched Jonas's lips.

"No, sir," Jonas answered flatly. Jonas forced himself to breathe normally as Stosh Kowalski's eyes measured his worth. A sigh of released tension whispered through his lips when the older man grinned.

"Okay, Jonas." Stosh nodded his head once, decisively. "I'll give you a try. I usually come in around eight so I can get some uninterrupted work done in back before opening the store at nine-thirty. What time could you start?"

Jonas considered a moment, taking his own measure of Stosh Kowalski, then he decided to lay all his cards on the table. "I've been working for over a year at the Sunrise Diner on the other side of town. I work the grill for breakfast and finish at eight-thirty when the lunch and suppertime cook comes in. I could be here by ten minutes to nine, if that would be all right?"

"You want to work both jobs?" Stosh frowned.

"Yes, sir," Jonas said firmly.

"I'd want you to stay until six most nights. What time do you start at the Sunrise?"

"Four-thirty."

"Four-thirty!" Stosh exclaimed. "You're talking one hell of a long day, kid. Can you handle it?"

"Yes, sir."

Something in his tone convinced Stosh, for, after giving Jonas a long, hard stare, he shrugged, then grinned. "Okay, Jonas, I'll give you a try. You can start tomorrow morning at nine o'clock."

"Thank you, sir."

"I appreciate the 'sir', kid, but it's not necessary. We're going to be working together all day. Call me Stosh."

When he left the shop some ten minutes later, Jonas was so buoyed by the idea of earning more money for his college fund that he almost missed seeing Lynn standing under the tattered awning of a tiny dress shop two buildings away. As he drew alongside her she said, pertly, "Did you get the job?"

Yanked out of his own thoughts, Jonas turned to face her and felt the blood begin to pound through his body again. Gosh, she was pretty!

"Yes." He grinned idiotically.

"Good." Lynn grinned back, starting to walk up the street. After only several steps she stopped and jerked her head in a beckoning motion. "How about a coke to celebrate?"

Jonas felt his heart sink. "I don't have any money," he said tightly.

"That's okay." Lynn grinned. "I have a whole dollar. It'll be my treat." When Jonas hesitated, she teased, "Come on, dopey, I've been waiting for you to come out for what seems forever. I'm hot and thirsty. Let's go."

Completely enchanted, Jonas went, feeling as though he'd been blessed by heaven. Even the teasing "dopey" sounded enchanting.

Jonas was hardly aware of his none too clean surroundings as he sat across the table from her in a booth in the corner of a small luncheonette. And afterward he never could remember what they talked about. All he knew was that she was the prettiest thing he'd ever seen and he wanted to touch her gold hair and kiss her red mouth. He didn't, of course. At least, not that afternoon.

"Are your parents dead, Jonas?" Stosh asked quietly five minutes after he'd reported for work the following morning.

"My mother is. She died while I was being born,"

Jonas answered stiffly. "I don't know about my father. She was alone when she had me. I'm a bastard," he finished starkly.

The bright blue eyes resting on his suddenly harsh-looking face flickered with compassion. "Were there no grandparents or relatives willing to take you in?" Stosh asked in astonishment.

"No." Jonas shook his head slowly. "She wasn't from Tamaqua. In fact, no one could find out where she was from. She just showed up at a rooming house across town one day and rented a room. She worked as a waitress somewhere up until a couple of days before I was born. Apparently she never saw a doctor and if it hadn't been for the owner of the rooming house who heard her muffled screams and sent for his own doctor, she probably wouldn't have lived long enough to deliver me." Jonas paused, amazed at himself for offering the information so freely. He'd never told anyone about his history before, and yet, there was something about Stosh's shrewd blue eyes that instilled the urge to confide. With a fatalistic shrug, Jonas ended his story. "She lived long enough to name me, but I don't know if Thorne was her name or the name of the man who fathered me. When they couldn't find out anything about her I was made a ward of the court and placed in a foster home." As had happened the afternoon before, Jonas' lips twisted cynically over the word "foster." "I've been in five different homes in seventeen years."

"Bad, huh?" Stosh probed.

"A couple of them were okay." Jonas lifted his shoulders in an unconvincingly careless shrug. "Mostly the people just wanted the money they were paid for my keep."

"And the people you're with now?" Stosh probed deeper.

Jonas hesitated, then, looking him straight in the eyes, said bluntly, "He's a brutal slob and she's a shrew."

Stosh was not altogether successful in masking his surprised shock at the open disgust in Jonas's tone.

"That's a strong condemnation, son," he said quietly.

This time Jonas's shrug *was* careless. "Not saying the truth out loud doesn't change it. The day I turn eighteen, I'm getting out." His mouth curled in a sneer. "They'd probably throw me out anyway—that's when the money stops."

"Have they treated you very badly, Jonas?" The slow, measured tempo of Stosh's question revealed the outrage he was feeling.

Jonas shook his head slowly. He was done talking. There was no point in complaining about the physical abuse he'd taken from the heavy-fisted man, or the shrill, vocal abuse he'd been subjected to from the strident-voiced woman. Or even the long hours he'd had to work on the small farm his foster parents owned. Jonas had always been too thin for his long frame and the authorities had genuinely believed that the fresh country air would be beneficial to his health when they'd placed him at the farm. And, in truth, it had been. At least, physically. For, even though he still appeared undernourished, the seven years of hard physical labor he'd put in on the farm had toughened his muscles to tempered steel. The last time his foster-father had struck him—just two months previously—Jonas had curled his large hand into a fist and knocked him flat. Jonas hadn't been abused since. The memory brought a satisfied smile to his face.

Stosh frowned, wondering at the meaning behind the young man's unpleasant smile, but, prudently, he did not probe any further. Leading Jonas into the workroom behind the shop, he said, "Okay, kid, let's get started."

For Jonas, that day was the beginning of a lifelong love affair between his mind and everything electrical. While he was on the job he lost himself completely in his work. During the other hours of the day and night, he was consumed with thoughts of the golden-haired Lynn.

Unwittingly, Stosh himself arranged their second meeting a little over a week after Jonas began working for him.

Although it was not yet nine o'clock that Saturday morning in late July, it was steamy hot. The unusual length and intensity of the heat wave had left even the most hardy residents of Tamaqua wilted and gasping. A humid haze hung like a pall over the city and in every dip and hollow of the heavily mined mountains surrounding it. Even the ugliness of the slag banks was softened by the shimmering heat waves.

Jonas entered the shop as Stosh was putting the telephone receiver in its cradle.

"You remember what I showed you about replacing the timer in a refrigerator on Wednesday?" he asked.

"Yes."

"Do you have a driver's license?"

"Yes," Jonas repeated.

"That was the wife I was talking to when you came in." Stosh indicated the phone. "She called to tell me the fridge is acting up." Stosh grimaced. "And in this weather, too. From the way she described it, I think the timer went. Do you want to take a shot at fixing it?"

"Yes, *sir*." Jonas grinned.

"You're on." Stosh grinned back. Digging into his pocket he withdrew a ring of keys and tossed them to Jonas. "Take my car. There's a replacement timer in the parts case in the trunk." He gave Jonas directions to his small ranch house on the outskirts of town, then waved him off with a warned, "Take your time. I want it done right."

Jonas had no trouble at all finding Stosh's home. He did have trouble with his breathing when Lynn opened the door seconds after he rang the bell. She was dressed in tight shorts and a halter top that barely covered her small breasts, and it was obvious she'd been sunbathing —her body was covered by a mixture of glistening suntan oil and perspiration.

"Hi, dopey," she said disspiritedly. "What do you want?"

"Your dad sent me over to fix the refrigerator," Jonas managed to articulate without stuttering. To an older, more experienced man, Lynn's moody eyes and pouting lips would have been a clear indication of her sulkiness. To Jonas, however, her eyes looked sexy and her lips wet and inviting.

"I didn't even know the dumb thing was broken." She shrugged, pulling the door wide as she stepped back. "I was lying in the sun. Come in." As Jonas walked past her she said, "I hope you know what's wrong with it, 'cause Mom's not here to tell you; she went shopping."

"I know what's wrong with it," Jonas assured her, his

eyes following her every movement as he trailed her to the kitchen.

Plopping herself onto a kitchen chair, Lynn chattered at him the whole time he worked, her petulant tone changing to one of interest as she observed the play of previously unnoticed muscles in his broad shoulders and long arms. She left the kitchen while he was washing his hands at the kitchen sink after the fridge was again running smoothly.

"Jonas, can you come in here and help me, please?" Lynn's voice floated to him as he dried his hands.

"Sure," he answered, wandering out of the kitchen and into a short hallway. "Where are you?"

"In here," she called from a room about halfway along the hall. Jonas walked to the open doorway and stopped dead when he saw it was her bedroom. "I can't get this knot open. Will you see if you can untie it?" Lynn was standing beside her unmade bed, her back to him, her fingers tugging at the knot closing of her halter top.

His pulses hammering, Jonas crossed the carpeted floor and with trembling fingers brushed her hands away and went to work on the knot. The second the cotton ends fluttered apart, he dropped his hands to his sides.

Before he could move, Lynn swung around to face him, curling her arms up and around her golden head as she turned. Jonas sucked air into his suddenly tight chest as the swathe of white cotton dropped to the floor.

Chapter Six

$\mathcal{A}$ part of Jonas's mind knew he should get out of that room, that house, but a bigger part wanted to feast his eyes on the perfection of her small, round, upturned breasts. The bigger part won.

"Do you want to touch me?" Lynn asked softly, teasingly.

"Yes," Jonas answered in a croaking whisper.

"Well, do it then, dopey," she laughed.

Raising an arm that felt weighted by lead, Jonas reached out and touched the tips of his trembling fingers to the smooth skin at the outside curve of one breast.

"Oh, you dopey," Lynn chided. "You call that touching?" Lowering one arm she caught his wrist with her hand. Following the pull of her fingers, he cupped the silky mound with his hand. The hard little nipple seemed to poke at his palm, sending a sweet stab of pain shooting into his loins.

His fingers clutching convulsively, Jonas bent his head to hers, his mouth opening as it made contact.

The feel of her small tongue sent a shudder along the length of his spine. Lynn's hand still grasped his wrist and when she sank onto the rumpled bed she pulled him down on top of her. His lips were dislodged from hers when they hit the mattress and Jonas heard the breath go out of her body.

Concerned that the force of his body striking hers might have hurt her, he rolled over, then pulled her tightly against him. His hips thrust against Lynn's body in automatic urgency.

"Ohh, dopey," Lynn whispered thickly, wriggling her own hips slowly. "Aren't you going to kiss my breasts?" she half demanded, half pleaded.

"God, yes," Jonas groaned, the very idea of placing his lips against her skin exciting him further. The feel of her oiled skin on his lips set his body on fire, and taking the hard little nipple inside his mouth, stroking it with his tongue, was exquisite torture.

Without even being aware of the motions, his hands moved down her slippery body to tug and yank at her shorts. Lynn's hands brushed his away impatiently.

"I'll do it," she whispered. "You worry about your own."

Fumbling in his haste, Jonas got to his feet. After yanking open the snap on the waistband of his worn jeans, he undid the zipper. His shorts followed his jeans to the floor and he stepped out of them.

Jonas was a virgin. Lynn was not. And so, it was Lynn who guided him at first, teaching him the art of lovemaking until instinct took over. And it was in her soft embrace that Jonas gained a knowledge of full manhood.

Summer limped along, and Jonas's life seemed suddenly comprised of highs and lows. The highs were reached simply by stepping into the workroom behind the appliance shop. The lows were caused by the fact that seeing Lynn proved not only difficult, but nearly impossible. He knew she was dating another guy, because he had seen them together. And that knowledge only increased his frustration.

As the weeks of unusually hot humid weather melted one into the other, Jonas burned in two ways: on the outside from the heat of the sun, and on the inside from the constant rage of desire.

That rage was appeased briefly at the very beginning of September. An organization Stosh belonged to was having a Labor Day clambake and when Stosh asked Jonas if he'd like to go as a family guest, Jonas accepted eagerly.

Jonas had never been to a clambake, and although he enjoyed the early part of the day, and the food, he did not enjoy the party's deterioration as the sun trekked westward. Laughter grew shrill and voices grew raucously louder as more and more beer was consumed. At seventeen, Jonas did not like the taste of beer. At eighteen, thinking it adult and sophisticated, Lynn did.

Jonas was not the only one to frown in Lynn's direction when she asked for her third glass of beer. In fact, Marge Kowalski did more than frown. Although she spoke softly, Jonas heard Lynn's mother's words of rebuke.

Jonas had spoken to Marge several times when she'd stopped by the shop, and he liked her. She was friendly in a soft-spoken, quiet way that appealed to him. If one were allowed to *choose* a mother, Jonas would have chosen Marge without hesitation.

Lynn did not share his opinion. Spoiled by Stosh, who indulged her slightest whim, she resented every attempt Marge made to control her.

At Marge's cautionary words about the beer, Lynn

drained her glass, slammed it onto the wooden picnic table, and flounced off fuming. Jonas trailed behind her like a devoted puppy.

Ignoring everyone who called out to her, Lynn stormed away from the picnic grounds into the wooded area of the foothills. Up until that point Jonas had followed her quietly, but it was growing dark, and he was afraid he'd lose sight of her.

"Lynn, where are you going?" he called out.

"None of your business," Lynn snapped peevishly. Then, as his lengthened stride brought him alongside her, she whined, "Go away. You're as bad as she is. I saw your face when I took that last glass of beer."

"I don't know how you can drink that stuff," Jonas observed mildly.

"I *like* drinking that stuff." Lynn pouted. "It makes me feel good." Coming to an abrupt stop she turned on him angrily. "So what?"

"Oh, Lynn, let's not fight." Jonas sighed longingly.

His tone was not lost on her. With a lightning change in mood, she pouted prettily, suggestively, "Can you think of something better to do?"

Desire, never far away, licked through Jonas's body. Slowly he leaned toward her. With the touch of his lips on hers, Lynn took the initiative from his far less experienced hands.

Clasping her arms around his waist, she arched her body up against the hardness of him. Jonas stopped thinking entirely. Allowing himself to be led, he obeyed her dictates with hands that shook in his eagerness to learn. Even in his inexperience Jonas realized, jealously, that someone with a certain degree of expertise had been tutoring Lynn.

* * *

Jonas started back to school the day after the clam-bake. Soon his time was completely taken up with his studies and work in the appliance shop and he saw even less of Lynn.

One day near the end of November he found her waiting for him in her father's car when he left the shop.

"I have to talk to you," she said tersely the minute he'd folded his long frame into the passenger seat. Not a hint of premonition gave warning of the bald statement that followed.

"I'm pregnant, Jonas."

Everything froze inside him—his muscles, his blood, his mind.

"Did you hear me?" Lynn cried, breaking into the numbness that gripped his mind. "I said I'm going to have a baby. What are you going to do about it?"

What was he going to do? What could he do? His dreams of college and a career in electronics dissolving in his mind, Jonas answered steadily, "I'm going to marry you."

They drove directly to her home, Lynn's nervousness apparent in the restless movement of her hands on the steering wheel. Jonas was every bit as nervous, though he succeeded in hiding it. He hated the thought of facing Stosh and Marge with his betrayal of their kindness.

The telling was every bit as bad as Jonas had feared it would be. Stosh was at first shocked speechless; then he was very vocally furious. Marge, ever quiet, sat motionless in stunned disbelief. The expression on her face hurt Jonas far more than Stosh's angry tirade. When, finally, Marge did speak, her quiet words surprised them all.

"Stosh, that's enough." Marge's tone held soft command. "What's done is done. At least *Jonas* is willing to marry Lynn." It would be months before Jonas would understand the emphasis she placed on his name and the knowing look she ran over her daughter. "But I think it would be a mistake for him to quit school in his senior year."

Jonas had declared that he'd leave school at once to work full time at the shop. Listening to Marge, hope for his future was reignited.

"As a matter of fact," Marge continued, totally ignoring Jonas's attempted protests, "I see no reason why he should not go on to college as planned."

"Now, Marge, be practical," Stosh began heatedly.

"That is exactly what I am being." Marge cut him off with unaccustomed sharpness. "One of Jonas's teachers is an acquaintance of mine. When she found I know Jonas she told me that, in her opinion, Jonas has a brilliant mind and if he did not continue his education after high school it would be a sinful waste."

Jonas learned two things about Marge that night. First, that when she took a stand she could not be budged. And second, that she could not be intimidated. Nothing moved her, not Stosh's anger, not Lynn's tears, and not Jonas's own persuasive tactics. Marge set down the rules, and the rest of the family meekly carried them out. Lynn and Jonas would be married at once. They would make their home with Marge and Stosh. Jonas would stay in school.

Jonas and Lynn were married in a private ceremony conducted in the rectory of the church the Kowalski family attended. After the wedding Jonas went back to school and back to work. The only difference in his life was that now when he left the shop at night he went to a *real* home, and to the accommodating body of his wife.

For the first three months of their marriage, Jonas delighted in their lovemaking, firmly ignoring the realization that his bride was well versed in the art—too well versed. With satisfaction came doubt. And with doubt came the cooling of his ardor.

In late February an ugly suggestion made to Jonas by one of his classmates sent him home in a rage. Slamming into the house, he ordered a startled Lynn into the privacy of their bedroom where he demanded, hotly, "How do you know that kid's mine?"

"W-what do you mean?" Lynn stuttered, obviously frightened.

"I was just informed that the only reason you married me was because the guy you tried to trap into marriage wouldn't have you." Jonas yelled. "Is it true?"

"No, no—I," Lynn's denial dissolved into tears, but Jonas could read the guilt in her pretty face. Sick at heart, he cried, "Who is he?"

"His name is unimportant, Jonas." The answer came from Marge, who had entered the room unnoticed. "He has looks, and money, and a very bad reputation. Lynn fell for his line and became infatuated with him."

"I love him," Lynn screamed at her mother.

"Although it breaks my heart to admit it, Lynn," Marge said sadly, "I truly think you are incapable of loving anyone but yourself."

"What do you know about anything?" Lynn screamed.

"I know you've treated Jonas unfairly," Marge retorted. "Whether this is his baby or not."

"Unfair!" Lynn exclaimed shrilly. "He's getting what he wants!"

Jonas had heard enough. Brushing past Marge, he left the house. He did not go to work that day. Hands jammed into his jacket pockets, shoulders hunched against the bitter cold wind, he walked the streets for hours. By the time he returned to the house whatever it was he'd felt for Lynn—love, physical attraction, fascination with her lovely face—it was all gone. He did not hate her. He just didn't feel anything for her at all. Entering the house through the back door, Jonas found Marge waiting for him.

"Jonas, about the baby," Marge began timidly.

"I'll raise it," Jonas interrupted. "Whether it's mine or not." The smile that curved his mouth brought tears to Marge's eyes. "I know what it's like to be a bastard."

Though he slept beside her every night, Jonas never again touched his wife in a personal way. Made cautious by the new, unyielding set to his features, Lynn did not question him.

Jonas turned eighteen three days before his graduation from high school. Two weeks later Lynn was delivered of a baby girl. With his first look at her, Jonas knew the child was his. Marge knew it also.

"Oh, Jonas," she whispered in awe. "I'm so happy for you."

"Poor thing looks just like me," Jonas murmured, emotion clogging his throat. Gazing in mute adoration at the tiny life he'd created, Jonas vowed that never would she want for anything. Not as long as he lived, and even after, if he could arrange it.

Seven weeks after Mary Beth's birth, and one week after her christening, Lynn ran away with the man she claimed to love.

Jonas came home from work to find Stosh and Marge waiting for him in the living room. The baby clasped protectively in her arms, Marge sat rocking back and forth, tears chasing each other down her cheeks.

In silence, Jonas read the note Lynn had left for him.

Jonas,
Please try to understand. I'm too young to be tied to a man who hates me and a baby I don't want. I want to see something of the world. I want to have some fun. And I want to be with Leon.
Lynn

"This Leon," Jonas said when he'd finished reading. "Is he the one with the looks and money and reputation?"

"Yes," Marge sobbed.

"Okay," he sighed then, straightening his shoulders. "I'll leave as soon as I can find a place to stay and someone to keep Mary Beth."

"Leave?" Marge and Stosh repeated blankly. "Keep Mary Beth?"

"Yes, I don't expect—" Jonas began, only to be silenced by his in-laws, both speaking at once.

"Where would you go?"

"What about college?"

"I'll have to forget college," Jonas said flatly.

"You'll do nothing of the kind." Marge snorted. "And you will not take my granddaughter out of this house." Clutching the baby even closer to her body, Marge jumped to her feet. "Now you listen to me,

Jonas Thorne. You are going to stay right here. Both of you. And you are going to Lehigh as planned. You've worked too hard to have your future snatched away now. Do you understand me?"

Jonas glanced at Stosh as if seeking guidance. Stosh, holding up his hands, avowed, "I'm not going to argue with her. You better do as she says, son."

In September Jonas went to Bethlehem and Lehigh University. In mid-December Stosh suffered a series of massive strokes. Two days after Christmas, Stosh died in his sleep.

Once again Jonas declared his intention of leaving school. And once again Marge refused to let him.

"When you go back to school in January, I want you to look around for an apartment for the three of us," she told him calmly. Before Jonas could protest, she went on, "I'm going to put the house and business up for sale. With Stosh gone there is nothing to keep me in Tamaqua."

Even though Lynn's name was not mentioned, Jonas knew Marge was thinking of her. They had heard nothing at all from his wife. It was not even possible to inform her of her father's death.

Settling Stosh's estate took longer than expected and it was June before the move to Bethlehem was made. The apartment Jonas had rented was far from elegant, but it was large and located in a quiet neighborhood. And the rental was within the budget Jonas had worked out.

With the college grant he'd obtained and the money he earned from his new job at Bethlehem Steel, Jonas figured they could squeak through his school years. Ignoring every one of Marge's pleas, Jonas remained adamant in his refusal to take the money she offered him, claiming she was doing more than her share by taking care of Mary Beth.

For Jonas, life consisted of study and work. He saw very little of his daughter, and was, at intervals, amazed at the rate of her growth. After his fiasco with Lynn, he stayed away from women altogether, remaining celibate by choice.

They heard from Lynn for the first time shortly after Mary Beth's third birthday. Luckily, Jonas was at work when she called. As though history was repeating itself, Jonas came home from work to find Marge in tears. Understandably, he jumped to the wrong conclusion.

"Is something the matter with Mary Beth?" he asked at once.

"No, she's fine," Marge sniffed.

"Then what's wrong?" Weak with relief, Jonas drew Marge into his arms. "Why are you crying?"

"Lynn called from California today, Jonas." Feeling him stiffen, she rushed on. "She wants you to divorce her so she can get married again."

"She can go to hell," Jonas snapped. "If she wants a divorce, let her get it."

"On what grounds?"

"That's her worry, not mine."

"Do you still love her, Jonas?"

"I never did *love* her." Suddenly realizing that he was speaking to Lynn's mother, Jonas sighed. "I'm sorry, Marge, but—"

"Don't apologize, Jonas, I understand." Brushing at her tears, Marge moved out of his encircling arms. "I told her what time you'd be home. She'll be calling back soon."

"How did she know where we were?"

"She called my lawyer." Eyeing him nervously,

Marge said, carefully, "I think you should tell her you'll get the divorce."

"What!" Jonas couldn't believe his ears. "Why should I?"

"For Mary Beth."

Jonas shook his head in bewilderment. "I don't understand, Marge. What has Mary Beth got to do with it?"

"Jonas, think," Marge urged. "If *you* file for divorce you can charge Lynn with desertion and claim sole custody of Mary Beth. If the divorce is granted on those grounds, Lynn would probably have a fight on her hands if she ever tried to take Mary Beth away from you."

"She'd have a fight on her hands in any case," Jonas vowed.

"Do it, Jonas," Marge advised earnestly. "Let her marry this producer or director, or whatever he is."

"Producer or director?" Jonas sneered. "What happened to Leon?"

"I don't know—" she shrugged tiredly—"and I don't care. All I'm concerned about is Mary Beth's future. Do it, Jonas."

Marge's pleading tone set off warning signals in Jonas's head. Studying her carefully, he asked, "Did she threaten to take Mary Beth away if I don't jump through the hoop?"

Marge didn't have to answer, her stricken eyes gave her away.

"Damn," Jonas snarled. "If she were here I'd break her neck."

"Jonas, please," Marge cried. "When she calls back tell her you'll do it. I couldn't stand it if she came and took the baby away."

"She'd have to go through me to reach her," Jonas said grimly, then, his tone gentling, he soothed, "Calm down, Marge. No one's going to take our baby, I promise."

Blinking back fresh tears, Marge looked up at him hopefully. "You'll do it?"

"Marge," Jonas groaned. "I don't have the money, you know that."

"I do," she replied quickly.

"No."

"Jonas, you can think of it as a loan. I don't need it. I do need Mary Beth." Marge's voice had dropped to a pleading whisper. "Please, Jonas."

And so, the divorce paid for with borrowed money, Jonas became a free man again at the advanced age of twenty-one.

After graduation the following year, Jonas did not have to go out and walk the streets looking for work. Finishing very near the top of his class, he found himself much sought after by prospective employers.

He considered each and every offer very carefully and then, to the confused surprise of Marge and the few friends he'd made, he accepted an offer from a relatively small company. But there was a very definite method to Jonas's seeming madness. After a careful evaluation, he had reached the conclusion that though the firm was solvent, it was stagnating. All it needed, he decided, was someone with innovative ideas and enough energy and guts to make them work. Jonas had ideas, energy, and guts in abundance.

The owner of the company was a fifty-six-year-old childless widower with an ulcer eating away at his insides. He was smart enough to realize his company needed to gear up if it was not to sink slowly into oblivion. He was also smart enough to be aware of his own limitations. The field of electronics was booming, and he no longer had the strength to keep up. When he interviewed Jonas, he had known this was the man he wanted. But not for even one euphoric second had he thought he had a chance of getting him.

By the end of Jonas's first year with the company it was well on the road to expansion and recovery, and Jonas was treated like a much-loved son. By the end of his second year, the owner made him a full partner. And when the owner retired five years later, he was a millionaire with a completely cured ulcer. At the time of his retirement, the company's name was changed to J. T. Electronics. Its former owner didn't mind—Thorne was his sole heir anyway.

By the time Jonas went striding by his thirty-second birthday—which he would not have remembered had not Marge and Mary Beth insisted on celebrating—he was well on his way to being a very successful, very rich man. Yet his on-going love affair with electronics continued.

His self-imposed celibacy had naturally ended long since. There had been a succession of several different women in his life. From the first, though, he was extremely selective. While still in college he had vowed that he would never again be trapped by a scheming female.

Not long after he took control of the company, Lynn reappeared on the scene, fresh from Mexico and her third divorce.

She was even more lovely than she'd been at eighteen. And it very quickly became apparent to anyone who observed her that she was looking for another husband and hoped to make it Jonas.

Lynn made all the right moves. She thoroughly fascinated her very impressionable teenage daughter. She reestablished a tenuous relationship with her mother. She completely charmed Jonas's small circle of friends. And she flirted with her former husband in a way that had other men aching to be in his shoes.

Jonas had not reached the position he was in by being stupid. He was very well aware of her game plan. He just couldn't decide if he wanted simply to ignore her or to throttle her. In the end he decided to pay her off and ship her out. She finally left, still pouting, for a small villa in the south of France—for which Jonas had paid a very healthy sum of money.

The money didn't bother him. What did was having to agree to allow their daughter to visit her periodically. Seeing Mary Beth off the first time she visited Lynn was one of the hardest things Jonas had ever done in his life. But at least he had his work. For Marge, there was nothing but an empty house until her granddaughter came home again.

The last time Mary Beth had gone away it was not to visit her mother but to attend a finishing school in Switzerland for a year.

And now the year was six weeks' shy of being up. She was coming home! What had happened, Jonas wondered, to her plans to spend a few weeks with Lynn sailing around the Aegean?

A buzz from the intercom prevented further speculation. Still lost in his thoughts, Jonas flipped the switch and growled, "What is it?"

Valerie's brief, but telling, hesitation brought him fully alert.

"There's a long distance call for you from Paris. A Mr. Barres," Valerie said stiffly.

"Put it through."

As he reached for the receiver, Jonas asked himself how he expected to evoke a positive response in her if he snarled and snapped at her all the time.

You were right the first time, he thought wryly. You are an arrogant fool!

Chapter Seven

After putting the Paris call through, Valerie sat glaring at the intercom. She would have to be insane to even consider Jonas Thorne's preposterous proposal. She could count on one hand the times she'd witnessed any sort of softening in him. Of course, there was that heart-wrenching smile of his.

The mere memory of that smile shortened Valerie's breath. Disgusted by her involuntary response to him, she swiveled around to face her typewriter. He probably practices that damned smile in front of his mirror, she thought nastily.

She resumed typing where she'd left off when the Paris call came, working furiously for a few minutes before coming to an abrupt stop.

Paris. Etienne.

She couldn't marry Jonas Thorne! She couldn't marry anyone. Until those back-to-back thoughts hit her, Valerie had not wanted to admit to herself that she *was* seriously considering his preposterous proposal!

But how could she! How could she give *any* kind of consideration to it? Jonas Thorne was hard, and he was cold. He was almost impossible to work with. What would he be like to live with? Oh, no, she couldn't, could she?

Trying to view the situation objectively, she imagined herself in the role of his wife. What would it be like, being Mrs. Jonas Thorne? A derisive smile curled her lip. I'd probably see less of him then I do now. Now, there's a thought!

"Valerie."

Valerie jumped at the sound of her name coming from the intercom.

"Yes, sir?" For some obscure reason she jumped again when Jonas chuckled softly.

"You sound a little—uh—nervous," Jonas soothed. "Why don't you go home—Val?"

The pause he'd made before whispering her shortened name had been deliberate, Valerie knew.

"Can I leave my problems here if I do—" she paused in retaliation, "sir?"

"You think you have problems?" His tone went a notch lower. "Come into my office, I'll give you problems."

Was he serious? Did he want her in there to work—or . . . ? Valerie shook her head; no not that, not in the office.

"Should I bring my pad?" she asked coolly.

"Is it big enough for two?"

Her cool melted. Damn him. He was being deliberately provocative. Teasing her the way he had teased Loretta and the others that night at the Drop Inn. Well, not in exactly the same way. Biting her lip, Valerie stared at the intercom suspiciously. Nothing. He was letting the silent seconds work on her composure.

"Valerie."

Valerie blinked in confusion. Never could she have have imagined him capable of achieving that—that almost caressing tone.

"Are you going to come in here?" he asked very, very softly.

"Mr. Thorne—I—I—"

"Either you come in here, or I'll come out there," he warned. "What's it going to be?"

"All right," Valerie sighed. "I'll come in."

"I thought you might," Jonas drawled.

Fighting the urge to run out of the office and into the elevator, Valerie slowly stood up, straightening her waistband and smoothing down her skirt automatically. Eyeing the closed door to his office warily, she drew a deep breath, walked over to it, and stepped inside.

"Tell me you're afraid of me," Jonas chided disbelievingly as she approached his desk with obvious reluctance.

"I'm afraid of you," Valerie obliged.

His smile, *that* smile, flashed like sunlight through a passing storm cloud. "Like hell you are," he grinned.

She couldn't help it. She grinned back.

"I like that." His glance indicated her grin. "Oh, yes, I do like that. I was beginning to wonder if you knew how to smile."

In marked contrast to his manner earlier that morning, he now appeared completely relaxed. Hardly able to believe her eyes or ears, Valerie decided to find out if his mood was real or assumed.

Lowering her eyes, she perched on the chair beside his desk. Then, raising her lids slowly she gazed directly into his eyes and laughed softly. "Oh, yes. I know how to smile. When there is someone to smile at."

"Watch it, Jonas," he warned himself aloud. "The woman's out to trap you." A slow smile, surprisingly sensuous, curved his lips, changing their usual harsh line into an exciting invitation.

Good heavens! Valerie thought wonderingly. They were all right. All those women who had said he was very, very sexy; they were right! In an effort to hide her reaction from him, Valerie again lowered her eyes.

"I think—" her lashes swept up. "I think it would be unwise for a woman to try to trap you, Mr. Thorne."

"Mr. Thorne," Jonas repeated musingly without denying her assertion. "A few hours ago I managed to articulate a proposal of marriage." His tone, though easy, held a definite warning. "Do you think you could possibly say the name Jonas?"

"I—" Valerie hesitated, unsure of herself now. "You are my employer," she protested lamely.

"Under the circumstances *that* argument could hardly be described as valid." He paused briefly, his eyes alert for her reactions. "I no longer wish to be your employer. I want to be your husband."

Valerie felt as though a wide band was being drawn tightly around her chest, slowly squeezing all the air from her body. She had to reply to him, say something. But what? Jonas broke the silence.

"I don't quite understand why you hesitate," he observed quietly. "Not only in accepting the use of my first name, but in the acquisition of my surname, as well." He paused long enough to light a cigarette, and to let his words sink in. "You've told me what you want out of life. I'm prepared to fulfill those wants. Much more than adequately, as regards a home and financial security."

"Financial security!" Valerie gasped. "I've placed no price tag on myself. I'm not up for grabs, or for sale."

"There's a saying that everyone has a price," Jonas retorted.

"It became a saying because it's probably true,"

Valerie retaliated. "But the price does not necessarily have to be paid in money."

"You don't like money?" Jonas ridiculed. "You'd be the first woman I've ever encountered who didn't."

"Yes, I like money," Valerie snapped, goaded to anger by his tone. "And I like all the lovely things I can purchase with it. I'd have no objections to having scads and scads of money. But not if I have to sell myself to get it."

"I'm not suggesting you do that, Valerie," Jonas said tightly.

"Aren't you?" she mocked. "It certainly sounded like you were. And offering yourself as the highest bidder."

"If it were that simple, we wouldn't be having this discussion," he assured her coolly. "I *would* be the highest bidder—you can be sure of that."

"Your conceit is exceeded only by your arrogance," Valerie snapped, jumping to her feet. She was shaking with anger, humiliation, and a jumble of other emotions she couldn't begin to identify.

"Sit down, Val," Jonas sighed. Then, his lips twitching suspiciously, he teased, "Feisty when you're riled, aren't you?"

Feeling suddenly foolish, Valerie sat down again.

"Aren't *you?*" she returned defensively.

"Yes," he admitted, laughing easily again. "I really think you should accept my offer, Valerie, for your own good."

"My own good?" Valerie frowned. "I don't understand. Why—for my own good?"

"I've drawn more emotion, more animation from you in the last few hours, than you've been reputed to have shown in the last year." Jonas's eyes were steady

126

on hers. Ignoring her soft gasp, he drove the nail home. "At least, with me, you'd know you're alive."

"Jonas, please," Valerie whispered pleadingly.

A wry smile curled his mouth. "Amazing." He shook his head slowly. "I had to hurt you to get you to say my name." The wry smile settled in place. "It's true, you know. We may lock horns, often. You may get hurt, but even feeling pain is part of being alive. Say yes, Val. Not only to me, but to being alive."

Everything he'd said was true. She *did* feel more alive than she had in over a year. She no longer clung to a subconscious death wish. She wanted to live again! Without giving herself time to think, to consider the enormity of the step she'd be taking, Valerie gave in.

"All right, Jonas. I accept your proposal."

The stillness that seemed to grip him puzzled her. Had he been playing some sort of game? she wondered, confused. Or testing her in some way? Had she answered incorrectly? Made a dreadful error?

He studied her face for a moment longer, then came around the desk to take her hand into his.

"You agree to the child as well?" he asked softly.

"Yes." Her answer was equally soft, if strained. "That was part of the proposal, wasn't it? You give me what I want in return for what you want."

"Yes," his eyes bored into hers. "I just wanted that point understood." Swinging away from her, he decreed, "I'm sending you home."

"But—" Realizing protest would be useless, Valerie closed her mouth. He was already holding the telephone receiver to his ear and punching out the numbers of a familiar extension.

"I want Lyle to have my car at the exit in five minutes

for Miss Jordan." As he replaced the receiver he turned to study her again. Apparently her pale cheeks and her trembling hands told him how nervous she felt, for he asked, "Are you all right?"

"Yes," she answered. "At least I will be when I get used to the idea—I think."

Once again she was treated to the radiance of his smile. "Go on," he urged. "Get out of here. I have several long distance calls to make, and something I want to discuss with Charlie. Do you think you'll be up to seeing me this evening?"

"Yes, of course."

"Of course," he mocked, glancing pointedly at her trembling hands. "Go on, beat it. I'll stop by the apartment tonight. That is, if you get out of here and let me get some work done. We'll talk then."

"Oh, but—"

"Go," he ordered, striding to the door to open it for her. "Lyle will be waiting."

Valerie went; not quite at a run. At the soft click of the door closing behind her she came to an indecisive stop. She breathed deeply a few times to calm her racing pulses, then walked to her desk. She was removing a sheet of paper from her typewriter when the phone rang. Lifting the receiver on the second ring, she gave her automatic response.

"Mr. Thorne's office."

"What time do you think you'll be ready to go to lunch today, Val?" Janet sounded alert and efficient— the complete opposite of how Valerie felt.

"I'm not going to lunch today. I'm being sent home."

"Being sent home!" Janet exclaimed. "Why, are you sick?"

Valerie sighed. She'd have to tell Janet, of course,

NO COST! NO OBLIGATION TO BUY!
NO PURCHASE NECESSARY!

PLAY "LUCKY 7"
AND GET AS MANY AS SIX FREE GIFTS...
HOW TO PLAY:

1. With a coin, carefully scratch off the silver box at the right. This makes you eligible to receive one or more free books, and possibly other gifts, depending on what is revealed beneath the scratch-off area.

2. You'll receive brand-new Silhouette Special Edition® novels. If you enjoyed Silhouette Classics, you'll be sure to love Silhouette Special Editions. When you return this card, we'll send you the books and gifts you qualify for *absolutely free*!

3. Unless you tell us otherwise, every month we'll send you 6 additional novels to read and enjoy. If you decide to keep them, you'll pay only $2.49* per book—that's 26¢ less per book than the cover price! There is **no** charge for shipping and handling. There are no hidden extras.

4. When you subscribe to Silhouette Books, we'll also send you additional free gifts from time to time, as well as our newsletter.

5. You must be completely satisfied. You may cancel at any time simply by writing "cancel" on your statement or returning a shipment of books to us at our cost.

*Terms and prices subject to change without notice.

PLAY "LUCKY 7"

Just scratch off the silver box with a coin.
Then check below to see which gifts you get.

YES! I have scratched off the silver box. Please send me all the
gifts for which I qualify. I understand I am under no obligation
to purchase any books, as explained on the opposite page.

235 CIS RIXZ

NAME

ADDRESS   APT.

CITY   STATE   ZIP

7	7	7	WORTH FOUR FREE BOOKS. FREE BRACELET WATCH AND MYSTERY BONUS
🍒	🍒	🍒	WORTH FOUR FREE BOOKS AND MYSTERY BONUS
⬤	⬤	⬤	WORTH FOUR FREE BOOKS
🔔	🔔	🍒	WORTH TWO FREE BOOKS

DETACH AND MAIL CARD TODAY

DETACH AND MAIL CARD TODAY

but not here, not over the phone. "No, Janet, I'm fine. But I can't explain now, Lyle's waiting for me."

"Lyle?" Janet repeated sharply. "Val, honey, why is Lyle—"

"Janet, I can't talk now," Valerie interrupted anxiously. "I'll explain when you get home to—" Valerie saved her breath; Janet had hung up.

After replacing the receiver, Valerie filed the work she'd been transcribing, covered her typewriter, and, draping her new spring raincoat over her shoulders, left the office. The elevator doors hissed apart to reveal a frowning Janet.

"You must be sick," she decided aloud as Valerie stepped into the elevator.

"No," Valerie denied. "I'm not sick, Janet. I—he—" she stuttered, not quite sure how to begin.

"Valerie, you didn't quit?" Janet cried. When Valerie shook her head, she gasped, "Jonas didn't fire you?"

"No, he asked me to marry him."

"He— What?!"

"He—" Valerie broke off as the elevator came to a stop and the doors slid open. "We can't talk here, Janet," she concluded, stepping out.

After a stunned hesitation, Janet hurriedly followed her.

"Lyle's waiting, Miss Jor—" Steve began as Valerie walked toward the exit. Janet cut him off with a tersely ordered, "Call Jonas, Steve. Tell him I'm going home with Miss Jordan."

"Will do, Janet." Steve's reply was punctuated by the door's closing behind them.

Lyle was waiting beside the open door of the silver-gray limo. "Morning, Miss Jordan—Janet."

"Good morning, Lyle," Valerie and Janet answered in unison, Janet adding, "We're going to my apartment, Lyle."

With a short nod of his head, and a smiling, "Okay, Janet," Lyle swung the door closed.

As soon as she was seated, Janet touched the button that operated the glass partition and the minute the window was in place between the front and back seats, she turned and demanded, "Now what's going on?" Not even pausing to give Valerie time to respond, she rapped out, "Were you serious about Jonas asking you to marry him?"

"Yes, I—" Valerie was interrupted by an unfamilar sound that was not quite a ring, yet not quite a buzz either. In confusion, she glanced around trying to locate the sound.

"I should have expected it," Janet sighed, sliding back the top of the center arm rest to reveal a phone nestled inside. Casting Valerie a knowing smile, she lifted the receiver and said, "Yes, Jonas?"

Valerie's eyebrows went up in questioning surprise as Janet's eyes studied her face.

"Yes, she's all right," she said quietly. "A little pale, but all right. I haven't been able to make much sense out of what she's told me, Jonas." Janet's tone invited clarification. She was quiet a moment, then she answered, "Yes." Again she listened, longer this time. "She did!" Her eyes flew to Valerie. "Well, you have my overwhelmed congratulations." Her pause was very short this time. "Well, of course I mean it, Jonas. I've been very worried about her." Pause. "Yes, I will, all right, Jonas."

"What was that all about?" Valerie asked suspiciously. "And why have you been 'very worried' about me?"

"*That* was Jonas." Janet grinned.

"Surprise, surprise," Valerie drawled. "And?"

"*And,*" Janet sobered, "you must have looked a little green around the gills to Steve. Jonas was concerned—" she shrugged—"hence the call." Her voice elaborately casual, she went on. "Jonas said you've agreed to marry him."

"Yes," Valerie concurred. "I have."

"Uh-huh—" Janet wasn't quite successful in masking her injured feelings. "We share the same apartment," she muttered, "and I don't even know you've got a thing going with the boss." Shooting Valerie a hurt look, she complained, "You said you didn't even like him."

"I don't," Valerie protested. "I didn't. Oh, hell, Janet, we don't have, haven't had, a 'thing' going. It's—it's—" Valerie's voice faded. How could she explain? She wasn't sure she fully understood the situation herself.

"Well, I certainly am glad you cleared that up," Janet said dryly. "But don't think for a minute that bunch of gibberish got you off the hook. Prepare yourself for the third degree after we get home."

An hour later Valerie decided Janet would have made a fantastic interrogation officer. Janet probed gently, but persistently, until Valerie gave in and told her about Jonas's unorthodox proposal.

"How like Jonas." Janet smiled wryly. "He does love a challenge. Women of all shapes, sizes, and colors willing to do anything, and I do mean *anything,* to get their well-manicured hands on him—and his money—

and *he* decides to produce an heir through a gal who is emotionally asleep."

"Janet!"

"You're going to tell me you're not?" Janet's eyebrows shot up. "Honey, do you have the vaguest idea what you are letting yourself in for? Jonas could devour you."

Valerie shook her head. "Janet, I don't know what you're talking about."

"That's what I was afraid of," Janet sighed. "Val, the man you're going to marry is not your everyday ordinary guy next door."

"I know that," Valerie cried indignantly. "The guy next door doesn't have loads of money."

"It's not the money," Janet retorted. "It's the man. In the first place, he's a bastard."

"Janet!" Valerie protested.

"I mean," Janet explained soothingly, "his mother and father were not married. He was also an orphan from day one and I've always had the feeling that he never had much of a childhood. His background made him tough and it made him hard. But that isn't what makes him different." Janet lifted her shoulders in a helpless shrug. "He isn't just ambitious. It's more than that. Jonas has a light in his head, a neon sign that spells out 'electronics. It consumes him. Everything and everyone else comes second."

Valerie shivered. She had always thought of him as machinelike, but Janet's confirmation of her opinion was unsettling. "You make him sound inhuman," she murmured, uncomfortably aware that she had also considered him so.

"Oh, no," Janet denied. "At least I don't mean to. Jonas is very human. When he's hungry, he eats. When he's tired, he sleeps. And when he feels desire, he takes a woman to his bed. He adores his daughter. All very natural, normal things—but he *is* different. That difference draws the females like a magnet. That's where my concern for you comes in." Janet shrugged again. "I've seen your reaction to the effect he has on women. Having a wife will not lessen that effect. Can you handle it?"

"Why not?" Valerie asked. "It's not as if I had any feelings for him."

Not fooled for a minute by Valerie's brave words, Janet sighed. "Val, no woman with any pride is going to sit by calmly while other women fall all over her husband, whether or not she has any feelings for him. It would more than annoy anyone, and you more than most. I've been a witness to it countless times. Quite often the play is none too subtle."

Janet thought of the dinner party she'd attended with Jonas at Edouard Barres's elegant home outside of Paris. The young actress had been embarrassingly obvious in her pursuit of Jonas. Janet sighed again at the memory of the actress running to the plane—and Jonas. She grimaced. "A few years ago, even his ex-wife got into the act."

Valerie felt an odd thrill of apprehension jump in her stomach. Something about Janet's tone unnerved her. Why? Why should the mention of Jonas's first wife make her feel shaky and even more uncertain?

"For a while there it looked like Jonas had finally been corraled." Janet's musing voice cut across Valerie's thoughts. "What a production." She grinned. "A novice to the game could have gained an education by taking notes."

"What happened?" Valerie asked unwillingly.

"Who knows?" Janet laughed. "He's an elusive devil. All I know is that one day she was here, living in his house, and the next day she was gone."

"Living in his house!" Valerie exclaimed softly.

"Yes." Janet nodded. "And she gave everyone the impression she was there to stay. I don't know." Janet's shoulders went up, then down. "She was fresh from a divorce, her third. Maybe she decided it would be more interesting to play the field for a while."

"She's been married three times?" Valerie's eyes widened with astonishment.

"Yep." Janet nodded. "Each one richer than the last. Of course—" she grinned—"that wouldn't have taken much for number two. Jonas didn't have a dime back then. But, as I understand it, her second had lots and lots of dimes, all of which he was eager to spend on his beautiful new bride."

Valerie's spirit nose-dived. "She was beautiful?"

"She *is* beautiful," Janet corrected. "Blonde, blue-eyed, and golden-skinned."

Suddenly very tired, Valerie didn't want to hear any more. But how to shut Janet up? Food! Of course, how much talking could Janet do if she was busy eating? Rising quickly, Valerie started toward the kitchen.

"I don't know about you," she tossed over her shoulder, "but I'm ready for lunch."

Janet followed, chiding, "In other words, you want me to button up, right?"

"I'd appreciate it," Valerie drawled.

"I'll go you one better," Janet laughed. "I'll clear out tonight so you and Jonas can have your discussion in private."

"But where will you go?"

Janet's smile was teasing. "Dining, dancing, romancing. All that same old dull stuff." Laughing at Valerie's surprised expression, she added, "Actually, I have a date. So don't worry about me, okay?"

Since Janet didn't volunteer a name, Valerie bit back the questions on her lips. That didn't stop them from tumbling through her mind. Was there a man in Janet's life? Who was he? And why hadn't Janet mentioned him before?

"What time do you expect Jonas?"

Janet's question wiped all idle speculation out of her mind. Jonas! Biting her lip, Valerie tried to shrug unconcernedly. "He didn't give a time, just said he'd stop by tonight."

Janet's laughter filled the kitchen. "I swear, there is no one in the world like that man."

That, Valerie thought uneasily, is what I'm afraid of.

A secret smile curving her mouth, Janet left the apartment shortly after seven, dressed to demoralize most men and all women. Feeling somewhat dowdy in comparison, Valerie changed her clothes three times, finally settling on a dress Janet had insisted she buy in Paris. The soft, almost weightless material clung to her full breasts and caressed her hips and thighs at her slightest movement. Although its dusky pink color lent a glow to her pale cheeks, Valerie, not at all satisfied with her appearance, frowned at her reflection in the dresser mirror. Her eyes, purpled by anxiety, stared back at her, and she sighed, then jumped at the sound of the doorbell. Trembling hands smoothing the material over her hips, she walked with forced steadiness to the door.

Jonas, looking cool and relaxed, and supremely sure of himself, stood at ease in the hall, a bottle of champagne in his hand. His eyes ran over her, coming to rest on her face. "May I come in?" he drawled when she made no move to open the door further.

"Oh! Yes . . . of course," Valerie blurted out, stepping back hastily.

The moment he was inside, he held the bottle aloft, chiding, "Do you think you could find some glasses? This is chilled and ready to drink."

Biting back a retort, Valerie turned and walked into the kitchen. Breathing deeply in an effort to calm her jangled nerves, she retrieved two fragile-looking wine glasses from the cabinet above the sink, then nearly dropped them when she turned to find Jonas standing behind her.

"Where's Janet?" he asked dryly, peeling the gold foil off the top of the bottle.

"She had a date," Valerie replied shortly. "Why, did you want to see her?"

"Hardly," Jonas drawled, easing the cork from the bottle. "Shall we adjourn to the living room? Or would you prefer to drink to our future here in the kitchen?"

Sarcastic brute! Spinning on her heel, Valerie marched into the living room. Depositing the glasses on the coffee table, she sat down on the sofa and watched as Jonas poured the wine before seating himself beside her.

"To the gratification of all wants." Jonas lifted his glass and touched it lightly to hers before raising it to his lips.

Valerie's entire body was suffused with heat at his sardonic tone. Well, one could hardly accuse Jonas Thorne of being trite or predictable! Valerie lowered her eyes in embarrassment as she lifted her own glass. One sip and she was transported back to Paris and the last time she'd had champagne—the night before Etienne's accident.

Etienne. Etienne.

Valerie was unaware that her trembling hand had placed the glass safely back on the table, or of the man who sat next to her watching her every move through narrowed lids. His tightly controlled voice jerked her into the present.

"Wake up, Valerie," he advised warningly. "You are here now—with me—Jonas," he gritted, leaving her in no doubt that he knew her mind had flown back in time, to Paris and Etienne. "Pick up your wine and drink to your future, with me, beginning in a few weeks' time."

A few weeks' time? Valerie's head jerked up and she froze as the full meaning of his words registered. Her eyes took in his tall frame and her skin crawled at the idea of that body's touching hers. A memory of the night she'd spent in Etienne's arms filled her mind and she had to bite her lip to keep from crying aloud: I can't. I cannot bear the thought of another man replacing Etienne in that way.

"Damn it, Valerie, come back," Jonas commanded harshly.

"What?" Valerie blinked, suddenly aware that she had superimposed Etienne's image onto Jonas's sprawling form.

"*I said come back,*" he muttered darkly. "You cannot live in the past. You cannot exist on memories. You can starve to death on dreams and wishes." Standing abruptly, he pulled her up in front of him. "We will be married in two weeks. *That* is a reality you can rely on."

"No!" Valerie hated the puny weakness of her protest even as she admitted her own meager store of strength was no match for his. Wetting fear-dried lips, she tried again. "Jonas, please, I—I can't—I—"

"You can and you will." His assurance sliced through her stuttering. "You cannot go back. You cannot stand still. That leaves only one direction—forward. I will make it as easy for you as I can—but I will not let you out of it." His hand opened to slide around the back of her neck, holding her still. "Face it, Val. I will allow no kind of retreat."

His promise held a distinctly ominous undertone and Valerie sighed with relief when he released her. As he turned away she drew a quick breath. Without thinking, she condemned herself with her opening words. "Mr. Thorne, please . . . I . . ."

"Damn you!" Jonas turned on her, his eyes blazing. "If you call me *Mr. Thorne* in that tone one more time I swear I'll hit you. Two weeks, Valerie. You have two weeks to come to terms with yourself and the facts of life."

The facts of life. Why, Valerie wondered distractedly, was it so important that she face life? She didn't want to face the facts of life; they hurt. She didn't want to face the reality of this hard man glaring at her. She wanted to be left alone. Her thoughts fragmented at the insistent prodding of Jonas's harsh voice.

"Do you understand?"

"I loved him."

Valerie bit down on her lip. She hadn't wanted to say that. She hadn't wanted to say anything. A chill feathered her body at the way Jonas's face settled into harshly defined lines.

"I know," he said tightly, through rigid lips that

barely moved. "But he's dead, and you're alive—at least partly so." Ignoring her wince of pain, he went on, roughly, "Life is too precious to waste, Valerie, and I'm not going to let you waste any more of yours."

Escape! It was not a conscious thought but an urge that consumed Valerie's entire being. Jerking away from him, she took off at a run. She didn't know where she was going; all she knew was that she had to get away from this man who used his cold voice and his cruel words to inflict torture.

She didn't get very far. With two long strides he caught up to her, his big hand reaching out to tighten painfully around her upper arm.

"There's only one place left to run to, Val," Jonas grated as he pulled her around to face him. "And that is to me." Grasping her other arm, he held her still. "I don't want to hurt you Val." His voice softened. "And I won't unless you force me to. You accepted me this morning. I'm going to hold you to that acceptance."

Valerie stared at him, violet eyes bright with moisture, confused by his swift change from monster to human. She was behaving like a hysterical teenager, and she knew it. What he'd said was true. She *had* accepted him, and he had every right to hold her to it. Defeat settled heavily on her shoulders.

"Jonas, please." Valerie could not manage more than a whisper. "I'm so tired."

"I know that, too." Although his hands loosened their hurtful pressure, he did not release her. "This weariness dragging at you is unnatural, don't you see that?"

The sense of defeat deepening, Valerie nodded dully. "Yes, I guess so."

Jonas's fingers gripped, then eased again. "Don't

guess—know," he urged softly. "Will you keep to our bargain?"

The tension in his body was transmitted to her through his fingertips. Valerie could actually feel it, and it unnerved her.

"Jonas—"

"Will you keep to it?"

Valerie wet her lips and wondered at the brief but sharp pain caused by the convulsive dig of his fingers. "Yes."

He was very still for a moment and now Valerie imagined she could feel the tension flow out of his body. Shaking her head to dispel the fanciful thought, she murmured, "Jonas, please—"

"I know," he interrupted. "I'm going now." He hesitated, leaning toward her slightly. Then, as if catching himself, he released her arms and stepped back. He hesitated again at the door. "Are you coming into the office tomorrow?"

"Yes, of course." Valerie frowned. "Why shouldn't I?"

A sardonic smile played around the edge of his mouth. "There are going to be a lot of questions." He shrugged fatalistically. "And a lot of speculation."

Valerie grimaced. "The first of the facts of life I'm going to have to face?"

Jonas nodded once, sharply. "The first of many, I'm afraid."

"So am I," Valerie admitted. "Afraid, I mean."

Chapter Eight

Two weeks later, en route between the East and West coasts, Valerie was no longer merely afraid: she was scared to death.

A narrow gold band gleamed on one of the hands gripping the arm of her seat. The entrapping circle of gold had been slipped onto her finger less than four hours earlier, along with a diamond solitaire so large she felt a jolt of shock every time she looked at it.

Valerie shivered and forced her fingernails out of the plush upholstery. Jonas was not in the compartment. Just before takeoff he had stood over her until she'd fastened her seat belt. Then he'd left her with a terse: "I'm going forward for a little while. Try to get some sleep, you look exhausted."

The way I look doesn't tell the half of it, Valerie thought now. Sleep—how she longed for it! It had evaded her since that night in Janet's apartment. Remembering that night, Valerie shivered again. She had felt the trap closing then, yet she hadn't had the strength to break free of it. Maybe, if she'd had another month or so before Jonas commenced his onslaught she would have been strong enough to refuse him—but she hadn't had that month.

God, he scared her! That was one fact she'd faced without any prodding from anyone. She had wanted—

no, ached—to tell him to go to hell, but, she simply did not have the nerve. She was filled with self-loathing. What a sniveling little coward she was! A pitiful creature without a backbone, bending in whatever direction Jonas Thorne dictated. She had been defenseless and he'd known it. He'd taken advantage of her weakness ruthlessly.

What did a man like Jonas Thorne want with her, anyway? She had asked herself that question over and over during the last two weeks. And she knew she was not the only one asking it.

Valerie was not disliked at J.T. Electronics. She knew that. But speculation had run rampant through the staff, just as Jonas had predicted it would. Valerie would have had to be deaf, blind, and unconscious not to hear the whispered remarks, see the calculating glances, or be aware of the hum of avid interest that permeated the entire office complex.

How it had affected Jonas, if at all, was just another question Valerie did not have an answer for. Jonas could, and did, don a mask at will. A mask in which his cool eyes observed everything, while revealing nothing.

Luckily, for Valerie's peace of mind, the pace of business in the office the last two weeks had increased considerably. There had been a number of transatlantic telephone calls between Jonas and Edouard Barres in Paris. The results of those calls seemed to electrify Jonas, who, in turn, galvanized the entire staff into action.

Except for Charlie McAndrew, no one, including Valerie, knew as yet exactly what it was all about. All that *was* known was that an office was being readied on the executive floor for someone, presumably from France, who was to work closely with Jonas on something. Valerie was grateful for this new source of gossip—it shifted the spotlight off her precipitous engagement to Jonas. But for all the speculation, the details of whatever was brewing remained securely locked away inside Jonas Thorne's head. He certainly hadn't confided in her!

Giving up all pretense of trying to sleep, Valerie sat up and gazed out the window. The incredible expanse of blue sky went unseen as she reviewed the events of the preceding two weeks.

The morning following Jonas's first visit to Janet's apartment, he had made known his intention to marry simply by leaking the information to the company grapevine via Charlie's secretary, Eileen. Before lunchtime Valerie had had at least a dozen interoffice calls, all with the same query: Was it true?

In the office Jonas was all business. When they were alone he was terse, edgy, and impatient with her lack of enthusiasm for any suggestions he made about their wedding. And the more impatience he revealed, the more tense she became until, finally, near the end of that first week, feeling boxed-in and panicky, she shouted, "I don't care what you do. Make any plans you wish." She had shocked herself with the outburst, yet, once started, she had not been able to stop. Shaking all over, she had released her nameless fears by lashing out at him. "You're the one that insisted on this farce, do as you please."

"I always do."

If he had raised his voice, or even sounded angry, Valerie might have made a bid for freedom. Jonas did neither. Instead, he seemed to close up before her eyes. He stared at her so frigidly she felt her blood run cold.

"I must be out of my mind," he said quietly, as if to

himself. "All right, Valerie, I'll allow you to play the role of Sleeping Beauty a little longer. I was considering *your* feelings by asking your preference in the proceedings." He was quiet for several minutes, his eyes steady on her pale face. He continued dispassionately. "Friday morning we'll apply for the license and get the medical requirements out of the way. I have a friend on the bench who, I'm sure, will be delighted to marry us in his chambers—I'll let you know what day." This last was drawled sardonically. "And by the way, we're having dinner with my mother-in-law on Sunday."

"My mother?"

"I said my mother-in-law," Jonas replied tiredly. *"Your* mother is my *future* mother-in-law, Val. I'm referring to my daughter's grandmother. She wants to meet you."

Valerie hadn't appreciated his tone of weary boredom. She hadn't particularly enjoyed having her stupidity pointed out either. Nonetheless, she tried to use a reasonable tone when she inquired, softly, "Why should your former wife's mother want to meet me?" She knew she'd failed the moment the question was voiced, for irritation, not reason, colored her tone.

"Why indeed?" After his previous self-control, Jonas's sudden flare of anger startled her. "I suppose she thought it might be nice if you two became acquainted before the marriage takes place—seeing as how you are going to be living in the same house."

"You live with your mother-in-law!" Valerie exclaimed.

"No, she lives with me," Jonas corrected.

"But why?"

"Because I choose to have her do so."

Valerie had been rendered speechless by the blatantly cool arrogance of his statement. She had also been made uncomfortably aware of the fact that Jonas did not welcome questions about his motives.

Valerie had followed his directives unquestioningly as they applied for their marriage license on Friday. At the end of that very long, tiring day, one bit of information remained sharply defined in her mind. Jonas Thorne was only thirty-eight years old!

He had not missed her expression of surprise when he'd marked that bit of information into the date-of-birth blank on the license application.

"You thought I was older?" he'd mocked her softly. "Well, console yourself with the thought that I will be before too long. I'll be thirty-nine in two months."

There were times, many times, during that two-week period when Valerie questioned her own sanity. How else could she explain her rash, ill-considered acceptance of Jonas as a life partner? He was cold, he was mocking, he was derisive—except, she was to find, when he was in the presence of his first wife's mother. To Marge Kowalski, Jonas was charming, and considerate, and very gentle. Somehow, his attitude toward her hurt Valerie, even while she asked herself why it should.

Valerie had looked forward to the dinner with rigidly concealed distaste—well, there *was* something very odd about a thirty-eight-year-old bachelor living with his ex-mother-in-law, wasn't there? But it proved to be a relaxing, enjoyable affair.

In fact, the evening turned out to be surprisingly enlightening. What had she expected? Moving her head restlessly, Valerie examined the plush interior of the expensive aircraft. A mansion. What she had been expecting the previous Sunday was a mansion—and possibly a matriarch in residence.

What she had found once they had left behind the two huge iron gates that guarded the entrance drive was a large, rambling natural stone and glass house. It had drawn a gasp of appreciation from her.

"Does that strangled sound denote approval or dismay?" Jonas asked as he pulled on the hand brake.

"It's absolutely beautiful," Valerie breathed softly.

The late afternoon sun bathed the house in gold, its massive windows reflecting the rays back to the ball of near red hovering on the horizon. She could feel Jonas's eyes studying her rapt expression, but at that moment she didn't care, for what she was experiencing was close to love at first sight. Jonas's amused tone broke into her enthrallment.

"I'm relieved," he drawled. "I'd have hated to give it up."

Marge Kowalski was almost as dramatic a surprise as the house itself.

Having only Janet's carelessly delivered, "You'll like Marge," to go on, Valerie had drawn her own conclusions about what her future husband's mother-in-law would be like. After only a few minutes, she knew that the conclusions she'd reached were wrong.

At sixty-one Marge was, if Valerie but knew it, exactly as she had been when Jonas first met her, at least as far as her personality was concerned. Her expertly arranged hair was completely white and she wore the age lines on her face as proudly as any soldier ever wore a medal of honor. Having, she claimed, earned every white hair and wrinkle, she was comfortable with them.

"Mary Beth, being her father's daughter, kept me

running while she was growing up," Marge said easily as she gave Valerie the grand tour of the house before dinner. "I think credit for more than a few silver threads go to the cracker as well." An expression of pure love lit her face as she indicated Jonas, sauntering along, drink in hand, behind them.

"You worked in the mines?" Valerie asked him, vaguely remembering someone else referring to him as a coal-cracker.

"No." Jonas gazed indulgently at Marge. "But it amuses Marge on occasion to call me a coal-cracker simply because I come from the coal regions." His smile turned into a soft laugh. "But, she forgets that she came from the same place as I do, so she must be a cracker too."

"Lady residents of Tamaqua are not crackers," Marge teased him. "Only male residents hold that honor."

"You made that up," Jonas bantered back. "Admit it."

Marge laughed up at him. "Okay, I admit it. So sue me!"

For some unfathomable reason, their affectionate exchange caused a strange, almost painful sensation in Valerie, possibly, she theorized, because it had been so long since she'd been exposed to the warmth of this kind of affectionate wordplay. Turning away, she concentrated on following Marge up the short, curving stairs that led to the third level of the house.

The lowest level had consisted of a small enclosed area that housed the heater and central air-conditioning units, a good-sized laundry room, and a huge family room—in which the largest TV Valerie had ever seen held pride of place.

The second level was comprised of a beautiful, compact kitchen, a large dining room with one wall made of glass, a living room of a size equal to the dining room, four good-sized bedrooms, two large, full bathrooms, and a powder room.

As she mounted the stairs Valerie hesitated to even guess what would be on the final level. What she found was her future home—with evidence that Jonas had been in residence for some time.

The apartment was self-contained and could be made completely private by the simple act of closing the door directly across the carpeted landing at the top of the curving staircase. Except for the master bedroom, the rooms here were smaller than on the floor below, and sliding glass doors led off the bedroom onto a wide redwood deck, at the end of which was a flight of steps that descended to the three-car garage. The furnishings were contemporary and expensive; warm and welcoming. Had she been viewing it with the idea of renting the apartment, Valerie would have jumped at the chance to live in it. But the prospect of sharing it with Jonas was daunting, and took the edge off her pleasure.

The evening was an unqualified success. By the time Jonas drove her back to Janet's apartment Valerie felt sure she was going to like Marge Kowalski very much. The woman was warm, friendly, and obviously willing to do anything to ensure Jonas's happiness.

Numbering her days like a condemned prisoner, Valerie had grown steadily more tense as her wedding day approached. With each passing day she grew more quiet and withdrawn, leaving Jonas obviously irritated, and Janet very worried. And even though she knew her behavior was far from mature, Valerie could not shake the feeling of dread.

And last night! Valerie grimaced. Last night had seemed a never ending torture. Not wanting to disturb Janet, Valerie had remained in her room, in her bed, caught up in a wide-awake nightmare. She had a wild desire to jump up, fling some clothes into a suitcase, and run for her life.

She couldn't and she didn't, of course, but now, her eyes shifting to the vivid expanse of blue just beyond the small window, she wished that she had.

Everything had gone off like clockwork. With Janet as her attendant, Valerie had met Jonas, Marge, and Charlie McAndrew at the exact time Jonas had stipulated. They were in the judge's chambers for exactly sixteen and a half minutes. From there they went directly to the Kona Kai, where a table, complete with hovering waiters, had been prepared for an elegant luncheon. Toasts were given and accepted. Valerie ate, drank, talked and smiled, all the time acting on reflex alone.

Jonas had not lingered over his food. As soon as the meal was eaten and the contents of two bottles of Dom Perignon consumed, he announced: "Time to go."

With the assurances of Janet and Charlie that they'd see Marge back to the house, Jonas led Valerie out of the hotel and into the silver-gray limo. The drive to the airport had been made in total silence.

"I'm going forward for a little while. Try to get some sleep, you look exhausted." Those had been Jonas's first words to her since they had left the hotel. Glancing at her watch, Valerie smiled wryly; Jonas's little while had stretched to two hours and ten minutes.

Though she knew they were going to California, she had no idea of their specific destination—nor did she care. At the moment she didn't care if the plane's wheels never again touched down on a landing strip.

A chill touched her spine as Valerie heard again the echo of the judge's low, melodic voice reciting the traditional marriage ceremony. Her nails dug into the arm rest as she again felt the warm touch of the entrapping circle of gold that Jonas had slipped onto her icy finger. And her entire body jerked with a shudder of remembrance at the cold, thin-lipped kiss Jonas had brushed across her mouth.

That . . . that insult of the lips had brought her previous feelings of dread to the point of smothering panic. After Etienne's gentle tenderness, how had she allowed herself even to consider this union with a man so totally devoid of emotion?

The sound of Jonas's voice preceded him into the compartment, giving Valerie the precious seconds needed to lower the seat back and close her eyes in pretended sleep.

Her feigned sleep soon became real and Valerie knew no more until she was wakened by the touch of his hand.

"It's all right," Jonas murmured when she stiffened. "I'm sorry I disturbed you, but your seat belt had to be buckled. We're coming in to land." The buckling completed, Jonas moved back to his own seat. Minutes after he'd latched his seat belt the plane banked and made its approach to the landing strip.

San Francisco! Valerie had often longed to see this city, considered by some to be the most beautiful city in the world. She had longed to see it, but not with Jonas Thorne! Nevertheless, her eyes were glued to the window of the plane as they made their descent.

Had she been in a frame of mind to be impressed, the

elegant hotel would certainly have impressed her. But Valerie viewed the elegant spaciousness of the lobby, the exquisite merchandise displayed by the many shops, and the expensively clad patrons through eyes dulled by fatigue.

Mutely, she walked beside Jonas, first to the registration desk, then, following the bellhop, to the elevator, and finally along a carpeted hall. As she was ushered, with something of a flourish, over the threshold to their suite her ennui was dispatched by the blatant luxury of the rooms.

A wry smile curving her lips, Valerie silently surveyed the small sitting room. Bemused by the opulence surrounding her, she was unaware of the door's closing or of Jonas's eyes watching her.

I don't know why I should be surprised, she told herself cynically. After his house, the private jet, the cars—her eyes rested on the open doorway to the bedroom, which was also sumptuously elegant—what in the world did I expect, a tiny, rustic motel room in some backwater town?

"Well?" Jonas prompted dryly. "What do you think?"

"Lotus-land," Valerie replied coolly, disparagingly.

"A suitable setting for the princess of never-never land?" he retorted.

Stung, Valerie spun to face him, her eyes showing life for the first time in weeks. "It's positively immoral," she retaliated. "I can't imagine what it must cost just for one night."

"As I have no intention of telling you," Jonas drawled, "there's no need for you to tax your imagination."

The amusement gleaming in his eyes sparked flashing

anger in her own and gave her tongue a sharp edge. "The French kings never knew this kind of indulgence," she snapped, indicating the suite with a condemning wave of her hand.

"Ah, but then," he literally purred, "the French kings never earned an honest dime—or heard of capitalism."

"That—that's exactly what *you* are—a capitalist." Valerie flung the words at him, fully expecting a quick denial. Wasn't everyone ashamed of the title today? Apparently not. At least, not Jonas Thorne.

"To my back teeth," he admitted easily. "Capitalism has made me a rich man." Now he glanced around the room, waved his hand encompassingly. "I'm not ashamed of my money," he informed her seriously. "I didn't inherit it. I didn't steal it. I *earned* it." Hard arrogance underlined every word. "I'll spend it any damned way I please, without anyone's permission—including yours."

"I never—" Valerie began in protest.

"Stop," he interrupted sharply. "Your prim, shocked expression has made your disapproval of my self-indulgence as clear as any tirade would have done."

Bewildered by his harsh accusation, Valerie cried, "I told you once, I have no objection to money."

"Only mine," he sighed striding away from her into the bedroom.

Feeling unfairly accused, Valerie retreated into hurt silence. Moving listlessly, she walked to the wide window to stare out at the city she had yearned to see with sightless eyes. Oh, God, she thought despondently, what have I let myself in for? This—pretense can't possibly work. I can't even talk to him. How could I have thought I could bear to have him touch me? I can't, I can't, she thought wildly. She spun around, and her eyes fastened on the door to the hall. I have got to get away. Her legs moved to put her thought into action. Where she would go, what she would do were unimportant at that moment, for now, her only objective was getting through the door. She was brought to an abrupt stop by a clipped order issued from the bedroom.

"Come in here, Valerie."

Valerie had heard and responded to that same command so many times over the last month that she did so now without conscious thought. It was not until she was inside the room that she paused to wonder why she had obeyed him. Annoyed with herself, she attacked him.

"Who do you think you're ordering around?" she demanded imperiously. "I'm no longer your secretary, remember? I'm your wife."

"Oh, I remember," Jonas said softly. "It was *your* memory I was concerned about."

Valerie didn't have the vaguest idea of what to say to him. That he had seen her move toward the door was pretty obvious. What *could* she say? I'm sorry, Mr. Thorne, but the very idea of your hands on me makes me sick to my stomach? Hardly. His reaction to a statement of that sort would very probably be swift—not to mention painful.

"I—I haven't forgotten," she whispered.

"No? Then where were you going?"

"I don't know," she admitted.

Jonas's lips twisted wryly. "You were just going to run, huh?" He shook his head. "To what? To where? Val, you are twenty-seven years old—when are you planning to grow up?"

Stung, Valerie lashed out at him wildly, thoughtlessly. "I'm getting pretty tired of hearing from you how immature I am. I *am* grown up. Just because the idea of being married to you doesn't appeal to me, that doesn't mean—"

"That's enough," Jonas barked. "No one twisted your arm or kidnapped you. And, whether I appeal to you or not, you're stuck with me, and I'm stuck with you." He grimaced. "So I guess you'll have to bite the bullet and bear it."

"As you will," Valerie taunted.

"Yes," Jonas sighed. "As I will." He stood rigidly a moment, just staring at her, then he shrugged. "This is getting us nowhere, Val. What's done is done. I'm not about to back out and I'm not going to let you renege, either." The tautness went out of his face and his tone softened. "So, what do you want to do?"

"Do?" Valerie repeated nervously.

"Yes, do." The wry smile was back. "It is now—" he shot a quick glance at his watch—"four-twenty. Would you like to do a little sightseeing? Or would you rather start fresh in the morning?"

"I—" Valerie hesitated, thrown off balance by his offer. "You're willing to take me sightseeing?" she asked disbelievingly.

"Well, of course I'm willing," Jonas snapped in exasperation. "We *are* on our honeymoon," he added dryly. "Were you afraid I'd planned to confine you to the bedroom?"

His chiding shot hit home and Valerie blushed, her color deepening when he laughed softly.

"You're really a winner," he jibed, still laughing.

"What, exactly, is that supposed to mean?" she demanded.

"You're so transparent." He shook his head wonderingly. "You ought to win a prize for surviving so long with your eyes firmly closed to reality."

Reality—again? Valerie's flush of embarrassment changed to a flash of irritation. "Watching the man you love die is very real, Mr. Thorne, I assure you." For a few sweet moments she had the satisfaction of watching his face fall, but only for a *very* few short moments. His expression grim, he took one step toward her, then stopped.

"Mr. Thorne?" Jonas gritted. "I'm warning you, *Mrs. Thorne,* don't *Mr. Thorne* me again in that tone of voice. Do you understand?"

"Yes," Valerie gritted back. "If you understand I will not be talked down to. I am sick to death of being treated like a child."

"I was not talking down to you, Valerie. Nor was I implying you are a child," Jonas said patiently. "What I *was* implying is that you are a coward."

Biting her lip, Valerie turned to move away; Jonas moved faster. Crossing the room in a few long strides, he grasped her arm with one hand and her chin with the other, forcing her to look at him.

"I know it took courage for you to watch him die," he said softly. "But I'd be willing to bet you have displayed precious little since. You can't run away from the truth, Val. Sooner or later it will catch up to you." Then all the patience and softness left his tone. "He's dead," he went on brutally, ignoring her gasp of protest. "Nothing is going to change that—*ever.* You are here, and so am I. Accept that fact—and me—and you'll know what is real again.

"I—I can't accept it," Valerie cried.

"You will," he promised grimly. "You have my word on that."

155

Chapter Nine

$\mathcal{F}$or one terrifying second Valerie thought he was going to draw her into an embrace, but then he released her and stepped back.

"I think we'll leave the sightseeing till tomorrow," he said decisively. "Even though it's early here, it's past dinnertime in Philly and I'm hungry." His eyes flicked over her. "You barely touched your lunch. I suggest we have dinner here in the hotel and call it a day."

Valerie dawdled over her dinner, convinced Jonas's blandly stated "call it a day" meant one thing—bed. That he was fully aware of the growing tension inside her was made perfectly clear when, after she asked for yet another glass of wine, he chided sardonically:

"If you are deliberately trying to drink yourself insensible in the hope I'll postpone the inevitable, forget it."

His words sent a chill of certainty through Valerie. There was no way she could avoid what was ahead of her, and she knew it. Still she tried.

"Jonas, I—I can't," she whispered pleadingly.

"You can," he stated flatly. "And you will. You were fully cognizant of what was expected of you." He lifted one eyebrow mockingly. "Unless, of course, you know of another, less physical, way of producing an heir?"

Controlling all but a tiny tremor in her fingers,

Valerie carefully placed her glass on the table, and with equal care, moved her chair back. Jonas was at her side by the time she stood up and no amount of willpower could prevent the shiver that rippled through her when his fingers curled around her elbow. Holding herself stiffly erect, she allowed him to lead her out of the large, nearly empty dining room and across the lobby to the elevators. On entering the suite, Jonas went directly to the fully stocked drinks cabinet provided by the management.

"I'll have a brandy while you shower," he said tonelessly. "I'll be in when my glass is empty—whether you're out of the shower or not."

Valerie walked into the bedroom with cool dignity, but all pretense ended with the closing of the door. With frantic haste she tugged and yanked her way out of the pale lilac dress Janet had insisted she buy before leaving France. As her fingers fumbled with the hooks at the back of her bra her eyes settled on her still closed and locked suitcase.

"Oh, no," she muttered, digging through her handbag for the key to her case.

Finally, divested of her clothes and with nightgown in hand, she dashed into the bathroom and under the shower. She was hastily rubbing herself dry when she heard Jonas enter the bedroom.

Grimacing at the outrageously expensive white chiffon gown Janet had given her that morning, Valerie slipped it over her head and reached for the doorknob. It was suddenly yanked away from her fingertips.

"Perfect timing," Jonas drawled as she scurried past him.

Panic rising in her throat, Valerie searched out her hairbrush and tried to calm herself by the age-old method of slow, repetitive brushing. She had no success.

I can't. I can't. The chant repeated itself over and over in her mind as she stood, still as stone, staring through the window at the fog-shrouded twilight.

"Etienne."

Whispering his name aloud called forth a plan. Jonas had repeatedly accused her of not facing reality. Well, now she would deliberately suspend reality. By the simple process of superimposing Etienne's image over Jonas's, she would not only enable herself to get through the coming ordeal, she might even enjoy it.

And so, when she heard the bathroom door open, Valerie turned calmly to face her husband with a warm smile of welcome.

Her smile faltered as her glance encountered his naked body. Concentrating fiercely, she dredged up her recollection of Etienne's form. The image wobbled and refused to stay together.

Etienne. Etienne. Etienne. Valerie repeated his name in time with Jonas's steps in a desperate effort to reassemble the fading image and hang on to her crumbling plan.

It was impossible, for in no way did this tall, lithe, powerful-looking man resemble the fiancé her memory was having such a hard time picturing.

Why couldn't she remember him more clearly? Why now, when she needed. . . .

"It won't work, Valerie." Jonas's softly taunting voice scattered her thoughts.

"Wha—what won't work?" she stuttered.

"Your little game," he grated. "Your smile was the tip-off." His voice dropped to a threatening growl. "I *will not* play stand in for a dead man, Valerie."

Intimidated by his tone and his overwhelming presence, Valerie moistened her suddenly hot, parched lips. Before she could form words of denial, he confused the issue by lifting his hand to finger the gossamer material of her gown, asking softly, "Are you trying to make a statement with this frothy bit of virginal white?"

"No!" The disclaimer was out before she could even consider her chances of getting a reprieve by avowing purity. "The—the gown was a bridal gift from Janet," she finished softly.

Gathering great folds of the chiffon into his hands, he drew it up her body. "In that case I'll remove it very carefully." The material caressed her skin as he lifted it over her head, and it fell to the floor soundlessly when he tossed it aside.

"Jonas, I—Oh!" Her breath caught with a gasp in her throat at the feel of his palm against her breast.

"Your heart's pounding away like mad," he murmured. "Don't be afraid, Val."

Valerie's eyes closed when his mouth brushed her forehead.

"I'm not a brute, you know. I do know how to be gentle."

As if to prove his claim, he dropped feather-light kisses across her forehead to her temple. When, in trembling reaction to his touch, she attempted to move away from him, he grasped her around the waist with a softly cautioning, "No."

Holding her still, Jonas proceeded to cover every inch of her face with light, teasing kisses; every inch, that is, except her quivering lips. He kissed his way with excruciating slowness down her neck, across both shoulders and then, even more slowly, to her breasts.

159

Valerie's trembling increased while her breathing grew slow and labored.

Feeling her senses beginning to swim, Valerie strove to recall her plan. Etie—, Oh, Lord, what is he doing! Eyes flying open in disbelief, she watched Jonas drop to his knees and lower his head to her breast. Raising strangely heavy arms, she gripped his shoulders to push him away, then dug her nails into his flesh at the riot of sensations his nibbling teeth exploded inside her body.

Oh, God!

All thought was swept away in the tide of sensual pleasure that flowed through her being. Jonas's tongue, flicking like the tip of a whip, teased first one then the other of her nipples into hard, aching arousal before his lips continued on their downward trek.

Following the dictates of her clamoring senses, Valerie let her head fall back, and she moaned softly when Jonas's hands arched her body to his mouth. Driven by a need she was beyond questioning, she moved her hands over his shoulders to the back of his head, the tips of her fingers pressing him closer.

When the hard tip of his tongue stabbed into the small hollow of her navel a shudder of surrender went rippling through her body. As if her shudder was the sign he was waiting for, Jonas tightened his hands, and, using her body as leverage, rose lithely to his feet. Sliding one hand to the center of her back and the other to the base of her spine, he drew her body to the hardness of his own.

Valerie was now aware that Jonas had deliberately by-passed her mouth in anticipation of this moment, but she no longer cared. As he lowered his head her arms curled around his neck, and with lips parted she lifted her head to meet him halfway.

The shock of his mouth sent her over the edge of reason and into the hot, swirling depths of desire. Never would she have believed those thin, hard lips capable of creating such total devastation. Hungrily they devoured her lips while his tongue explored the recesses of her mouth.

Plastered against him, she moved when he did, sinking onto the mattress without protest. With hot, openmouthed, plunging kisses and gently caressing, teasing hands, Jonas brought Valerie to quivering readiness. When his searching fingers found the moist core of her desire, she gasped and cried aloud with pleasure as she parted her thighs in invitation.

Curving his hands around her hips, Jonas moved into position between her soft thighs. Lifting her hips slightly, he entered her carefully, then paused as if savoring the moment of possession. His movements slow, exquisitely sensuous, he drew her with him into the heady realm of passionate expression. Trembling, moaning softly, she clasped his hard body to her until, consumed in the flame of desire, they moved as one. The flame flared higher and higher until Valerie, feeling as though the tension would never end—and not even sure she wanted it to—shuddered with release and cried:

"Oh, God, Jonas!"

"Yes." Jonas drew the word out in a hard tone, deep with satisfaction. "Jonas."

Adrift in an ocean of contentment, she was hardly aware he'd spoken. For an hour, or mere minutes, buoyant with fulfillment, she floated carefree in the nether world midway between sleep and wakefulness.

As her feeling of euphoria faded, reality returned and she was once again conscious of the not unpleasant weight of Jonas's relaxed body. Her left shoulder, where his head rested, and her side from the waist down, were numb—oddly, that too was not unpleasant.

How was it, she mused sleepily, that this man who held the exclusive power to annoy, frustrate, frighten, dismay, and enrage her, all within the short span of a few hours, also held the power to unleash—from deep within her—a powerful, passionate nature she had been ignorant of possessing?

In mute acceptance she faced the realization that Etienne had lacked that power. He had never caused in her a bubbling cauldron of seething emotions. She had believed she loved him passionately. But now, after experiencing Jonas Thorne's passion, she knew better. Comparing the two was like trying to make a comparison between a gentle rain and a deluge. The only similarity was the fact that they were both wet—as Jonas and Etienne were both men—end of comparison.

The introspection created confusion, and was much too much like work. Lazily replete, Valerie simply was not up to the task.

Later, she promised herself drowsily. I'll work it all out later. For now, the temptation to smooth the disheveled strands of Jonas's hair, gleaming silver in the eerie half-light, was too great to resist.

Sliding her fingers through his hair proved very exciting. The silky strands caressed her palm sensuously, triggering a curiosity about how the rest of him might feel. She slid her hand very slowly down the side of his face, testing the feel of his sharply defined cheekbones, the shallow hollow beneath, and the hard line that comprised his jaws.

Very nice—but inconclusive. Further investigation

was definitely called for. Tinglingly alive to every nuance of sensation, her hand slipped over the edge of his beard-roughened jawbone and down the corded column of his neck.

The skin covering his shoulder was moist and surprisingly satiny, beckoning her hand to further study of the subject matter. Engrossed in her exploration, Valerie was unaware of the subtle change in Jonas's breathing, or the very stillness of his supine frame.

His back was an education in muscular development, his hips and flanks a doctoral degree in bone and sinew. Her fingers traced the line of his leg to the knee, hesitated, then trekked up the inside of his thigh; there *was* still the texture of his stomach and chest to measure.

Her hand moved around to his hip and paused again. Dare she continue? She wondered shyly.

"Oh, God, Valerie," Jonas growled softly into her ear. "Don't stop now."

Made brave by his hoarse plea, Valerie slid her palm over his protruding hipbone and across his taut, flat abdomen, enjoying the feel of his muscles contracting under her hand. Her hand moved up, over his navel and onto the slightly concave area between his ribs, and at that moment his ribs expanded as he drew a deep, ragged breath.

Her own breathing becoming quick and uneven, Valerie allowed her hand to caress the breadth of his chest. The hair her fingers slid through was more coarse than that on his head and it tickled her palm. Valerie decided she liked the sensation.

"Oh, sweet heaven." Jonas's groan was echoed by a gasp from Valerie as his tongue slid down her neck and his hand began stroking the inside of her thigh. As his lips slowly kissed a path to her breasts, Jonas shifted his weight, easing his body between her thighs.

"Mmm." His warm breath caressed her lips. Valerie's arm coiled around his neck as his mouth crushed hers. The downward search of his mouth began again, and Valerie lost her hold on reality as his body slid lower on hers. Moaning aloud, she arched her back when his teeth nipped playfully at her hard nipples, but he ignored her silent invitation. Not one spot on her torso was left unkissed.

Whimpering, mindless with desire, her fingers raking through his hair while her body writhed and arched against his lips, Valerie felt on the point of bursting into flames when he finally edged himself up the length of her body. He kissed her mouth, hard. Then, lifting his head, he ordered, "Look at me, Val."

Valerie's tightly closed lids, heavy with passion, opened slowly to reveal desire clouded eyes.

"In our bed there will be no barriers, no shame, no holding back. I will know you and you will know me. Now bring me to you, Val."

"Jonas, I—" Her breath was pushed back into her throat by his thrusting tongue.

His mouth still on hers, he groaned, "Guide me in, Val."

She obeyed him simply because she *wanted* to obey him; she wanted to touch him, and, most of all, she wanted to feel the life of him inside, filling her again to completion.

"Who?" he demanded as that completion was attained.

"Jonas," Valerie gasped.

"Yes,—Jonas, and don't ever forget it."

* * *

The insistent ringing of the phone roused Valerie. Jonas's low curse as he left the bed brought full wakefulness. Rubbing her eyes sleepily, she watched him snatch up the receiver.

"What is it?" Jonas lifted his hand to rake spread fingers through his ruffled hair and Valerie's mouth went dry at the sight of his naked form. In the darkness his body had felt hard and sinewy against hers. In the midmorning light he looked magnificent.

"Okay, I'll take the call." Jonas's hard tone drew her eyes to his equally hard, set features. A chill slid down her spine as her gaze came to a halt on his lips. A shiver followed the chill when his lips twisted into an unpleasant smile.

"This better be good, Charlie." Jonas's tone held a definite threat and Valerie was feeling sorry for Charlie McAndrew when she saw Jonas's eyes sharpen an instant before his lids narrowed. Apparently Charlie's reason for disturbing his employer was very good.

"For God's sake!" Jonas exploded. "Why did you even agree to see him?" He paused, listening, then growled, "I don't give a damn about Trans Electric, they dug themselves into the hole with inefficient management, and they can climb out by themselves." Again he paused to listen, longer this time. "I don't give a damn about them either," he snarled.

Valerie could hear the excited tones of Charlie's voice all the way over on her side of the bed. Something had definitely gone wrong in the last twenty-four hours. Jonas's expression had become positively grim when he turned to run his eyes over her. For a fleeting instant conflicting emotions were evident in his gaze, then his expression locked and he looked away.

"All right, Charlie," he snapped. "Call Caradin in Washington and tell him to get up to Philadelphia. I'll be there in—what the hell time is it, anyway?" He drew a deep breath. "Okay, I'll be there as soon as I can." He practically threw the receiver onto its base. Before it even stopped rattling he snatched it up again.

"Desk, please." There was a pause. "This is Jonas Thorne. I'm checking out. Will you get my bill ready and send the bellhop up in a half hour? Thank you."

This time he replaced the receiver carefully before turning to look at her fully for the first time.

"I'm sorry, Val, but I have to go."

"All right." Valerie heard the disappointment in her tone and cursed herself for it. But—she had so wanted to see San Francisco.

Dropping onto the bed beside her, he caught her face in his hands. "I'll bring you back, I promise." His kiss began as a gentle seal on his promise and quickly changed to a rough, hungry demand. By the time he lifted his mouth from hers her pulses were pounding and she was gasping for breath. His left hand caressed the right side of her body restlessly before honing in on the dark triangle between her legs.

"Jonas!" Valerie protested, even as she arched her body to his hand. "Charlie—Caradin, they'll be waiting for you! And the bellhop will be here. . . ."

"First things first," Jonas whispered. "I'm the boss, remember? Let them wait."

Less than two hours later Valerie was once again strapped into the velour-covered chair, and the Gulfstream was airborne—heading east.

"Come over here."

Jonas's soft command drew her eyes from the small pane of glass to his reclining form.

"What?"

Wedging his body tightly against the arm rest, he patted the small area of exposed seat. "Come here."

His eyes looked heavy-lidded and smoky and Valerie felt her heart thump; oh, yes, they had all been right—he was very, very sexy.

"Come."

She went. After she was settled beside him—very tightly beside him—she found the nerve to risk a question.

"What's going on, Jonas?"

Jonas made no pretense of misunderstanding. "You knew an office was being prepared for someone, didn't you?" Valerie nodded. "That office is for a representative from Edouard Barres. He's coming to work with me on a project Edouard and I are beginning."

This was the first Valerie had heard about any new project, and as Jonas's former personal secretary she felt slightly miffed at being excluded.

"Is this project a secret?" she asked suspiciously. Jonas slanted her a wry glance.

"Not anymore," he replied disgustedly. "The thing started when I was in Paris," he explained. "Edouard was speculating on the feasibility of a smaller, less expensive communications system for space exploration. The idea intrigued me, as I'm sure Edouard had intended it would. I began playing around with it—and came up with a practical solution."

"But—" Valerie frowned. "What does that have to do with Charlie's call?"

"I'm getting to that." Jonas grimaced. "You are also

aware, I assume, that Trans Electric has been having some serious financial trouble?"

"Yes." Valerie nodded again. "Everyone in the industry is aware of it."

"Yes," Jonas repeated. "But so far the general public is not, and Trans Electric is scrambling to find a way to improve the situation before it becomes common knowledge." He smiled, the same unpleasant smile that had twisted his lips earlier. "Somehow—I don't know how, but I'll find out—" he inserted grimly, "The president of Trans got wind of the project. Trans wants a piece of my action and they sent their chief negotiator, a fool by the name of Parsons, to tell us so."

"While you were out of the office," Valerie murmured.

"Hell, yes!" Jonas snorted. "They knew damned well I'd throw him out."

"But," Valerie shook her head, "I don't understand. It's your project. Why would they even dream you'd consider letting them in?"

"Why? Because the president of Trans has friends in high places, of course," Jonas enlightened her. "And not an hour after Charlie showed Parsons to the door, he had a call from Washington. The lyrics had changed, but the tune was the same. It went something like this: Trans could be of great assistance to us while we put this show together. Besides we couldn't possibly let a reputable firm like Trans go under—bad for the economy, you know. And, really, all they're asking for is a tiny slice of what could turn out to be an enormous pie. And—here is the zinger," Jonas sneered. "It has been brought to *someone's* attention that there are several government regulations J. T. Electronics is guilty of having ignored. If pressure were to be applied in certain quarters, a number of our projects could be tied up for an extended period, thereby dealing us a very costly, crippling blow."

Noting her somewhat awed expression, Jonas added, "They really talk like that. Names or specifics are never mentioned, but you know the screws are being applied just the same."

"And that's why you're bringing George Caradin up from Washington," Valerie surmised.

"That's what I pay him for," Jonas concurred.

Valerie was quiet a long time, appalled at the very idea of someone's trying to undercut Jonas in that way.

"Jonas," she said softly. "If nothing you or Charlie, or George, or anyone else can do works, you'll have to go along with Trans, won't you?"

"No." Jonas's tone held hard finality. "It's my pie, and I won't share even a thin slice of it with them. No one picks *my* brain, Valerie."

"But how would you stop them?"

Jonas smiled, crookedly. "I've only been working on this a few weeks. Even though *I* know it's feasible, what I've committed to paper wouldn't mean a thing to anyone else. The majority of the details are still in my head." His smile became strangely benign. "If we can't beat them at their game—I'll set a match to the plans."

"You wouldn't!" Valerie leaned back to stare at him in astonishment. His arm hauled her close to him again and he laughed.

"Watch me."

Chapter Ten

Placing her hair brush on top of the dresser, Valerie turned away from the mirror, then turned back again.

Was it too much? The dress—the makeup? Valerie had lost count of the times she'd run sharply critical eyes over the young woman the mirror reflected back to her. The dress, purchased especially for this day, was very simple, and very chic, the blending of colors from palest pink to deep amethyst complimentary to her white skin and violet eyes. The makeup had been painstakingly, if lightly, applied with all the skill she'd picked up in Paris. Her hair held the sheen of sun striking a raven's wing. Yet she was dissatisfied.

It was so very, very important that she look, if not perfect, then as close to it as possible.

Smoothing her hands nervously over the silky material covering her hips, Valerie let her eyes fasten on the flashing reflection of the diamond on her left hand. He'd be back soon. They would all be here soon. Jonas and Marge, and—Valerie spun away from the mirror— God, what would she be like, this daughter Jonas was bringing home? Would Mary Beth accept her?

Standing perfectly still, hands clenched at her sides, Valerie slowly closed her eyes. She felt actually sick with nerves, and it was all his fault. Why, why, why had Jonas chosen to do it this way?

He had to have realized that his remarriage would be a shock to his daughter. Yet he hadn't told her a thing about it!

Valerie flinched, experiencing again the shock she'd received the night before. Naturally apprehensive, she'd been seeking reassurance when she'd asked him what Mary Beth's reaction had been to their marriage. Now, the memory of his reply still had the power to horrify her.

"I haven't told her."

Beginning to shake, Valerie dug her beautifully manicured nails into her palms. Somewhat hysterically, she pictured the scene at the airport. Marge would, of course, be teary-eyed. Probably Mary Beth would weep a little also. Then she heard Jonas' emotionless, confident voice saying, "Welcome back, Mary Beth. When we get home I'll introduce you to your new stepmother."

Valerie swallowed convulsively against the nausea that suddenly overcame her. Not again, she moaned silently. Clutching her stomach, Valerie ran into the bathroom. There was nothing, of course. Nothing but the dry, wracking heaves. Her stomach had relieved itself of its contents five minutes after she'd opened her eyes that morning. It was morning sickness, Valerie was certain. She didn't know quite how she knew, but know she did. She *was* pregnant. And so, added to the surprise of having a stepmother would be the news that Mary Beth was also to have a sibling.

Oh, why didn't they come so they could get it over with? The waiting was the hardest part. Moving jerkily, Valerie walked to the sliding door, blinking against the glaring brightness of the early afternoon sun. She didn't see the smooth expanse of green lawn or the delicate, new leaves on the surrounding trees, for her attention was directed inward, reviewing the past four weeks of her marriage to Jonas Thorne.

Perhaps, after the wedding night they'd had, if they'd been allowed a few short days—Valerie sighed. What use to think of that now? They had not had a few days, and the beginnings of closeness she'd felt while sharing his seat on the plane had been lost the moment they'd stepped off the craft.

Not one, but two cars had been waiting for them. Valerie had been installed in the one driven by Lyle, and dispatched without a backward glance from Jonas. She had, in all ways but one, remained dispatched.

Valerie shivered in the warm May air. Nothing, nothing that had occurred from the day she met him, had prepared her for the living dynamo Jonas became when he was embroiled in a fight. And his language! Talk about turning the air blue! If she had learned nothing else about him Valerie had learned one thing— Jonas Thorne swore like a seasoned trooper when he was mad. And Jonas had been mad for over three weeks!

Geared for battle, Jonas went almost nonstop. He was always gone in the morning when she woke, no matter how early that was, and it was always late before he retired. And even then he did not rest right away for, whether she was asleep or not, he always drew her to him. Lord, the man's appetite was insatiable!

Had she really ever had doubts? Had she really had moments when she'd wondered if he might lose? In retrospect, it seemed inconceivable that she had, for Jonas was a born winner. Even had he been forced to put a match to his plans, he would have won.

Valerie had known it was over when he'd come home early two days ago. And before he'd said another word she'd known that he'd won. The lines of strain were gone from his face and he'd favored Marge—who claimed falsely that she'd never had any doubts—with a devastating smile.

That night, relaxed for the first time in weeks, and victorious, Jonas had made love to her until she was nearly insensible with her need for him. Valerie shuddered now with remembered ecstasy, her whole body growing warm at the images that flashed through her mind. Turning away from the brightness of the light, Valerie let her gaze rest on the bed. Oh, yes, Jonas had won—more than he was as yet aware of. He'd won her admiration, and her respect, and whether he wanted it or not, her love.

Sighing softly, she walked out of the room. Exactly how little regard Jonas had for her, or her feelings, had been brought forcefully home to her with his cool statement last night.

At Marge's insistence they had been making a last minute inspection of Mary Beth's newly refurbished room, and Marge had stared at Jonas in shocked disbelief.

"You haven't told her?" Marge had finally blurted. "But I naturally assumed—Jonas, why didn't you tell her? It's unfair, not only to Mary Beth, but to Valerie as well."

Unperturbed, Jonas had shrugged. "I was busy here, and she was busy with winding everything up over there." Turning to the door he gave another, dismissive, shrug. "Anyway, I didn't want to tell her over the phone or in a letter."

"But Valerie told her mother over the phone," Marge persisted, following him.

"That's different," Jonas had replied smoothly. "Valerie's mother isn't coming back to the States. Mary Beth is."

Valerie paused halfway down the curving stairway, the conversation of the night before fading as she thought of that phone call to her mother. Why was it, she asked herself, that trouble always seemed to come all at once? It was over three weeks since she'd made that call and shock waves from it were still reverberating through her mind.

Her mother had taken the news of her marriage quite calmly, then had stunned Valerie with news of her own. She was pregnant! Her mother, at forty-six years of age, was pregnant, and happy about it, as well! And she was due sometime around the end of July!

Valerie grimaced and continued down the last few steps and along the hall to the kitchen.

Dorothy Fister, Jonas's housekeeper for over ten years, was at the stove preparing lunch.

"Everything under control, Dot?" Valerie asked from the doorway.

"Of course," the competent woman replied turning to run her glance over Valerie. "You look lovely, Valerie," she added quietly. Like so many of Jonas's other employees, Dot was on a first-name basis with the family. "Don't be nervous," she advised shrewdly. "Mary Beth is a nice girl. Things will work out."

"I hope so," Valerie murmured fervently, turning to leave.

"Oh, I've made up the guest room, just as you asked," Dot added.

Valerie's only reply was a sigh. Another problem, she thought tiredly as she wandered into the living room. With the tenuous relationship between her and Jonas, and Mary Beth's homecoming, the last thing they needed was a house guest. Yet, they were getting one, at least temporarily. Jonas had calmly informed them only yesterday that Barres's man would be arriving today, and as a suitable place had not as yet been found for him, he would be staying with them. Stifling a groan, Valerie stared out the front window.

It was some fifteen minutes later that she saw the gleam of the silver limo as it purred up the driveway. She reached the front door as the Cadillac glided to a smooth stop. Opening it, she felt a thrill of apprehension scurry down her spine at the set expression on Jonas's face as he alighted from the front passenger seat. Something was very definitely wrong, for although his face revealed nothing, Valerie somehow knew that he was very angry. What in the world now? she wondered silently. Not another problem? Then she felt shock stiffen her spine as not two, but three women got out of the car.

Marge was the first one out, and Valerie did not miss the anxious glance she shot at her. Behind Marge came a tall, slim, young blonde who anyone at a glance would know was Jonas's daughter. And after her came an older, equally slim blonde, who anyone would recognize as Mary Beth's mother!

Lynn! Disbelief froze Valerie in place.

Mary Beth's smiling face, and Lynn's smug expression, sent a pang of pure panic through Valerie. He hadn't told them! The truth of her deduction was proved by the curious glances both mother and daughter turned on her as they entered the house. The urge to run, anywhere, was squashed by Jonas's arm sliding around her waist.

"Val, I'd like you to meet my daughter, Mary Beth, and her mother, Lynn." Jonas's smooth tone revealed none of the anger being transmitted to her by his fingers digging into her waist. "Mary Beth, Lynn," his pause was infinitesimal, "my wife, Valerie."

For one instant there was total silence, and then Mary Beth and Lynn spoke as one.

"Your wife!"

Mary Beth was the first to articulate her reaction.

"Dad," she cried, looking directly at Valerie. "When did this happen? And why didn't you tell me?"

"I just did," Jonas answered sardonically. "And *this* happened almost a month ago."

"Really, Jonas—" Lynn began angrily, only to be silenced by her mother.

"Lynn, I don't think the foyer is the place for this discussion," Marge cautioned sharply. "I suggest we go into the living room."

Held in place by Jonas's restraining hand, Valerie stood mutely as they entered. After taking a few steps, Mary Beth turned to glance at them over her shoulder.

"Coming, Dad?"

"*Val* and I will be with you in a moment," Jonas assured her.

Feeling like an intruder, Valerie watched Mary Beth frown as she turned to follow her mother and grandmother.

"She's a lovely girl." Valerie wasn't even aware she'd murmured the observation aloud until Jonas agreed softly, "Yes, she is."

Glancing up at him quickly, Valerie caught the

softening in his eyes, the gentle smile that touched his lips. If he would only look at me that way, just once—Valerie shrugged the wish away, and the hollowness that had followed it.

"Yes?" Jonas's prompting made it clear he had not missed her scrutiny of him.

"Nothing," she said. Then, at the arching of one disbelieving brow, she temporized, "It sounds strange, hearing Mary Beth call you Dad." It wasn't a complete fabrication. It had sounded strange to her and had caused a strange, aching feeling as well.

"It sounds a little strange to me, too," came his surprising reply. "It's been so long since I've heard it." Releasing her, he turned as Lyle entered the house loaded down with suitcases. "Put the red cases in Mary Beth's room," Jonas instructed. "And drop the white ones here in the foyer for the time being."

Valerie eyed the white cases for several seconds after Lyle had retreated before lifting her eyes to Jonas. "Is she staying . . . here?"

"She has before," Jonas said dryly.

"But that was before. . . ."

"Dad?" Mary Beth's soft, but impatient call ended Valerie's protest.

"Coming," Jonas called back. Lowering his voice, he argued, "Her daughter and mother are here, where else would she stay?"

A hotel? A motel? Home? Valerie didn't voice her suggestions. Instead, she reminded him, "You have another guest coming today."

"I haven't forgotten, Val," Jonas assured her smoothly. "Now, shall we join the others?"

Her resentment flared at the note of command in his tone. Seething with impotent fury, Valerie allowed him to usher her into the room. The sight of Lynn's elegant body ensconced in Valerie's favorite chair set her teeth on edge. Damn him, if he'd wanted Lynn in his home why hadn't he remarried *her?* Valerie thought furiously.

Valerie was excluded from much of the ensuing conversation; whether the exclusion was deliberate or not she didn't know, and, at the moment, didn't much care. With cool detachment, she studied Lynn and Mary Beth in turn.

Janet had not been exaggerating when she had said that Lynn was beautiful. She had to be close to forty, Valerie knew, yet she showed none of the usual signs of aging. Valerie decided she hated her.

Mary Beth, on the other hand, was a lovely composite of her mother and father. Tall and slim, with the same high cheekbones and determined jaw as Jonas, she had the blue eyes, pert nose, and golden skin of her mother. Her hair color was strictly her own, being a shade between Lynn's gold and Jonas's ash-blond.

Her hand sliding over her still flat belly, Valerie wondered how her coloring would combine with Jonas's in their offspring. Her eyes grew misty as she contemplated a tall, slim youth with a shock of black hair and cool gray eyes. Suddenly she longed to hold the infant version of that youth in her arms.

"Valerie?"

The rough edge to Jonas's tone jerked her out of her pleasant daydreams of the future. "I—I'm sorry." Valerie blinked at him. "I didn't hear what you said."

"I asked if our guest room was in order?" Jonas frowned.

"Yes, of course." A sickening thought sent heat

flashing through her. He wouldn't install Lynn in the room next to theirs, would he? She had to ask. "Why?"

"That should be obvious," he rapped. "Our guest room is the only one available for Barres's man."

"If you don't mind, I'd like to go to my room and rest awhile." Lynn, one slim hand hiding a yawn, fluttered long lashes at Jonas.

"Of course," Valerie said crisply, gritting her teeth. "I'll show you to your room."

"Don't bother," Lynn purred oversweetly. "I know the way."

To a lot of bedrooms, I'll bet, Valerie thought nastily.

Rising, Marge reached for Mary Beth's hand. "Come along, young lady, I have a surprise for you."

During the ensuing confusion and chatter, Valerie escaped up the stairs, feeling unloved, unwanted, and totally unnoticed.

Although the third floor contained a kitchen and dining area, Jonas and Valerie had always eaten dinner with Marge in the larger dining room downstairs. That evening dinner was, for Valerie, an ordeal. Lynn kept up a constant stream of chatter, much of which was designed to make Valerie uncomfortable.

"You replaced Maria Cinnelli, didn't you?" the older woman began. "Tell me, is he as much of a bear at the office as he is at home? He's always had an awful temper, you know—" casting a sugary smile at Jonas— "swears like a dock worker, too."

Tell me about it, Valerie longed to purr cattily. Actually, by the time they left the table she longed to hiss and claw like a cat. Lynn was, she decided, an absolute witch.

Jonas, seemingly unaware of the battle raging between his past and present wives, was sublimely going about the business of getting reacquainted with his daughter.

Seating herself in an easy chair as far away from Lynn as possible, Valerie concentrated on the conversation between her husband and his daughter.

"By the way," Jonas quizzed Mary Beth, "what happened to your plans to cruise the Aegean this summer?"

"Well—" Mary Beth began, only to be interrupted by the tinkling sound of Lynn's laughter.

"I'm afraid I squashed those plans, Jonas," Lynn cooed. "We were supposed to go on a yacht that belongs to a friend of mine, but when this friend began talking about a match between his penniless nephew and Mary Beth, I decided I'd better bring her home to Daddy."

"Indeed?" Jonas drawled before arching a brow at his daughter. "Do you want to marry this young man?"

"Heavens no!" Mary Beth choked, roaring with laughter. "I'd probably have to share my allowance with him."

"No, you wouldn't," Jonas corrected dryly. "If you married a fortune-hunter you'd have no allowance to share."

That shot sobered Mary Beth. "You mean," she gasped incredulously, "if I marry a man you don't approve of, you'll stop my allowance?"

"That is exactly what I mean, honey-girl," Jonas drawled.

"But—" Mary Beth began.

"But, Jonas, that's ridiculous!" Lynn's shrill voice cut in.

Jonas's eyebrows shot up. "Why ridiculous? Strange, I was under the impression a husband was supposed to support his wife—not her father." His lids narrowed. "I intend to keep what's mine up till the last minute," he warned softly.

"Don't be silly, Jonas," Lynn snapped, obviously upset. "Mary Beth will get the majority of it eventually, anyway."

"Not the majority of it," Jonas corrected even more softly. "At least, not if there's another heir."

"Another heir?" Lynn and Mary Beth cried in unison.

"I see." Lynn's blue eyes glittered. "Is that the *real* reason you married a woman only a few years older than your daughter?"

Valerie steeled herself for Jonas's answer, but just as he opened his mouth to speak, the doorbell rang.

"Ah," he grinned. "Literally saved by the bell. That will be Barres's rep. I'll answer it." His grin widening, he got to his feet and sauntered out of the room.

With his departure three pairs of blue eyes were turned on Valerie. Lynn's in condemnation, Mary Beth's in confusion, and Marge's in commiseration. Unwilling to answer questions, or to withstand their stares, Valerie lowered her eyes. When she lifted them again Jonas stood framed in the archway, a man several years younger than he at his side. Hardly daring to believe her eyes, Valerie whispered:

"Jean-Paul."

Then, with a near shout, she jumped out of her chair. "Jean-Paul!"

"Valerie?"

Jean-Paul was no less surprised than Valerie and as he cried her name he opened his arms.

Unmindful of the tears that blurred her vision, Valerie ran across the room and into his embrace.

For several minutes the air was filled with babbling French.

"Oh, Jean-Paul, it's so good to see you."

"Little one, I've been out of my mind with worry about you."

"Never would I have dreamed you'd be the rep from Barres."

"My sweet girl, why did you leave without a word?"

"But I wrote to your parents!"

"They were visiting me in New York, then they went on to visit with *maman*'s sister in Quebec."

"You look fantastic, but you've lost a little weight."

"You are beautiful as ever, but you've gained a little weight."

"I see you've met my wife, DeBron." Jonas's cold English sliced through the noise of their happy reunion.

"Your wife," Jean-Paul answered, his eyes darting from Jonas to Valerie then back to Jonas.

"*My* wife," Jonas emphasized.

Jean-Paul shifted his eyes to gaze questioningly at Valerie.

"I'll explain everything later, darling," Valerie promised, not seeing the way Jonas stiffened at the endearment. "Please, come in."

Inside the living room, his voice tight, Jonas made the introductions.

"Jean-Paul DeBron—my daughter, Mary Beth."

"*Mademoiselle.*"

"And her grandmother, Mrs. Kowalski."

"*Madame.*"

"And her mother, Lynn Varga."

"Enchan—her mother?" Jean-Paul shot a puzzled look from Lynn to Valerie.

"Yes, Mary Beth's mother." Lynn's honeyed tone drew Jean-Paul's eyes back to her. "I'm Jonas's *first* wife," she purred.

"I assume," Jonas spoke with deceptive softness, "you met my wife while she was living in France?"

"But of course," Jean-Paul replied, still looking puzzled.

"Jonas," Valerie said quietly, "Jean-Paul is Etienne's brother."

Valerie stood under the shower spray as long as she dared. Jonas was angry. Wrong. He was furious. In fact, he had seemed to be in a black fury for most of the last month, ever since Jean-Paul had arrived, come to think of it. Wasn't Jean-Paul's work up to Jonas's expectations? Was that why he had been constantly on the edge of anger all these weeks? And tonight she had pushed him over the edge.

Valerie sighed. Why, why had she risen to Lynn's taunting and allowed herself to ruin Jonas's birthday dinner by lashing out the way she had? He had seemed so genuinely pleased, too. You're a fool, she chided herself. But, even a fool can take only so much torment. And Lynn had made sure Valerie got more than her fair share.

Four weeks of snide remarks and veiled innuendos had proved to be Valerie's limit. It was Lynn who had so carelessly told her that Maria Cinnelli was back in Jonas's good graces *and* in his office. It was Lynn who inferred that Jonas was paying the rent on Maria's apartment. It was Lynn who hinted that Jonas had dropped several obscure remarks to the effect that he was now sorry he'd married so hastily. But the real topper came when Lynn slyly suggested that, should Valerie waken one night to find herself alone, she should check Lynn's room first. It was because of Lynn that Valerie had not yet told Jonas that she thought she was pregnant.

And then, tonight, something had just snapped inside of Valerie. Again she sighed. I could have taken it for myself, Valerie thought angrily, but why did she have to start on Jean-Paul? God! The memory of Mary Beth's striken face made her want to weep. Hadn't Lynn seen the love growing between Mary Beth and Jean-Paul? How could she have missed it? But then, Valerie knew Jonas had not seen it either. But, of course, that was different. Jonas was much too busy to see anything as unelectronic as love. He hadn't even seen his own wife's love for him!

Which still doesn't answer that question of why I had to ruin Jonas's dinner by flying to Jean-Paul's defense when Lynn made that disgusting remark about how she'd heard somewhere that French brothers shared their women. Even though Lynn had laughed as if teasing when she said it, she had hurt two people who were close to Valerie: Jean-Paul and Mary Beth—who was now dear to Valerie *because* of Jean-Paul. So I told her to shut her filthy mouth! It was long past time *someone* did. The problem was, now she had to face Jonas.

With sudden determination she turned the shower off. What could he do, stand her against the wall and shoot her? The picture that formed from that idea—she could see herself against the wall, a blindfold over her eyes, a last cigarette dangling from her lips—was ludicrous. Valerie had to stifle a giggle. She didn't even smoke! A hand flew to her mouth to muffle her nervous laughter.

"Val, what are you doing in there?"

Valerie's laughter dried along with all the moisture in her mouth and throat. Squaring her shoulders she went to face the firing squad.

The first volly hit her as she walked into the bedroom.

"Does he look like Etienne?"

Valerie paused, controlling the urge to step back. "No, not much," she answered truthfully. "His voice and eyes are almost the same, though." Why, she wondered, had he waited till now to ask questions?

"You obviously got to know him very well."

Valerie didn't trust his tone. It was much too silky. Surely he hadn't taken Lynn's sick remark seriously? "What do you mean?" she bristled.

"You called him darling when he arrived. You flew to his defense tonight." He shrugged. "You're very fond of him?"

"Yes, very," Valerie admitted. Her voice grew husky. "He—Jean-Paul was very kind to me when—when. . . ."

"Never mind," Jonas cut into her throaty explanation. "I get the picture." He turned away, then swung back to face her, his mouth grim. "You must not let Lynn get to you. She loves shocking people." He shook his head. "I sometimes think she is less mature than Mary Beth."

"I'm sorry your birthday dinner was spoiled," Valerie said softly.

"Are you?" he asked with equal softness. "Well, in that case, we could celebrate the occasion right here."

Walking to her, he slid his arms around her and drew her close to his long frame. "Say, happy birthday, Jonas," he ordered in a near growl.

"Happy birthday, Jonas," Valerie repeated, smiling.

"Very good," he murmured close to her ear. "Now say, take me to bed, Jonas." His tongue, teasing the side of her neck, sent expectant shivers down through her body. His hands, tormentingly caressing the very outer curve of her breasts, removed her inhibitions.

"Take me to bed, darling." Valerie gasped when his fingers dug into the soft flesh of her breasts.

"Do you call all your lovers darling?" he demanded harshly.

"Jonas, you're hurting me," Valerie cried, holding her breath in an effort to relieve the pressure.

"I know." His fingers loosened but his arms tightened. "You make me *want* to hurt you." His lips brushed hers, the tip of his tongue urging them apart. "Say it again, Val, I want to hear it, even if it means nothing."

Nothing. Valerie closed her eyes against the rush of hot tears. It means nothing to him. Which means *I* mean nothing to him. Nothing deep, nothing lasting. I'm a convenience, a warm body that's nearby whenever the need arises. Dear God, I love him, and all he wants from me is an heir and the moaning, feverish words that attend the begetting of that heir. Meaningless. Nothing.

"Val."

Jonas's urgent groan pierced her mind, and her heart. Why not, she thought wildly. His teeth nipped her lower lip and she shuddered in response. Why not give him what he wants? It's his birthday. Curling her arms around his neck, she returned his playful bite.

Happy birthday, Jonas, she cried silently, you're going to be a father. Her voice, when she spoke, was thick from unshed tears.

"Take me to bed, darling."

It was late when Valerie woke, which was not surprising. Jonas had not let her sleep till near dawn. Groaning aloud, she stretched aching muscles. Lord, where did that man get his energy? He was gone. Hours earlier, she had been vaguely aware of his movements as he showered and dressed to go to the office. Had he invented some kind of machine that kept him charged electrically? Valerie would not have been in the least surprised to find that he had. And during the night he had transmitted some of that electricity to her. It had been like a charge running between them. Jonas had generated fresh sparks with each new impassioned endearment she had moaned against his mouth or skin.

Sliding her fingers into her tangled hair, Valerie swallowed against the tightness in her throat. Was this the way the rest of her life was going to be? Hours and hours of indifference followed by moments of sweet, hot passion? Shaking her head to banish the chilling thought, she jumped out of bed. She had to do something, anything that would keep her from thinking.

Two weeks later, Valerie visited a doctor. During those two weeks she had seen more of Jean-Paul and Mary Beth than of Jonas. In an effort to avoid Lynn, Valerie had spent more time away from home than Jonas had. Dear, gentle Jean-Paul, what would she have done without him? He had not only become her shield against Lynn, he had, in effect, given her Mary Beth.

Mary Beth had felt a natural resentment on coming home to find a stepmother in residence. Jonas's flat announcement about his hopes for another heir hadn't exactly endeared Valerie to her. But Jean-Paul's love had enabled Mary Beth to let her guard down enough to get to know her new stepmother. By the time Jonas celebrated his thirty-ninth birthday, Mary Beth and Valerie were friends—a fact that Jonas had not yet come to recognize.

Not having the slightest idea of which doctor to see, Valerie made an appointment with Dr. Milton Abramowitz, simply because Marge had mentioned having to see him for her six-month checkup soon after Valerie and Jonas had married.

It was not until after she was ushered into Dr. Abramowitz's office that Valerie learned he was a member of Jonas's small circle of close friends. By the time she left his office, Valerie was calling him Milt—at his request—and glowing at his confirmation of her condition.

Her euphoria lasted all the way home. Lynn burst her rosy bubble as soon as she entered the house by announcing, in a self-satisfied tone, that Jonas would not be home for dinner. Valerie had her foot on the bottom step of the stairs when Lynn added, sweetly, that she also would not be there.

For several seconds Valerie felt nothing but devastating disappointment. Then, suddenly, anger engulfed her. Who, she seethed, did this woman think she was? And, for that matter, who the hell did Jonas Thorne think *he* was? Lifting her head regally, Valerie stared coldly at Lynn.

"Let me assure you," she said icily, praying she could

back up what she was about to say, "Jonas *will* be home for dinner. As for you," she went on scathingly, "I couldn't care less if you *never* came back."

"Indeed?" Lynn sneered. "Well, *darling*," she simpered sweetly, "We'll see about that! When Jonas hears about this you just might find that you're the one who goes and never comes back. I've put up with this situation long enough," she snapped. "I think it's time Jonas put an end to this farce of a marriage."

Valerie, shaken by Lynn's complacency, hesitated a moment, and then, with far more confidence than she was feeling, she went to the phone.

"I'm afraid you are riding for a fall, young lady. A bad fall," Lynn opined condescendingly as Valerie punched out the number of Jonas's private line. Steeling herself against rejection and subsequent humiliation, Valerie forced her voice to a cool calmness as she replied to Jonas's impatiently snapped "Thorne."

"Jonas, this is Valerie," she said unnecessarily. "Lynn tells me you won't be home for dinner and I . . ."

"That's right," Jonas cut in harshly. "I called to tell you I had some work I wanted to finish up here, but Lynn told me you were out . . . again. Strangely, Jean-Paul had to be out of the office today also."

There was something disturbing in the way he emphasized his last statement, but, filled with the importance of her news and the fear that he would refuse the request she was about to make, Valerie shrugged aside her feeling of unease and plowed on.

"Jonas, I would—" She paused, searching for the right word. "I would appreciate it if you *could* get home. There's something I must t. . . ." She almost said "tell," but quickly changed her phrasing. "There is something I must discuss with you."

Valerie held her breath through the moment of silence that followed her request, letting it out slowly and soundlessly when Jonas finally spoke.

"Is this discussion—important?" he asked somewhat grimly.

"Yes," Valerie said quietly.

"All right, Val, I'll be home in time for dinner," Jonas said as quietly and then, without a good-bye, he hung up.

Schooling her features into an expressionless mask, Valerie turned to face Lynn. "Jonas *will* be home for dinner." She looked Lynn straight in the eye. "Perhaps *you* are the one riding for a fall."

"We'll see, little girl," Lynn spat, pure hate glittering in her eyes. With a dramatically sweeping motion she walked to the door. Pulling the door open she cast a withering glance over Valerie. "Oh, yes, we will see."

Suddenly exhausted, Valerie walked tiredly up the stairs and into the bedroom to drop limply onto the bed. Hours later the slamming of the bedroom door startled her awake. Jonas was standing just inside the door, his narrowed eyes fixed on her.

"You said there was something you had to discuss with me?" he prompted without preamble.

"Yes," Valerie whispered through parched lips. Why, she thought wildly, should telling him be so difficult? She was going to give him what he had wanted from her, wasn't she?

"I'm pregnant," she blurted out, then held her breath. She held it a long time, finally releasing it when he didn't respond. Why was he so still and quiet? Why didn't he say something? He *had* claimed he wanted an heir, so why was he so silent, so taut? When he finally did reply his voice had an odd, tense inflection.

"You're positive? It's been confirmed?"

"Yes, I saw Dr. Abramowitz this afternoon."

"This afternoon," he repeated softly. "I see."

What did he see? Valerie asked herself blankly. What was there for him to see? She was going to have his child and all he seemed capable of saying was "I see." Where was the tender concern she had hoped for? Where was the joy? Glancing up at him, Valerie stopped breathing altogether. Joy? His eyes were slate-gray with rage, his body stiff with the emotion. As she cringed, Jonas stode to the bed to stand over her menacingly.

"And did you really believe I'd support your fun and games?"

"Fun and games?" Valerie shook her head in confusion. "Jonas, what are you talking about?"

"You," he rasped. "And that damned Frenchman."

Frenchman? Jean-Paul? Me and Jean-Paul? No! She cried silently, he can't believe that Jean-Paul and I are. . . . The idea was insupportable, and in an effort to deny it she began, "Jonas, you can't—"

"*And* the burden you're carrying inside your body," he interrupted nastily.

His words, his tone, were shocking. His crudeness insulting. Enraged, Valerie flung herself off the bed with such force that Jonas was startled into backing up. "Burden!" she screamed. "How dare you! Why are you talking like this?"

"Very simple, Val," Jonas retorted. "What exactly are you carrying? A young Thorne—or another De-Bron?"

Another DeBron? The words echoed inside her head

191

as Valerie felt the color drain out of her face. Wide-eyed with shock, she stared at him in disbelief. He actually thought . . . ?

"I don't believe what I just heard." Although her voice was a rough whisper when she began, it rose steadily. "You . . . you think that I've been . . . like that? With Jean-Paul?" Gasping for breath, she controlled her voice enough to say, "You're nothing but a gutter-minded. . . ." she raked her mind for the most stinging condemnation she could think of, "bastard!" Valerie flung the word at him.

"Exactly," Jonas agreed quietly. "In every sense of the word." Valerie stared anew at the unfamiliar sound of contrition in his tone. "I'm sorry, Val." Turning away from her abruptly, he strode out of the room.

He was on the stairs before Valerie came out of her shock. She couldn't let him go like this!

"Jonas!" Galvanized into action, she ran after him. She heard his car start up as she reached the bottom of the stairs and in an effort to intercept him she ran out of the front door. Jonas was backing the silver Cadillac out of the drive alongside the house.

"Jonas!" Without pausing to think, she flew down the steps and along the front of the house toward the car just as he swung it back in her direction onto the curving drive.

The anguished shout was heard an instant before the car's back fender brushed her hip and spun her off her feet to land with a thud in a large privet hedge bordering the drive.

"Valerie!"

Chapter Eleven

*É*tienne's brother. Millions of Frenchmen in the world, and Barres sends me Etienne's brother. Oh Lord.

What will I do if she dies?

Damnit, why did I listen to Lynn? Jonas could almost hear her voice purring cattily—was it only yesterday? He could still see her wide blue innocent eyes.

"Jonas, really," Lynn had sighed. "If you don't care for yourself, will you consider your daughter?"

"Lynn, I haven't the vaguest idea what you're talking about," he'd snapped, asking himself why he'd let her into his office in the first place. "I don't have time for your innuendos. Either explain or get out of here."

"You know, there are times I wonder what any woman would want with you," Lynn retorted. "You are. . . ."

"Out," he'd cut in impatiently.

"All right," Lynn purred, as if satisfied with herself for making him angry. "I'm talking about your lovely *young* wife and the fact that she's been seen, by mutual friends, not only *with* Jean-Paul, but coming out of his apartment as well." Her purr became silky. "The apartment, I might add, that *you* pay for."

Why had he listened?

Face it, Thorne, you no more listened to Lynn than

193

you would any other idiot who might presume to advise you. The questions, the suspicions were there long before Lynn injected her dose of poison. In point of fact, the feeling of unease he'd been living with for weeks had begun when Etienne's brother walked into the house and Valerie called him darling.

Lord God, what will I do if she dies?

Had Valerie ever had the courage to ask him, Jonas could have—but probably would not have—told her he did not only swear when he was mad, but when he was upset, as well. And now, at six-o-three on a rainswept June morning, Jonas was not only upset; he was terrified.

The baby was lost. Jonas had faced that at once. He winced as he recalled her last faint words:

"Jonas, please, tell them to save my baby."

What he had told them was:

"You had damned well better save my wife."

He knew he couldn't back up his threats. Yet he'd made them, thereby straining the long friendship between himself and Valerie's obstetrician, Milton Abramowitz.

Jonas's clenched fist came down lightly against the windowsill, the very lightness of the blow betraying the self-control he was exerting over himself.

Had he really threatened Milt with a malpractice suit? Jonas shook his head in disbelief. For a few minutes there, right after they'd arrived at the hospital, he'd gone slightly mad.

A soft, steady stream of expletives rolled off his tongue, each more colorful than the last, before Jonas pulled himself up short. Hell, he was still slightly crazy. But it was the waiting that did it. The waiting, and the wondering, and the pure, stark fear.

God, how long have I been in love with her?

In an effort to escape the fear clutching at his guts, Jonas played a game in his mind, trying to pinpoint *the* day.

Was it the evening Etienne's brother came to the house that first time? Without even considering it, Jonas shook his head. No, it must have been before that—he'd reacted too strongly when she'd called Jean-Paul darling.

What would I give to hear her call me darling? And really mean it? All my money? Without question. My immortal soul? In a second.

What has that got to do with it anyway, you arrogant fool? Jonas derided himself. She hasn't asked you to give up anything. She doesn't want your money, or your soul, or your love either. His sigh sounded loud and harsh in the small, quiet room.

Not even Lynn's arrival had had much of an impact on her. The fist resting on the windowsill tightened until the knuckles turned white. Oh, she'd been angry, sure, but her anger had been swiftly forgotten with the advent of Jean-Paul. Etienne's brother, for God's sake. His lips twisting bitterly, Jonas remembered the way Valerie had gone after Lynn when she'd attacked Jean-Paul.

Suddenly realizing he was beginning to think in circles, Jonas turned away from the window impatiently. What was taking so long? Crossing the room in a few long strides, he dropped wearily onto the plastic covered torture-rack they dared to call a couch, and picked up the March issue of *Time*. Jonas had skimmed through the issue the week it came out, but that didn't matter, he wasn't reading anyway.

Was it on their wedding night? The day after?

Musingly, Jonas continued with his game. No, he gave a brief shake of his head. Not then. That he had been both eager and determined to consummate the marriage—and equally determined that she be fully aware of who was doing the consummating—pointed to his having been in love before that night.

The day he proposed to her in the office? He remembered how tense he'd become while waiting for her answer. And later that day, after he'd sent her home, he'd grown still more nervous, afraid she'd change her mind.

Did that nervousness indicate the presence of love? Jonas didn't know for sure, but he had a strong suspicion it did. Never having been in love before, he wasn't quite sure of the components that went into the emotion. Not knowing the language, how was a man supposed to read the signs? If those components included the desire to protect, possess, and pamper a woman, well then, he was definitely in love.

Under better circumstances it might even be enjoyable. Jonas grimaced. Damn Jean-Paul! Jonas's grimace changed to a half-smile of self-mockery. There was no earthly reason to damn Jean-Paul, and Jonas knew it. Jean-Paul was innocent—at least as far as Valerie was concerned. And Valerie was innocent as well. Why had he let his suspicions and his mouth run away from him like that? He had known the child was his from the moment the words "I'm pregnant" came out of her mouth.

His last thought propelled him out of the couch and back across the tiled floor to the window. He knew the child *had* been his, he amended thoughtfully.

That the child was lost he was certain. Jonas shuddered as his mind replayed the events of the evening

before. God, would he ever completely forget the fear
that had gripped him when he had glanced in the
rearview mirror and seen Val running into the back of
his car? Jonas shuddered, remembering how he'd
slammed on the brakes and flung open the car door to
run to her and lift her, white and shaken, out of that
hedge. Why was it, he fumed now, that doctors were
never available when you really needed them? After
carrying Val inside he had called Milt, only to be told
the doctor was in the delivery room. By the time Milt
returned the call, Valerie was ensconced in their bed,
her color restored, insisting that but for a few minor
scratches she was fine. Now, twelve hours later, Jonas
asked himself why he'd allowed her to dissuade him
from taking her to the hospital at once.

"Really, Jonas," she had pleaded. "I'm feeling much
better. I promise I won't get out of this bed before
tomorrow, and then only to go see Dr. Abramowitz."

And both he and Milt had listened! That was what
bothered him now. But, she *had* seemed all right!
Until, less than three hours ago, she'd called out for
him, wakening him from the light doze he'd fallen into
on a living room chair. Just thinking about it created
that same tightness inside that he'd experienced at the
panicky sound of her voice, and the same gripping fear
he'd felt on entering the bedroom to find her standing
beside the bed, white-faced with pain. If he lived
another hundred years he'd never forget the terror that
had momentarily frozen his entire mind and body at the
sight of all that blood! Her blood! In that frozen instant
he had been certain that the life was flowing out of her.
He was also certain that if she died, life would never
again hold any real value for him. Not even his work
could fill the void losing her would leave inside him.

She can't die! Damnit, I won't let her die! I can't give her up. I won't give her up! Not even to death. Why doesn't Milt come? What *is* taking so long?

Val, don't leave me!

Jonas stood very still by the window, shocked motionless by the intensity of his thoughts. Never had he experienced such agony of mind. Not even at the vulnerable age of seventeen when, for two months, he'd carried the anguish of uncertainty about whether or not he'd fathered the child Lynn was carrying.

The child! Once again his large, bony hands balled into fists. Had she lost his son? Jonas swallowed against an unfamiliar tightness in his throat. Valerie hadn't *lost* the child, *he* had robbed her of it!

No, his head moved in sharp denial. It had not been his fault. It had not been her fault either. It had been one of those stupid accidents that happen at times. And it *had* happened. No point in casting blame now.

Jonas was not a man to wallow in guilt or regret. What was done could not be undone. All he could do now was hope Valerie could have another child. *His* child.

If she lives.

She has to live, damnit. She has *got* to live!

What is taking so long?

Was this what *she* had gone through while Etienne had teetered between life and death? This sudden, new insight made him go still again. No wonder you withdrew, love, Jonas at last sympathized. The pain is close to unbearable.

Don't leave me, love. Mentally Jonas did what he would never be able to do aloud; he pleaded. Please, fight to hang on to your precious life, for if you die, living will be hell, but I cannot withdraw from it. Once again the words Jonas could not voice aloud screamed through his mind:

What will I do if she dies?

In an effort to escape the merry-go-round of his thoughts, Jonas jerked back the sleeve of his jacket to expose his watch. Had he really been here two hours? It seemed impossible, yet even as he gazed at the small face of the slim gold disc, the digital number changed from one to two. Six-twenty-two, and he had dashed out of the house with Val in his arms at around four-thirty.

It was a wide-awake nightmare. How often had he heard that phrase and dismissed it as exaggeration? Jonas shrugged. Live and learn. That's what life is all about, isn't it? What point in living if you *never* learn? And what have you learned, Thorne? That you are as capable as the next guy of feeling very deep pain and very real fear.

Your mind's meandering, Thorne. Jonas pulled his rambling thoughts together. You had better go back to the game.

Why bother? he asked himself scathingly. You *know* that what began as desire for her very quickly became love. What purpose in pinpointing the exact day, hour and minute? You love her. But *she* still loves a dead man—or his memory. She doesn't love you.

Impatience riding him, Jonas strode to the door and into the corridor. It was eerily quiet. Hadn't he always heard about how noisy hospitals were when the patients were sleeping? Where was everyone? Where was Milt?

He swung around and strode back into the waiting room. Reaching into the slash pocket of his jacket, he yanked out a crumpled cigarette pack, grimacing as he withdrew the last cigarette in the package. For an instant he contemplated going in search of the lunch-room or a cigarette machine. Then, with a shake of his head he decided to stay put. Surely Milt would come soon?

Some ten or fifteen minutes later, Jonas stood staring out at the lashing rain, his long fingers drumming a staccato beat on the windowsill, when a soft voice interrupted his thoughts.

"Dad."

Jonas turned to sweep his gaze over his daughter and frowned darkly.

"What are you doing here?" Jonas's tone betrayed his surprise.

"I came to be with you," Mary Beth answered quietly. "And to bring you some coffee." She held a stainless steel thermos bottle aloft. "Gram sent it."

"The coffee I could use," Jonas growled, walking to her. "The company I can do without." He plucked the bottle out of her hand.

"Dad!"

"What do you want here, anyway? Did you come to gloat?"

"How could you even think something like that?" Mary Beth reproached him softly.

"I can think that, because you have given me good reason to think it," Jonas retorted. "You would have resented the child, the same as you resent her. Very likely you resent *me* for marrying her in the first place." Turning away, he walked back to the window, opened the thermos, and poured the steaming brew into the steel cup.

"That's not true," Mary Beth denied.

Gripping the cup as if he'd like to crush it, Jonas turned to face her, controlling his anger with difficulty.

"Isn't it? Can you honestly tell me you're sorry the baby's gone?"

"I *am* sorry," she choked, her eyes pleading for him to believe her.

"Are you? Why?" Studying her intently, Jonas sipped tentatively at the hot coffee, apparently unmoved by her stricken expression.

Her eyes swimming, Mary Beth bit down on her lip. "Daddy, please," she cried, "don't be like this. I—I know I was cool to the possibility of a baby at first, but—well, I'm twenty, for heaven's sake. How did you expect me to react?" Jonas opened his mouth but before he could answer she went on, earnestly, "I've had *all* your love for those twenty years. I . . . I guess I thought of you as my exclusive property. But Valerie can tell you that over these last few weeks we have become friends, and, well, I was kind of hoping for a brother or sister." When he didn't reply, Mary Beth reached out to grasp his arm. No longer even trying to contain her tears she sobbed, "Daddy, you *have* to believe me. I never, never wanted anything like this to happen."

What she said was true, he realized. She *had* had his love exclusively—with the exception of Marge—for the entire time she had been on this earth. Her reaction to his remarriage, and to his statement about another heir, had been completely normal. You're lashing out in fear, Thorne, he told himself wryly. Placing the cup on the windowsill with one hand, Jonas reached out with the other to draw his daughter to him. "Okay, okay, honey, don't cry. I'm sorry I snapped at you, I'm a little worried and not thinking too clearly."

Her arms clasped tightly around his waist, her forehead resting against his knit shirt, Mary Beth was just beginning to feel secure again when his words registered. Swallowing a half-sob, she looked up at him wide-eyed. "What do you mean? Why are you worried? Valerie *is* going to be all right, isn't she?"

"I don't know, honey." Unconsciously his arms tightened around her slim form. "It's taking so damned long." Jonas sighed. "I just don't know."

Her eyes wide with amazement, Mary Beth stared up at her father in astonishment. "You're in love with her!" she exclaimed softly. "You really are in love with her!"

Jonas fully understood her astonishment; he had been acting like anything but a man in love. But that didn't mean he was going to share his thoughts with Mary Beth. Arching his oddly dark brows, he asked, "Had you thought I wasn't?"

"Well. . . ." She paused, then went on quickly: "Mother said that you were getting scared."

"Scared?" His brows went up further.

"About," Mary Beth bit her lip, suddenly sorry she'd mentioned her mother. "Well, about losing your youth."

"She said *what?*" Jonas laughed without humor.

"She said that you were probably getting edgy about getting close to forty, and that's why you married a woman so much younger than yourself. She said it happens to a lot of men, and that the marriages seldom work."

"And of course your mother's an expert on what it takes to make a marriage work." Jonas again laughed without humor.

"Well, kid, I've got a news flash for your mother. The threat of reaching forty bothers me not at all, and the difference between Val's age and mine never even entered my mind. And as far as our marriage goes, let me assure you, it will work." Brave words, Thorne, he chided himself. Yet he knew that if it was at all up to him the marriage would survive. If *she* does, he amended.

"Dad?" Mary Beth's soft voice broke into his thoughts. "Do you think we should call Gram? She's concerned too, you know. She really likes Val."

"I know." Releasing her he turned to pour more coffee into the steel cup. "I think we'll wait until I've talked to Milt. There's no point in getting your grandmother upset needlessly. For all I know about this sort of thing, *I* may be worrying needlessly." He raked his hand through already disheveled hair, then asked, "Do me a favor, honey, and go see if you can find me a pack of cigarettes."

As she swung out of the room Jonas drained the cup of coffee Marge had laced with whiskey and poured what was left in the thermos into the cup. Taking a sip he silently thanked Marge for the whiskey. It helped; but not much. What *was* taking so long? If he didn't hear something soon he'd start raising some hell. No, Thorne, he advised himself sternly, raising hell won't help a bit. And if she does die nothing is going to help.

Jonas moved uncomfortably, not liking the sensation of fear that gripped his insides at this last thought. He was making his fourteenth circuit of the room when Mary Beth came back.

"Still no word?" she asked unnecessarily.

"No," Jonas shook his head. "Nothing."

"I'm sorry I took so long," she apologized as he brought the flame of his lighter to the end of a cigarette. "But I took a minute to call Jean-Paul."

The sharp click of the lighter sounded loud in the

quiet room. "You did what?" Jonas asked in an ominously soft voice.

"I said I called Jean-Paul," Mary Beth repeated, missing the edge in his tone. "He loves her too, you know."

"I had an idea he did." Jonas's voice had become raspy. Drawing deeply on the cigarette, he thought of all the times she had been with the Frenchman during the last weeks. Had she, he wondered, transferred her love for Etienne to the brother whose voice and manner were like his?

Jean-Paul can't have her. The thought seared into his mind like a hot flame, only to be followed by one that chilled him: Can I keep her if she decides to go to him? A wave of fierce possessiveness swept over him and he dragged deeply on the cigarette to hide his reaction from Mary Beth. Lord, just thinking about her leaving gave him the shakes. She isn't only under my skin, he thought hollowly, she's in my blood.

"Dad?" Mary Beth's sharp tone broke into his circling thoughts.

"Are you listening to me? I said Jean-Paul asked if one of us would call as soon as we hear anything."

Jonas swore to himself savagely. I could strangle the idiot and he calmly requests that I call him. Call him? I'll fire him.

"Dad?" Mary Beth repeated worriedly, obviously thinking he had not heard her the first time.

Deciding to leave her in the dark, Jonas looked at her blankly. "What did you say?"

"I said Jean-Paul is very concerned and he asked if we'd call him when we hear something."

"Yeah, okay, if we ever do hear anything." Swinging away from her he strode to the door and shouldered his way into the hall. He was just in time to catch sight of a nurse as she disappeared into an office. Lord, the place was as quiet as a morgue. That thought sent him back into the waiting room.

"Dad, you're making me nervous with your prowling back and forth. Sit down and talk to me," Mary Beth coaxed.

"What do you want me to talk about?" Jonas grimaced as he lowered his long frame into a molded plastic chair.

"You, and Valerie." Jonas stiffened visibly and she went on hurriedly, "Don't close me out, Dad, please."

"What, exactly, do you want to know?" Jonas sighed.

"Well, for one, why didn't you make it plain from the beginning how you felt about Val?" Jonas moved to get up and she placed a staying hand on his tautly held arm. "Don't you see that if you had, I very probably would have accepted the news of your marriage a lot more easily?"

"Perhaps," Jonas conceded.

"And surely you realize that Mother would not have built up her hopes of a reconciliation with you if. . . ."

"Wait a minute," Jonas cut in sharply. "Are you telling me that's why she came to the States?"

"Yes, of course," Mary Beth insisted. "When she found out that you sent Maria Cinelli packing she. . . ."

"How did she find that out?" Jonas again interrupted.

"She said that a friend had mentioned it in a letter," Mary Beth explained. "Anyway, when she found out, she canceled our plans to go cruising. She told me she thought you were probably tired of the swinging life and were ready to settle down." At that point Jonas attempted to cut in again, but she held up her hand in a silent bid to be allowed to finish. "I guess I had myself convinced she was right and was all set for an announcement of your remarriage. That's why I was so shocked when you introduced Val as your wife."

"You should have known better," Jonas snapped in exasperation. "You know I don't love Lynn. If you want the truth, I never did love her. You're old enough to count. You know why I married her in the first place." At her pained expression he stood up and pulled her into his arms. "Honey, I've never been sorry you were conceived. But that doesn't change the facts. I never would have considered marrying her otherwise. I tolerate her for you and your grandmother."

"I suppose I always knew that." Mary Beth smiled tremulously. "And I'm really not sorry you married Val. I've come to like her very much these last few weeks."

Dropping his arms Jonas walked to take his place at the window. "I'm glad you like her, but it wouldn't have made any difference whether you did or not, I hope you realize that."

Mary Beth smiled ruefully. "I've known you a long time, remember? I've always known that you do exactly as you please, no matter what I, or anyone else, thinks." She hesitated a moment, then decided to brave his anger by asking, "Does she love you, Dad?"

"No." Jonas said bluntly, grimly. "But I knew that when I asked her to marry me." A teasing smile curled up the corners of his mouth. "Any other questions, nosey kid?"

"No." Mary Beth shook her head. "And I'm sorry, Dad, I wasn't prying, honestly."

Jonas smoked one cigarette after the other as the minutes dragged slowly by.

"Why don't you go on home, sweetheart," he told Mary Beth as he crushed out his fourth. Then, immediately lighting another, he rasped, "Where the hell is Milt?"

And at that moment, as if in answer to his question, Milt Abramowitz pushed open the waiting room door.

"She's all right," he said at once. "But we lost the baby. I'm sorry, Jonas."

Expelling his breath slowly, Jonas nodded. "I am too. Are you sure Valerie's going to be all right?"

Even though Milt heard the anxious edge in Jonas's tone, he snapped, "Do I question your knowledge of electronics? She is weak, but she will be fine."

"Okay, Milt, I'm sorry. But what took so long?"

"I work slow, but I work neat," Milt drawled in a tone that had infuriated more than one of his patients' husbands.

Jonas was not infuriated. Like Milt, he didn't like his judgment questioned by a layman either. "I said I was sorry, Milt. May I see her?"

"In a few minutes. And I'm sorry too," Milt sighed. "I sometimes get frustrated when I can't do anything to save a baby a woman wants very badly." He sighed again. "At least there was no permanent damage."

"She can have more children?"

"Yes," Milt assured Jonas, then cautioned, "But not right away. Be careful for a while."

He turned to leave and Jonas said softly, "Thanks, Milt."

Turning back, Milt threw him a wide, crooked-toothed grin. "You'll get my bill."

Chapter Twelve

*V*alerie lay unmoving on the bed ignoring the tears
that rolled down her face. Her baby was gone, leaving
in its stead an emptiness; not only in her body, but in
her mind, as well. She didn't move an inch when the
door to her room opened, but a spark of recognition
entered her eyes when Jonas crossed her line of vision.

"Valerie, why are you crying? Are you in pain?"
Jonas asked sharply.

His tone was too sharp; the flow of tears doubled.

"Valerie, answer me!" he ordered. "If you're in pain
I'll get Milt."

"What's wrong with me, Jonas?" Valerie whispered
as he reached for the button to ring for the nurse.

"Wrong?" Jonas repeated confusedly; surely she
knew that the baby was gone? "Nothing's *wrong,* Val.
Milt assured me, not ten minutes ago, that you will be
fine. All you need is rest."

"No," her head moved restlessly on the pillow.
"What's wrong with *me?* Why do I lose everyone I
love?"

"Valerie, stop," Jonas said softly. Bending over he
clasped her upper arms gently. "You can have
ano. . . ."

"First my father," she cried over his quiet, unheard

voice. Then my mother. Then my grandparents. Then . . . then Etienne," she sobbed, unmindful of the tightening of his fingers. "And now my baby." Gazing up at his blurred features, she cried, "Why, Jonas, why? What have I done that I must be punished this way?"

"That's nonsense," he said in a crooning tone. "You aren't being punished."

"Then why do I lose everyone I love?" she choked. "Even y—" Valerie caught back the word "you" just in time; she was distraught, but not *that* distraught. *He* had never been hers *to* lose. "Even my b—baby," she wailed.

"It was an accident," he soothed. "A stupid accident." Sitting down on the side of the bed he gathered her into his arms and held her shaking body close to his chest.

"Jonas, I'm never going to hold my baby in my arms," Valerie sobbed.

"*Our* baby," he admonished softly. His meaning was lost on Valerie, who was now sobbing uncontrollably. For a fleeting moment Jonas hesitated, then, kicking off his handmade loafers, he slid onto the bed beside her and pulled her tightly against him. "Hush," he crooned. "I'm here. Rest, Val. I'll hold you while you rest."

Slowly, comforted by his crooning voice and his hand gently smoothing back her hair, Valerie stopped crying. Secure in his arms, lulled by his even breathing, she was beginning to drift into sleep when the door opened and she heard a nurse exclaim:

"What do you think you're doing?"

"Get out of here, nurse," Jonas growled softly.

The nurse gasped then sputtered, "But you . . .

you can't lie on the bed like that. If you don't get up—at once—I'll have to call security and have you removed."

Stirring fitfully, Valerie felt tears come to her eyes again. It was childish, she knew, but right now his arms were a haven she needed very badly, a haven she was not yet ready to leave.

"Don't go away." Valerie's plea sounded every bit as insecure as the need that prompted it.

"I'm not going anywhere," Jonas assured her softly. Then he said with hard authority, "Nurse, call Doctor Abramowitz and tell your tale of woe to him. You can also tell him that I said I'm not moving. Now get out of here."

"But . . ." the nurse got no further, for Jonas was not about to argue.

"Out."

His bark sent the nurse into retreat with a rustle of her starched skirt and a grumble about arrogant men. That she *would* call Milt, Valerie had very little doubt. That Milt would more than likely tell her to keep out of the room, *Jonas* had very little doubt.

Loosening his hold on her, he murmured, "Move over," and when she had done so he settled his long length more comfortably in the narrow bed. Then, drawing her close to him again, he ordered softly, "Now go to sleep, Val. I'll be here."

When she woke, some three hours later, she was alone in the bed. Jonas was gone, leaving her to wonder if, perhaps, in her sedated, befuddled state, she had imagined he'd been there in the first place. Her mind now clear and alert, she found it hard to believe he had chosen to defy convention to the point of crawling into a hospital bed with her. Still weary in body, if not in mind, she pushed the speculation aside and rang for a nurse. She felt grubby; she wanted a bath and a hairbrush.

Determined to get well, if only to get away from the antiseptic smell of the hospital, Valerie recovered swiftly. Surrounded by an entourage consisting of Jonas, Mary Beth, Marge, and Lyle, Valerie left the confines of the hospital on a bright, warm morning in late June, eagerly breathing in the scent of flowers in the fresh air.

Buoyant with renewed energy, she breezed into the house with a confidence that was immediately shattered by the drawling voice of Lynn Varga.

"Well, the little near-mother is back. How—ah—nice."

"That's enough, Lynn." Jonas's voice, sounding at once both tired and indifferent, slashed across the gasps from Mary Beth and Marge and the muttered curse from Lyle. Turning his back on the elegant form of his first wife, he bent and scooped the now stricken-faced Valerie effortlessly into his arms. As he started up the steps he shot over his shoulder, "If you haven't enough manners to be pleasant to your hostess, then you'd better leave. Go spend some more of my money on something you don't need." He came to a full stop on the landing at the top of the short flight of stairs and stared down into Valerie's hurt-filled eyes, whispering for her ears alone, "My—*wife*—has no use for my money."

With those words, all the hope Valerie had allowed herself to begin harboring rushed out of her, leaving her feeling defeated and tired. When she looked away from him without response, Jonas sighed and continued into their bedroom to place her gently on top of the bed. "You'd do well to stay there," he cautioned, "at least for a day or two." With that he turned and left.

They were back to square one, Valerie decided morosely as she listened to the fading sound of his car's engine. By the end of her first full week at home she was forced to face the fact that things between them were worse now than they had been before her stay in the hospital. At least then they had shared a bed. Now, with her health restored and all physical restrictions removed, Jonas treated her like a guest in the house that was supposedly her home. He was polite. He was considerate. He was a stranger.

For two weeks Valerie tormented herself with thoughts of what she had thrown away. Over and over she relived the events of that afternoon. Repeatedly she heard his cold voice demanding, "What are you carrying? A young Thorne or another DeBron?" Another DeBron. Valerie shivered. He actually believed that she would . . . she shivered again. And over and over, the thought growing stronger each time it occurred, Valerie came to the decision that she could not stay with a man who believed her capable of that kind of deceit.

As the days changed from pleasantly warm to uncomfortably hot Valerie withdrew to the air-conditioned comfort of what was now *her* bedroom. Jonas had moved into the guest room on the day he brought her home from the hospital, saying he didn't want to disturb her rest with his comings and goings.

By the middle of July, feeling rejected, useless, and defeated, Valerie seldom came out of her bedroom. And then Jonas announced that he was leaving for Houston the following Monday and had no idea how long he would be gone. Her nails digging into her palm, Valerie turned away from him with a shrug, missing the expression of hopelessness that washed over his face.

The next morning Janet breezed into Valerie's bedroom without bothering to knock.

"Janet!" Valerie exclaimed, "What are you . . ."

"Val, honey," Janet cut her off impatiently. "I know losing this baby was a shock for you, but you absolutely cannot do this to yourself again."

Again? Do what again? Valerie, not thinking too clearly, didn't have the vaguest idea what Janet was talking about. "What do you mean?" she frowned.

"You know perfectly well what I mean," Janet retorted. "It's Paris all over again, isn't it? I knew it when Mary Beth called me and said you weren't seeing anyone, not even her and Jean-Paul." She sighed with exasperation. "Honey, I know how you must feel, but it's not the same as losing Etienne. You *can* have another baby."

Not by sleeping alone! Valerie thought bitterly. So, they all believed her to be in mourning for her lost child! Did Jonas believe the same? Did it matter anymore?

"Valerie, talk to me," Janet demanded. "Don't close yourself away like this."

"It's not only my baby," Valerie murmured, groping for a plausible reason for her attitude. Then a germ of an idea stirred. "I . . . I'm concerned for my mother. She's due any time now, and, well, she's not a young woman."

"Well for heaven's sake!" Janet cried. "If that's what's bothering you, go see her. I'm sure Jonas would understand."

I'm sure Jonas couldn't care less, Valerie retorted

silently. But Janet's suggestion was a good one. She *would* go to Australia, and maybe she'd just forget to come back.

"If I go now," Valerie said slowly, "I could be with her when the baby comes."

"And it would be the perfect time to go." Janet smiled, satisfied with Valerie's show of animation. "I mean, since Jonas will be in Houston for at least a week."

When Janet left, obviously much easier in her mind about her friend, Valerie coolly picked up the phone and punched out the number to Jonas's private line.

"Are you all right?" he said urgently the minute she said hello.

"Yes, I'm fine," Valerie replied, wondering if his show of concern was genuine. "I . . . I was wondering if you would be home for dinner tonight?"

"Are you eating dinner tonight?" he asked quietly. The question was not as strange as it might have seemed. Valerie's eating habits lately had been erratic and she and Jonas had not shared a meal in nearly two weeks.

"Yes," she sighed. "And, if you have time, there's something I'd like to discuss with you."

"I'll make time," Jonas promised. "In fact, I'll come home early."

As she hung up the receiver, Valerie smiled sadly at the thought that she actually had to make an appointment to talk to her husband.

As she waited uneasily for dinnertime to arrive, Valerie was prey to all sorts of doubts and regrets: What if she had carried the child full term, would his cool manner toward her have warmed? What if she had told him, straight out, that she was in love with him, would he have treated her less like the secretary she had been, and more like the wife she supposedly was? If they had discussed the loss of the child and what had precipitated it, would the strain between them have been eased? It was all a pointless exercise in frustration, as there was no way Valerie could answer any of her own questions. Only Jonas himself could do that.

Thoroughly sick of her own thoughts, Valerie heaved a deep sigh of relief when she heard his car come to a stop in front of the garage. Her pulse beginning to flutter with apprehension, she listened as he took the outside stairs two at a time and strode along the deck to their private entrance. Through the glass his form was bathed in a golden glow from the afternoon sun and she caught her breath in appreciation of the tall, deceptively slim-looking magnificence of him.

Was she completely out of her mind? she asked herself in wonder. He was a part of her now; the largest part. How could she face a life that did not include the sight of him each day? Oh, wasn't there some way she could remain with him?

Jonas began speaking even as he closed the door behind him.

"If you've called me home to tell me that you are pregnant again, I swear I'll strangle you, Valerie."

"That I'm . . ." Valerie gasped, totally missing the underlying note of fear in his voice. "Jonas, you know that isn't possible, we haven't even . . ." She came to an abrupt halt, her eyes widening. He had done it again! Not as crudely this time, but every bit as hurtfully. What did he hope to gain with these groundless accusations? Good Lord, she had only left the hospital a little over a month ago! She had not even been out of the house except to have lunch with Mary

Beth and Jean-Paul at the end of her first week home. Jean-Paul! He still believed that she and Jean-Paul . . . Valerie shuddered, refusing even to finish the thought. Biting back the outraged protest she longed to fling at him, she forced her tone into cool unconcern.

"The reason I requested a moment of your precious time," she managed acidly, "was to inform you of my plans."

"Plans?" Jonas repeated warily. "What plans?"

"I—" Valerie hesitated, then plunged. "I'm going to Australia to be with my mother when she delivers."

"You're worried about her?"

Why, she wondered, did he have to voice even the most simple of questions in such an arrogant, demanding tone? "Of course I'm worried," she snapped, refusing to let him see how his tone had hurt her. "She's past the *safe* childbearing age. If," she swallowed against the sudden tightness in her throat, "there *is* a safe childbearing age. She put on a good act the last time I talked to her on the phone, but she's scared, I know it, and I want to be with her."

"All right, Val." Jonas surprised her by agreeing. "You may go. I'll give you one month longer."

I may? Valerie seethed. I may? Big deal! Would this man never stop treating her like one of the employees? "I didn't ask for your permission, Jonas," Valerie flared. "I have reservations to fly to San Francisco tomorrow afternoon whether you approve or. . . ." Valerie's voice faded as his last statement registered. "What do you mean, you'll give me one month longer?"

"Exactly what I say," Jonas retorted grimly. "One month to the day that you walk out of this house I will expect you to walk back in again."

"But—" Valerie paused, searching for words. What was he up to now? They had barely spoken to each other in weeks. Was he attempting to exercise his authority over her now? The very idea angered her. "Why do you persist in speaking to me as though I was still your secretary?" she demanded. "I am leaving this house tomorrow. I will come back when I'm ready . . . if at all." Head up, back straight, she started for the door.

Long, hard fingers curled around her upper arm to bring her to a stumbling halt. Pulling her to him he slid the fingers and palm of his other hand along her jaw, holding her head still. "If you know what's good for you, you will do as you're told," he murmured menacingly, his fingers spearing into the hair behind her ear. "I said you have one month and that is exactly what I meant." Using the heel of his hand, he jerked her head up so he could see her eyes. "Do you understand?"

"You don't frighten me," Valerie lied, trying to pull her head away from his hand.

"No?" Jonas smiled humorlessly. Slowly, deliberately, he dug his fingers into her scalp, pressing against the side of her face with his palm. "You'd be wise to be a little frightened, Val." His hand exerted more pressure.

Sucking in a quick gasp, Valerie stared at him mutely, disbelievingly. Never before had Jonas used his superior strength to deliberately hurt her. Angry, stubbornly refusing to cry out against the pain, Valerie glared at him rebelliously. Jonas was obviously unimpressed.

"One month, Valerie," Jonas growled as he lowered his head to hers. "And if you are not here at the end of that month, I will come after you."

His mouth came down onto hers, driving the breath

back into her throat. For a second, panicked, Valerie struggled to tear her lips from under his. Releasing her arm, he slid his freed hand around her waist as he turned his body to hers. Spreading his fingers, he moved his hand down to the base of her spine, then, drawing her body against his, he coiled his long fingers around her neck.

His hand was still hurtful, but in a new, strangely sensuous way. The deep core of passion that only this man could tap answered the demand his hardened, aroused body was making on hers. Moaning softly, deep in her throat, she encircled his waist with her arms and arched herself to him.

"You will come back in a month, won't you?" Jonas demanded, dropping biting kisses on her lips as he spoke.

"Jonas stop," Valerie moaned, not even believing the command herself. Wildfire raced through her veins. Her arms tightened convulsively when his tongue caressed the spots his teeth had so recently bitten.

"Wh—why are you doing this—now?" Valerie gasped, her breath coming unevenly.

"I have given you time repeatedly, and still you ask for more," Jonas muttered. "This additional month has a price tag, a high one. If you want to go badly enough you'll pay it."

Her mind cloudy with the devastation his mouth was inflicting, Valerie didn't understand a word he said, but, at the moment, she didn't care either. Greedily, she opened her mouth to his tongue as her hands slid down his back to grasp his buttocks and pull him tightly against her.

"You must want to go very badly," Jonas murmured

thickly, confusing her even more. But then all thought fled at the electrifying thrust he made with his hips.

She had to have him. Nothing else mattered, nothing else had any importance. Valerie's hands slipped between their fused bodies to fumble shakily with his belt buckle. He liked that. Keeping his mouth clamped onto hers, he took a half-step back to allow her hands freedom of motion. Loosening his grip on her neck, he moved his hand slowly down the front of her body, wringing soft moans from her as he did so.

"Can you wait to undress?" he growled into her mouth. Valerie answered him by outlining his lips with her tongue. "Neither can I," he groaned, drawing her with him onto the floor. Always before he had come to her with a slowness that drew out the moment to exquisite torture. Now, he took her with a voracious hunger born of his overwhelming need. Somewhere in the depths of her consciousness Valerie knew she should protest his violence; instead she met it with an answering violence of her own.

"Remember, Val," Jonas warned softly as he lay spent beside her. "You have one month."

Lying wakeful and restless in the spare room in her mother's house in Sydney, one day before that month was up, Valerie could hear again Jonas's whispered warning, could feel his lips brush her skin as he spoke. A shiver feathered her shoulders and she pulled the blankets closer around her. But it wasn't the air from the cold night that had caused the chill, and she knew it. The memory of the near savage way Jonas had made love to her, drawing her to him again and again long into the early hours of the morning, had caused repeated shivers during the last four weeks.

Edwin and her mother, looking radiant with happiness, had welcomed Valerie with open arms as she staggered from the plane after the seemingly endless flight. Three days after her daughter's arrival in Australia, Celia had given birth to a squalling, healthy son.

Even though Valerie had filled her days to the limit getting reacquainted with her mother, helping to care for her captivating new brother, and sightseeing, the hours and days and weeks seemed to drag by. She missed Jonas more than she would have believed possible.

He had sent flowers in response to Valerie's telegram about the arrival of the baby, but she had heard nothing more from him.

Unable to sleep, Valerie fought a silent battle with herself. When she had driven away from Jonas's house, it had been with the intention of never returning. Yet, as each day passed without a word from him, her resolve wavered. Impatiently, she told herself she was a fool to even consider going back. Jonas was arrogant, infuriating, domineering. He was also straightforward, honest, generous, and, at times, gentle. And, whether she wanted to or not, she loved him.

Suddenly Valerie could see herself, years from now, drifting from man to man in the hope of finding one who could blot Jonas out of her memory. Shuddering at the vivid images her restless mind projected, she scrambled out of bed to stare out the window.

By the time she slid tiredly back into bed over two hours later, Valerie's mind was made up. She was going home. Jonas had told her, months ago, to face reality. For Valerie, Jonas *was* reality, and she was going to face him, be honest with him, and find out, once and for all, if there was a marriage between them.

Chapter Thirteen

*S*he's not coming back.

The words rang inside Jonas's head like a death knell. As he had months previously, Jonas stood, taut and tense, staring out the window behind his desk. And, in just the same manner, his fingers dug into the tight muscles in his thighs.

She is not going to come back, and I don't know what to do about it. Should I go after her? He knew the answer to that. *No.* If she was coming back at all, she was coming back because she wanted to, not because he had forced her. But, sweet Lord, he ached to bring her home.

Valerie was already two days over the one-month time limit he had given her, and every nerve in his body felt drawn to the breaking point.

Absentmindedly he slid his right hand out of his pocket and lifted it to his midsection, where he unconsciously began to knead the area over his stomach. Jonas became aware of the action of his hand at the same moment he became aware of the burning sensation in his stomach.

"Damn."

Muttering the word aloud, he spun about and yanked open the top drawer of his desk. Taking out a small bottle, he unscrewed the cap, shook out two tablets, and popped them into his mouth.

All he needed at this point was an ulcer, he thought, chewing methodically. Grimacing, he turned back to his perusal of the parking lot. He really could not afford to waste time staring blankly out the window. He knew it, and yet he made no attempt to move.

As the tablets began to have an effect and the burning sensation eased, Jonas let his hand drop to his side. There was no ulcer yet, but the doctor had warned him he was on the right track. Jonas's lips twisted wryly as he remembered the doctor's exact words.

"Jonas, the nerves in your stomach are working overtime. If you don't slow down they are going to work a hole in the lining of your guts." Mike Slater, internist, had always thought he was something of a comedian. "The rest of your body's not faring a whole lot better, either. Lord, you high-powered types are going to make me a very rich man some day."

Jonas had agreed to watch his diet and take the medication Mike prescribed. He refused to cut down on his working hours. That had been two weeks ago. No one, not even Mary Beth or Marge, knew that Jonas had had cause to see a doctor, and, as far as Jonas was concerned, no one need ever know.

If Valerie had been home he might have told her. The thought stiffened his back. Never in all his thirty-nine years had he considered confiding in someone else that way.

The pain was completely gone now, and still he made no move. Good going, Thorne, he charged himself scathingly. Every move you made was wrong, starting with that blundering excuse of a proposal, and ending

222

with that stupid ultimatum. No, scratch that, ending with the hell you put her through the last night.

A shudder of sexual excitement rippled through the entire length of his body and Jonas cursed softly. Lord, just thinking about that night brought him to aching arousal. The mere *memory* of her had the power to affect him more than the actuality of any other woman; Jonas had proof of that.

Lips twisting in self-mockery, Jonas called forth the memory of Maria's last day as his secretary. In his mind's eye he could see the confident smile she'd displayed when she'd strolled into his office. Had he given her reason to think he was ready for some extramarital fun and games? Jonas shook his head sharply; he had not. What was it with women, he wondered, that they insisted in living in realms all of their own creation? Again his head moved sharply. Valerie's fantasy land was populated by only one man, Etienne DeBron, the faceless enemy Jonas did not know how to fight.

Feeling his fingers curling into tight fists, Jonas forced his thoughts back to that last encounter with Maria just three days earlier. He had dictated several letters, and when he was through, Maria had caught her heel in the carpet on the way out of the office. Jumping out of his chair, he'd hurried over to her. With his arm supporting her, he'd helped her to the long white couch.

"Let's get that shoe off and have a look," he'd said, dropping to one knee in front of her and reaching for her left foot.

"Jonas, darling."

His name had whispered from her lips while her hand stole caressingly into his hair. Caught completely off

guard, he'd glanced up in surprise as she bent to him.
Not even to himself would he deny the stirring of
response he'd felt at the touch of her hot, red mouth,
her probing tongue. Yet, even as his body moved
toward hers and his hands reached for her, an image of
Val flashed through his mind. When his hands grasped
her shoulders it was to push her away instead of pulling
her close. It had been more than a month since he'd
made love to Val and he had need of a woman, but,
strangely, any woman would not do. He wanted just
one woman, and that one was surely not Maria. He
wanted Val, and only Val. What he would do if she
never came back to him, he couldn't begin to imagine.
Maybe, in time . . . Jonas closed his eyes against the
jolt of fear his own thoughts caused.

Damnit, it was an impossible situation. Opening his
eyes to narrow slits, he stared in disbelief at his
trembling hands. Why, he berated himself, why hadn't
he taken Maria right then and there? You know why,
you fool. Because that couch is reserved for one woman
only. And you love that woman with every inch of your
body, and every cell of your mind. Forcing his thoughts
away from the vision of his black-haired, violet-eyed
tormenter, Jonas recreated the scene that had followed
his rejection of Maria.

"What's the matter with you?" Maria had demanded
in a stunned tone. "It was always good for us, wasn't
it?"

"The operative word is *was* Maria," he'd replied
quietly. "I'm a married man now."

"Really?" she'd sneered. "So where's your bride?
Down under playing footsie with some rugged Aus-
sie?"

Getting to his feet, Jonas had stepped back to run his

eyes over her in cold appraisal. What had he ever seen in her? The answer was obvious. Maria was a good-looking woman, intelligent, clever, sometimes witty, in a biting sort of way, and a regular wildwoman in bed—which Jonas admitted without shame, had been her biggest attraction. What the hell, he was a man.

He was also fully aware of the fact that she had destroyed what little they had had going for them when she'd walked out on him. She had wanted the position of secretary *and* lover. Her mistake had been in thinking she could call the tune simply because he danced with her. She had not been the first woman to make that mistake. Jonas had *never* needed her. He didn't need her now.

"Clean out your desk and get out of here," he'd ordered her with deadly quiet.

"But—I. . . ." Maria had sputtered in disbelief; then her red lips twisted nastily. "Oh, I get it. You don't need me *or* your little bride, do you? Not as long as you have Lynn living in your house. No wonder sweet Valerie ran for her life." Before she walked out the door, Maria paused to fire a parting shot. "You're a fool, Jonas. Don't you know that every one of your friends has slept with Lynn? She's not at all particular where she finds her loving." Then she added pityingly, "What was the problem, Jonas? Did little miss innocent Valerie object to your *ménage à trois?*"

"Out."

Jonas had not raised his voice, but the cold disgust he felt for her was evident in his tone. That had been three days ago, and yet the memory of the scene still rankled. Still more unpleasant was the scene that had happened that same night after he finally got home around ten-thirty. Mary Beth was out, again. Marge had already retired, and Lynn was waiting for him—like a spider waiting for a fly, Jonas had thought at the time.

"You look tired," she'd begun innocently enough. "Why don't you sit down while I get you a drink?" Rising with studied grace, she'd gone to the portable bar. "There is something we'd better discuss."

"Yeah?" Jonas had been tired, and certainly not in the mood for more problems. Dropping into a chair, he'd eyed the mother of his daughter disdainfully. Was she really sleeping with *every* one of his friends? he wondered disinterestedly. He hadn't realized they were all that hard up.

"It's about our daughter," Lynn said sharply, obviously aware that his thoughts had drifted.

At once alert, Jonas had straightened in his chair. "What about her?" he asked warily.

"You mean you really don't know?" She'd arched her brows. "She's sleeping with the hired-help." Lynn had smiled at the shock her statement caused. "Your *wife's* friend, to be exact."

"Jean-Paul?" he'd asked very, very softly.

"Of course, Jean-Paul," she'd purred. "While you've been sleeping all alone in your empty bed, your daughter has been sleeping with your wife's lover." Her voice had then dropped to a whispered taunt. "One wonders, who is Valerie sleeping with?"

Furious, fighting the desire to slap her smirking face, Jonas had not answered. After several breathless moments, Lynn had offered, "You don't *have* to sleep alone, Jonas."

"You?" he'd asked quietly.

"Yes, of course. There's no reason why we shouldn't enjoy one another."

Come into my parlor said the spider to the fly. "You're out of your twisted mind," he'd laughed aloud. "I wouldn't touch you if you begged me for it." Getting up lazily, he'd smiled mockingly at her outraged expression.

"Where are you going?" she'd demanded as he sauntered to the door.

"Back to my office," he'd tossed over his shoulder. "At least there I don't have to worry about being disturbed by your lies."

Jonas blinked, refocusing his gaze out the window where the dusk-to-dawn lights were just beginning to dim as the pink light of morning touched the parking lot, empty of cars save for the lone silver Cadillac. He'd been right here in the office ever since, except to take his daughter to dinner the evening before.

As usual, he had come directly to the point. "Your mother tells me you have—ah—become involved with Jean-Paul. Is it true?"

"If you mean by involved, am I going to bed with him, then the answer is yes," Mary Beth answered with refreshing honesty.

"I see," Jonas murmured, noncommittally.

"I don't think you do, Dad." Mary Beth shook her head. "I love him and I'm going to marry him."

"Does he know?" he'd asked roughly, shocked by the mixed emotions her statement had stirred in him.

"Oh, that's cute, Dad!" Mary Beth's voice revealed the hurt his tone had inflicted. "Jean-Paul asked me to marry him weeks ago." She drew a shaky breath, then went on accusingly, "He wanted to speak to you about it at once, but, knowing the trouble you're having with Trans Electric, I asked him to wait." She held up a silencing hand when he would have responded. "Besides, I wanted to wait until Val came home . . . if she ever does."

"What do you mean, *if* she comes home?" he demanded harshly. "Did she leave you with the impression she was not coming back?"

"No," she denied at once. "But, well, it was pretty obvious to everyone that you weren't getting along. You . . . you do have a way of making your displeasure with someone felt without opening your mouth."

"What is that supposed to mean?" Jonas snapped.

"Dad, I . . . I . . ."

"Tell me," Jonas ordered.

"Well, you *were* giving her the cold shoulder," she said hesitatingly. Then she rushed on. "Were you punishing her for losing the baby?"

Mary Beth's question had literally struck him speechless. Was that what Val had been thinking when she'd decided to go to her mother? Had she run from his condemnation? Jonas had not answered Mary Beth's query. Instead he'd told her to ask Jean-Paul to come to his office in the morning.

Now, at six o'clock on a deceptively cool-looking summer morning, Jonas shook his head at the blunder he'd made in his campaign to awaken Valerie to reality. Totally unaware that at that very minute Valerie was landing at Philadelphia International Airport, Jonas mentally reviewed the debacle he'd made of his marriage. What had Mary Beth said? "You were giving her the cold shoulder." *He'd* thought he was being tactful and sensitive.

Sighing deeply, Jonas turned from the glare of the red sun and sat down wearily at his desk. He'd had very little sleep during the preceding two nights. He hadn't been able to sleep.

You've got to put her out of your mind, Thorne, and get to work; that is if you can still find anything in the mess that last girl left. Loretta had not yet been able to find a replacement for Maria and a different girl had occupied the outer office every day, each more incompetent than the last.

Valerie had been very competent. Jonas groaned aloud. Always it came back to Valerie. God, he missed her. Would she ever come back? Sliding down in his chair, he rested his head against the leather back. What should he have done differently? Everything, the answer came at once. But worst of all had been his attitude toward Etienne. Why had he taunted her about him? Because he had been afraid. And he still was.

Yes, he finally admitted to himself, he was afraid of the hold Etienne's memory had on her emotions. He could still hear her asking him why she lost everyone she came to love, his own name conspicuously absent from her list. He had known from the beginning, of course, that she did not love him. But he had honestly thought that he could make her aware of him as a husband in every sense of the word, not just in bed.

And sexually, their relationship had been extremely satisfying. Again the memory of their last night together rose in his mind to torment him. God, he had used her without compunction, and he had loved every minute of it. A sudden thought sent a thrill of excitement through his mind. What if he had made her pregnant again? Would that bring her home? Hope burned fiercely for a few moments before he recalled the agony of waiting for word of her condition when she'd miscarried. Milt had warned him about not getting her pregnant too soon! A cold sweat sprang out on his upper lip. God! I hope she's all right! Moving uncomfortably, Jonas heard her voice crying to him, felt her body trembling in his arms as she sobbed out her grief.

There's a reason your plan didn't work, Thorne. You are by far too damned arrogant. While *you* thought you were giving her time to get over the miscarriage, everyone else, very likely Val included, thought you were punishing her. While *you* assumed that, given time, she would welcome you back into her bed, she probably thought you had washed your hands of the marriage. Would she even consent to speak to him if he called her? Jonas doubted it. And he really couldn't blame her. Should he go after her? Try to make some kind of a deal?

Jonas shook his head in wonder at himself. He was actually thinking as though she were a corporation instead of a woman. Well, an errant grin slashed his thin lips, he wanted to merge, didn't he?

You're walking pretty close to the edge, Thorne, he advised himself seriously. Think about something else. But what? Mary Beth. Jean-Paul.

What would he say to the Frenchman when he came to his office later this morning? What *could* he say? Mary Beth was an adult; she didn't need his approval if she chose to marry a man he did not like. But then, he didn't dislike Jean-Paul. That had been part of his problem. Even when he had thought there was a liaison between Val and Jean-Paul he could not dislike the man. Lord, but he had wanted to.

So, you caution the man about the care of your

daughter, and then you shake his hand and wish him well. Nothing hard about that. And if he presumes to ask questions about Val and your own marriage? Simple, you control the urge to rap him in the mouth, and tell him nothing.

Beginning to fear for his sanity, Jonas pulled a folder to the center of his desk and opened it. Within minutes, the technical jargon had caught his attention. When he closed the folder over an hour and a half later his eyes ached with fatigue. Still mulling over the information he'd read, he rested his head against the soft leather back of his chair. Less than five minutes later he was sound asleep.

Jonas had had the dream several times over the last month. Sweating, his head moving restlessly, he fought to free himself from the coils of unwanted sleep. The dream persisted, and once again he stood at the window in the hospital waiting room, sick with fear for Valerie. At his feet was a large pool of blood and at the door Milt stared at him accusingly, while behind him a nurse screamed, "She's dead, and it's your fault. You should have left her in Paris. Then she'd still be alive." His eyes wide with horror, Jonas watched, unable to move as a stretcher was wheeled down the hall, and although the form on it was shrouded, he knew it was Valerie.

A brisk tapping sound brought him awake with a jerk. His body was damp with a coating of cold sweat, and his hands had a death grip on the soft leather covering of the chair arms. Ignoring the renewed tapping at his office door, Jonas pushed himself out of the chair and went into the bathroom. Grabbing a small towel, he wiped his sweat-sheened face, tossed the towel in the sink, then walked back into his office with a growled, "Come."

At his command, Charlie's secretary opened the door a few inches and poked her small face around it.

"I'm sorry if I woke you, Jonas, but there's a call for you on line one. I wouldn't have disturbed you," she hurried on at his frown, "but it's Caradin in Washington."

"All right, Eileen." Jonas smiled an apology for his frown. As the door closed he picked up the receiver and punched the first button. "All right, George, let's have it," he said without preamble.

"You've won again, Jonas." George Caradin's usually calm voice held a note of exaltation. "They're backing off."

A long, soundless sigh escaped through Jonas's lips before he rasped, "It's permanent this time? I don't relish the idea of having to play these games every couple of months."

"No." George's tone was confident. "I'm sure they realize the game is definitely over."

"Okay, George, thanks for the hours you put into this. Now it's back to business as usual."

"I was only doing what I get paid for, but you're welcome, Jonas." George chuckled, "I know it held you up, but I rather enjoyed the fight." He paused, then said seriously, "I'm glad I'm on your team, Jonas. You really know how to fight dirty when it comes down to the clinch."

Jonas's tone was dry as dust when he replied. "They grow them tough in the coal regions. Talk to you later, George."

George's news had completely banished the nightmare and a smile of satisfaction curved his lips as he hung up the phone. Then he went still, his hand still on the receiver. For several seconds he fought a silent battle within himself. The temptation to lift the receiver and make flight arrangements to Australia fought with his need to get back to work. Australia won. He lifted the receiver, then replaced it, sighing softly. He couldn't force her to come back. He'd tried to force her into facing life again, and instead he'd driven her away from him. He'd give her a little more time, he decided, and then, if she still had not returned, he'd go after her.

But a moment later he was snatching up the receiver and calling the airport; when he hung up again some fifteen minutes later he was booked on the late-night flight to San Francisco. The hell with it, he thought grimly, I'm bringing her home.

Jonas was still staring pensively at the phone when Eileen tapped at the door again.

"Do you want to dictate now, Jonas, or can I go take Charlie's?" she asked brightly.

"Go back to Charlie and catch up on some of your work there." Jonas waved her away. "I'm sorry about running you back and forth like this, Eileen." He smiled ruefully. "I don't know why Loretta's having such a hard time replacing Maria but until she finds someone you're going to have to do double duty." Then he favored her with a rare grin. "I'll make it up to you in your paycheck."

"I don't mind, Jonas, really. I just hate to see everything get backed up like this." Eileen sighed over the mess the files were in. "I'll come back after lunch." With that she closed the door again.

Jonas picked up a sheaf of blue-line sheets and

was engrossed in checking over them when there was another tap on the door. Wondering how he was supposed to get any work done with all the interruptions, he called, "Come in."

This time it was Jean-Paul who poked his head around the door. "You wanted to see me, *monsieur?*"

"Yes, Jean-Paul, come in." Jonas waited until he was inside the room and seated before continuing bluntly, "Mary Beth tells me you have asked her to marry you."

"Yes, sir," Jean-Paul responded at once. "I wanted to speak to you at once, but she thought it best to wait until this business with Trans Electric was cleared up." Jean-Paul gave a very Gallic shrug of his shoulders. "I . . . I did not like seeing her without your knowledge but," again his shoulders lifted, "I also did not wish to lose her."

"Well, don't lose any sleep over it." Jonas smiled. "My daughter knows exactly what she wants, and apparently, that is you. Oh, by the way," he added, "that business with Trans *is* cleared up. We can get down to some serious work again."

"But that is wonderful news!" Jean-Paul exclaimed. "And I get your—ah—drift?" His eye brows inched up his forehead. "I will get out of here and get to work."

"DeBron," Jonas said softly as the younger man reached for the doorknob.

"Monsieur?"

Jonas walked to within a foot of him. "You *do* love her, don't you?" he asked in the same soft tone.

"Mary Beth has become my life," Jean-Paul answered quietly, his eyes steady on Jonas's watchful blue-gray ones.

"Good enough." Jonas extended his right hand. "You may tell her she can set the date." He liked

Jean-Paul's strong grip. "I hope you will be happy . . . Jean-Paul."

Jonas's concession was duly noted by Jean-Paul, who grinned and assured him, "As long as I have her, I will be . . . Jonas."

What is the news of their engagement going to do to Valerie? The thought jumped into his mind as the door closed behind the Frenchman. Valerie had seemed to cling to Etienne's brother. Would she, he wondered, resent Mary Beth now? Telling himself he'd find out soon enough, he headed for the bathroom.

Uncomfortable from the fine film of sweat his dream had drawn from his body, Jonas stripped down for a shower. Stark naked, he stood in front of the medicine cabinet mirror to shave off the overnight growth of beard and brush his teeth. The pre-shower ritual completed, he stepped into the shower stall.

After a quick scrub-down in hot water, Jonas slowly turned the hot water tap off. The tepid, then cool water cascaded over his body, bringing him to tingling life and sensuous awareness. Closing his eyes, Jonas had a wide-awake dream of Valerie, equally naked, stepping into the stall with him. With very little imagination, he could feel the silky touch of her skin against his own, could see her wet lips lifting to meet his hungry kiss. The low groan that was torn from his throat startled him and he turned the water off with a violent motion. Grabbing a large towel, he dried himself from head to toe as he walked into the adjoining dressing room.

Fifteen minutes later, dressed in a pristine white shirt, charcoal-gray suit, and a very conservative blue-and-silver-striped tie, Jonas took one step into his office and came to a dead stop.

At the doorway to the front office, looking crisp and bright, and incredibly beautiful, stood the black-haired, violet-eyed temptress who tormented his every thought. Jonas was barely aware of the raspy sound of his own voice.

"Valerie."

Chapter Fourteen

*W*hat would she say to him? Valerie had considered and discarded at least a dozen different opening lines. Now, with her hand raised to knock on his office door, she still had no idea what she *could* say. Somehow, a simple "Hello" wasn't enough. She had been away over a month, and they had barely spoken to each other for weeks before she left. No, "Hello" was not nearly enough. Hoping that something brilliant would pop into her mind at the sight of him, Valerie rapped her knuckles against the door. Nothing. No growled "Come," no softly muttered curse, nothing.

Janet had spent hours convincing her that coming to the office was the right thing to do and he wasn't even in! Her hand falling limply to her side, Valerie made a half-turn away, then stopped. Could there possibly be a clue to his whereabouts on his desk? Before she could change her mind, she turned the knob and pushed the door open. She took two hesitant steps inside the room and came to an abrupt halt. Either he had left the water running or he was in the shower—and Valerie knew he had not left the water running. Mortals did dumb things like that, not Jonas Thorne.

He was here. In that bathroom. And she still did not know what she would say to him. For a delirious instant

Valerie had the wild urge to rip off her clothes and join him under the spray. The urge died as quickly as it had sprung to life. Supposing he didn't want her, or worse yet, supposing he was not alone! Valerie did a quick inventory of the large room. The desk was in its usual state of disarray, cluttered with loose papers, folders, and blue-line drawings. Nothing significant there. Compared to the desk, the rest of the room looked stark in its neatness. Her sharp-eyed perusal found no sign of a woman, which still did not prove there was none.

Well, she thought, at least I'm prepared for a surprise, *he* isn't. Then, in self-disgust, she took herself to task; it is not yet nine o'clock in the morning—of course he's alone. The urge to retreat subsided, but she did not move out of the doorway. Glancing over her shoulder she gave the front office a quick survey. It looked neat enough, yet Janet had said it was in a mess. Had she lied to get her to come in?

Leaning back against the door frame, Valerie recalled the events of her morning from the time she'd left the airport around six.

Unsure of her welcome at home, she had decided while still on the plane that she would go to Janet's apartment first. After the long flight the cab ride to Janet's had seemed amazingly short. Janet welcomed her with a delighted smile and opened arms.

"Val, honey!" she'd exclaimed, after hugging the breath out of her. "Why didn't you let me know you were coming home? When did you get in?" But before Valerie could answer, Janet saw the suitcases in the hall. "Good grief! Haven't you been home?"

"No." Valerie shook her head. "I . . . I don't know yet if I'm going back h . . . to the house."

"Get in here at once," Janet ordered. When the door

was closed she said grimly, "What do you mean you aren't sure? You aren't thinking of leaving Jonas, are you?" But again she didn't give Valerie time to answer as she drew her into the kitchen with another question. "Would you like some breakfast?"

"Just coffee, please, I had breakfast on the plane. And, to answer your question, I don't know what to think about Jonas," Valerie said steadily.

Placing a cup of steaming coffee in front of Valerie, Janet frowned. "I don't understand, why don't you know what to think about Jonas?"

"Just that." Valerie shrugged. "I don't know if he *wants* me to come back to the house. I haven't heard a word from him since I left, Janet."

"Nothing?" Janet asked sharply.

"Oh, he sent flowers to my mother after I telegraphed the news of the baby's arrival, but he never wrote or called."

"You telegraphed!" Janet exclaimed. "Why in the world didn't you call?"

"Because I didn't know what to say," Valerie replied calmly.

Janet was far from calm. "Val, that doesn't make sense. Jonas is your husband. He . . ." Her voice faded, then came back in a whisper. "Had you left him? I mean, for good?"

"I . . ." Valerie hesitated before admitting, "Yes."

"Oh boy," Janet sighed. "Do you want to tell me why?"

"It just wasn't working," Valerie answered defeatedly. "We were barely speaking to each other when I left. I . . . I had to get away, Janet."

"And now?" she probed.

"Oh, I don't know." Valerie sipped at the hot drink.

"I had some wild idea about trying to talk things out but—"

"Go on," Janet insisted. "But . . . what?"

"But I guess I'm afraid of what he might say." Valerie shook her head.

"You won't know, though, unless you do talk to him," Janet urged. "Go see him, tell him how you feel." A crafty smile curved her lips. "And I have the perfect plan of action for you to follow."

"What plan?" Valerie asked warily.

"He needs a secretary." Janet grinned.

"Why do I get the feeling that this is where I came in?" Valerie groaned. "What do you mean he needs a secretary? What happened to Maria?"

"She's gone." Holding up a silencing hand, she added, "I don't know why or how but she is gone. She took off a couple of days ago." Her grin widened. "Jonas has scared away two or three stand-ins since then. The way I hear it, the front office is a shambles. Added to that, Trans Electric is pushing again."

"He's in the middle of another go-round with Trans and he hasn't got a secretary?" Valerie cried.

"No secretary," Janet murmured complacently, her eyes correctly reading Valerie's outrage.

"How is the fight with Trans going?" she demanded.

"Who knows?" Janet shrugged. "With no regular secretary in the office, the information from the high-rent district is pretty sketchy."

"Jonas must be unbearable by now," Valerie muttered. "Remember how awful he was the first time Maria left?"

"How could I forget?" Janet smiled, watching her closely. "And, as I said, he has already scared a couple of girls into running for cover, so I can imagine how unbearable he is by now." She paused to let her words sink in, before adding, "Valerie, he needs you."

"In the office." Valerie laughed bitterly.

Janet sighed in exasperation. "You don't know that, and anyway, that's as good a place to start as any other. Better, actually, because he spends more time there than anywhere else."

"Oh, Janet, I don't know." Valerie sighed. "Before I left Mother's I'd decided to have it out with him. Find out exactly what, if anything, I meant to him. Somehow that prospect seemed relatively easy from a distance of thousands of miles. But the closer I get to him, the more difficult facing him becomes."

"Do you love him, honey?" Janet eyed her consideringly.

"Do you think I'd be here if I didn't?"

"Well, then what are we doing sitting here?" Janet asked. "Let's go."

"Now?" Valerie asked nervously.

Janet smiled in understanding. "Putting it off won't make it any easier, Val."

"But . . . I feel grubby, I need a shower and clean clothes," Valerie hedged. "You go on, I'll come in after I've changed."

"I'll wait." Janet grinned.

"But you'll be late and. . . ."

"If I'm late, I'm late." Janet cut her off decisively. "I'm an executive, remember?" Lazily waving her hand in a shooing motion, she drawled, "Run along, I'll wait."

"Valerie."

The raspy sound of her name shattered her reverie. Glancing up, Valerie felt her breath catch in her throat and her legs go weak. He looked clean, and handsome, and sexy as the devil, and she had to bite her lip to keep from crying his name aloud.

Swallowing the lump in her throat, she managed a steady, if somewhat whispery tone. "I hear you have an opening for an experienced secretary."

"When did you get home?" Jonas asked in that same raspy voice.

"Early this morning."

"Why didn't you let me know you were coming?" Jonas demanded in sudden, relieved impatience. "I'd have been at the airport to pick you up."

"You mean you'd have sent Lyle," Valerie snapped, first hurt, then angered by his tone. What had I hoped for, she despaired, that he would welcome me with open arms? Yes, she knew that was exactly what she'd been hoping for. Disappointed, she added, "Exactly as you sent Lyle to take me to the airport."

"Val, you know—" Jonas began, feeling his elation deflate.

"Do you want my help or not?" she interrupted with a soft sigh.

"Yes." Jonas also sighed. You irascible idiot, he berated himself, are you trying to drive her away again? Moving slowly, he walked across the room to her. "I can't find a damned thing." He indicated the room behind her. "Those kids Loretta sent to me just messed everything up in there. And that phone never stops ringing."

Just then, as if to prove the truth of his complaint, the phone rang shrilly. Without a word Valerie walked to his desk and lifted the receiver.

"Jonas Thorne's office," she said briskly.

There was a pause, and then, "Valerie?" Charlie McAndrew exclaimed into her ear. "Is that you?"

"Yes, Charlie, it's me." Valerie smiled.

"Thank God," Charlie said fervently. "Maybe now the cracker will calm down and put the whip away."

She laughed wryly. "Don't hold your breath, Charles."

"I think I could," he returned seriously. "Does Janet know you're back?" he asked.

"Yes, as a matter of fact she drove me in this morning." Valerie could feel Jonas hovering behind her. "I'll see you later, Charlie, here's Jonas," she said, handing the receiver to him.

"What is it, Charlie?" Jonas asked, then paused to listen.

Valerie closed the door quietly and went to the desk that had once been hers. Everything was indeed a mess, and the files were in a positive shambles. With a sigh of acceptance, she got to work on the confusion of papers on top of the desk. Where, she asked herself two hours later, had Loretta found the girls she'd sent up—in a nursery?

Jonas had been on the phone for the majority of those two hours, with long distance as well as local calls. As yet he had not called her back into his office, either for dictation or anything else. Valerie couldn't decide if that was a good or bad sign.

She was working on the last of the file drawers when Janet sauntered into the office.

"Is Legree going to let you go for lunch, or should I bring you a sandwich?" she drawled.

The dry voice that answered came from the doorway to Jonas's office. "You can have someone in the cafeteria bring up two sandwiches, and a pot of coffee," Jonas ordered quietly. "And two pieces of apple pie, if there is any."

"What kind of sandwiches?" Janet glanced from Jonas to Valerie.

A wry smile curving her lips, Valerie attempted to let Janet know she had not yet found the courage to do any straight talking with Jonas. "Chicken salad," she murmured tonelessly. The matching smile she received from Janet told her her meaning was taken.

"I'll have the same," Jonas said in answer to Janet's questioningly raised brows. The slant of his own brows made Valerie uneasy. Could he possibly have read her meaning? Valerie glanced at him quickly, but his expression was unreadable. "Come in and take a break," he invited after Janet had sauntered out again. "We could both use one."

Valerie followed nervously at his heels, wondering if she had the courage to confront him. What was she going to say to him? Everything had seemed so clear-cut way down in Australia, but now that she was here, well, this was for real. Valerie suddenly felt actually sick. Positive she would not be able to handle it if he told her there was no hope for their marriage, Valerie went weak with relief when the phone rang again.

"Oh, hell," Jonas muttered, indicating that she should answer it on his phone. "I'm not in," he added tersely.

Valerie answered the phone, then, placing her hand over the mouthpiece, said softly, "It's Edouard Barres."

Jonas cursed again but took the receiver from her to say in a surprisingly pleasant tone, "Hello, Edouard, what can I do for you?"

Once again Valerie retreated to the front office. Jonas was still on the phone when the girl from the cafeteria brought a tray bearing their food. Relieving her of her burden, Valerie carried it to his desk just as he was saying, "Right, Edouard, within the week. Of course, hold on and I'll have the call switched to his office. You bet, good-bye." He punched out the numbers to transfer the call, then said, "I have your boss on the line, Jean-Paul. He wants to talk to you." He listened a moment, then hung up. Standing up, he took the tray out of her hands and strode to the white couch. "We may as well be comfortable while we eat." When she hadn't moved by the time he set the tray down he shot her a questioning glance. "Are you coming over?" he asked very softly.

"Y—yes, of course," Valerie answered nervously, running suddenly damp palms down over her hips.

"Relax, Val," Jonas advised softly. "I'm not going to jump on you." *You stupid fool*, he accused himself at the nervous flicker of her lashes, *now you've put her on guard. What would she do*, he wondered, *if I grabbed her and took her here and now?* Although he would have liked to do just that, Jonas cautioned himself to go slowly. *Don't spook her now, go easy*, he told himself. *She's showing signs of fright, and you don't want to put her on the run again.* With cool deliberation he dropped his voice to a soothing tone. "Come sit down, Val. I give you my word that I won't touch you."

Eyeing him warily, Valerie crossed the luxuriously thick carpet and seated herself on the opposite end of the couch. Even with five feet of couch between them she didn't feel any too safe. There was silence for several minutes, as both of them discovered exactly how hungry they were. Glancing up to feast her eyes on

245

him, her gaze collided with the sensually warm one he was casting at her, and Valerie felt every one of her senses go haywire. With sudden clarity she heard again Charlie's words of early that morning, "Maybe now the cracker will calm down and put away the whip." Could it be possible that Jonas cared for her? The thought was a heady one, and her mind whirled with visions of what life with him would be like if he did. The "if" in her thinking was the only thing that kept her from sliding down the length of the couch and into his arms. If, if, if. How do I go about finding out? I can't just look him in the eye and say bluntly: Do you love me?

Meanwhile, Jonas was having similar thoughts about her: Why this sudden shy attitude? Even at the very beginning of their relationship she had revealed no shyness. Anger, disapproval, yes. And on their honeymoon, she had shown real fear—but shyness? Is it possible she feels something for me? Is that why she came home?

During the long afternoon the air in the two offices was heavy with tension. As the day wore on Valerie became more and more edgy, certain that something was about to happen. And while she sat beside him taking dictation the atmosphere was so heavy she felt stifled and breathless.

What was going through his mind? That question plagued her all afternoon. His voice was cool, his manner quietly polite, and yet his eyes were telling her things she was afraid to believe. It was nerve wracking . . . but it was also exciting.

Late in the afternoon Janet called her and asked with absolutely no tact at all: "Has he cornered you yet?"

"Of course not!" Valerie exclaimed indignantly. "This is a business office!" Her indignation was completely false. Actually, the idea of him seducing her held an inordinate appeal. "Jonas wouldn't dream of doing that." Darn it.

"Oh no?" Janet laughed. "If Thorne decided he wanted to badly enough, he'd take you anywhere he pleased."

Sounds interesting. Valerie shocked herself with her own suddenly erotic thoughts. Reminding herself that this was indeed a business office, she said, coolly, "Look, Janet, I'm very busy, why did you call?"

"I already told you," Janet teased. "I was curious as to whether you were still dancing around each other, or if you had decided to waltz together."

"Good-bye, Janet," Valerie said repressively. As she hung up the receiver she heard Janet chuckle.

Unknown to Janet, her call had achieved her intended purpose—it made Valerie wonder if both she and Jonas weren't behaving a little childishly. Why couldn't they discuss their relationship, past and present, rationally? Why couldn't *she* make the first move? What did she have to lose? Pride? What good was salvaging her pride, if she lost him?

Quitting time came, and went, and Jonas kept working. By seven o'clock Valerie decided enough was enough, and gathering all the courage she possessed, she covered her typewriter, straightened her desk, and strolled into his office.

"Are you going to buy me dinner or not?" she asked, dropping into one of the chairs in front of his desk.

Jonas glanced up sharply at her aggressive tone, his eyes narrowing on her tiredly slouched body. "Of course I'll buy you dinner . . . if that's what you want."

"Am I to infer from that that you are willing to buy me *anything* I want?" Valerie asked softly.

"Yes." Jonas's tone was equally soft. "If you're willing to provide me with what I want."

"A . . . and that is?"

"You know damned well what *that* is." His eyes raked the length of her body. "I want you, now, on that couch."

Straightening her shoulders Valerie stood up slowly. "It'll cost you," she murmured, starting to unbutton her blouse.

"You're serious!" A small smile tugged the corners of his mouth, changing his rather harsh expression to one of devilment. "You're willing to take all your clothes off here—and now?"

"It'll cost you more," Valerie warned, an answering smile pulling at her own lips. She had never indulged in this kind of sexual teasing, and excitement made her feel a little light-headed.

"I can afford it," he assured her, beginning to loosen his tie. "Name your price." The tie dropped onto his desk and his fingers went to work on his shirt buttons.

Valerie went cold. Name your price! What was she doing? This wouldn't solve anything! Would it?

"Val?" Jonas's voice, sounding strangely strained, drew her startled eyes to his equally strained face.

"Jonas . . . I . . ."

"Name it," he ordered tersely.

"Lynn has got to go," Valerie blurted out, her eyes pleading with him to stop this farce.

"You've got it," he promised. Swinging away, he strode to the desk. "She'll be gone by tomorrow morning." Snatching up the phone, he began punching out a number.

"Jonas! Darling, stop!" Valerie ordered frantically.

She couldn't go on with this game! She just couldn't. To her surprise, Jonas froze in place. Then, very slowly, he turned to her.

"What did you say?" he whispered.

"I . . . I said . . ." Valerie faltered at the expectant look on his face. What had she said? "You don't have to call her now, I mean . . ."

"Not *that*," Jonas's hand sliced the air, silencing her as he walked to stand mere inches from her. "What did you *call* me?"

"Dar . . . darling?" Valerie murmured, wetting her lips.

"Yes, darling." Lifting his hands, he grasped her waist. "You called me that once before, at my command. I decided then that I didn't want to hear it again unless you meant it." Valerie bit back a gasp as his fingers dug into her flesh. "Do you mean it?" Jonas demanded harshly.

"Yes!" Valerie released that gasp on a strangled note. "I meant it then, Jonas!"

"Oh, God, Val." Burying his face in the side of her neck, he slid his arms around her to enclose her in a rib-jarring embrace. "If you knew . . ." His groaning words were lost as his mouth came down on hers.

Which one of them made the first move? Valerie didn't know, nor did she care. Within minutes, divested of her clothes, she found herself beneath him on the couch, wildly responding to his driving urgency.

"Darling . . . darling . . . darling!"

Later, when they lay entwined in one another's arms, Jonas whispered, "Lord, that was good. It was never that good with any other woman." She stiffened and his lips brushed her shoulder. "Easy, my love," he murmured. Lifting his head, he smiled down at her. "And that's the reason it was never as good. I didn't love any one of them."

"Oh, Jonas," Valerie choked, clasping his face in her hands. "Do you love me, really? Because, if you don't then don't say you do. I couldn't bear it if . . ."

"Will you shut up?" He grinned. Jonas could no more stop grinning than he could stop breathing. It was either grin, he thought wryly, or laugh like an idiot. With her big violet eyes staring up at me all misty with tears, I could easily whoop like a demented wildman.

"Yes, I love you." The grin was gone, replaced by a look so intent Valerie shivered. "God, how I love you."

As he lowered his mouth to hers, Valerie slipped her arms around his neck. His kiss was so gentle, so tender, that the hovering tears spilled over her lids and trickled down her cheeks.

"Now it's your turn," Jonas prompted as his mouth reluctantly released hers.

"I love you, Jonas Thorne. I didn't want to, but I do."

"You're not sorry are you, Val?" Jonas frowned. "I mean that I forced you to leave the dead alone and join me in living?"

"No." She smiled, then gasped. "Are you telling me every move you made was planned?"

"Most of them," he admitted, shifting his weight so that he lay beside her. He drew her into his arms. "Of course, I hadn't planned on your leaving me to go to Australia, or . . ." He became quiet.

"Or what?"

"Of for you to lose our child."

"Jonas, I'm so sorry about . . ."

"Stop!" he ordered roughly. "It wasn't your fault."

His arms tightened protectively. "Dear, God, you had me worried there, love. I was scared to death I was going to lose you."

"But you didn't, and you won't." Valerie drew a quick breath, then rushed on. "When can we start another baby? Did you have that planned?"

"How about in the next couple of minutes?" he teased.

"What's wrong with right now?" she challenged.

"Right now, my love—" Jonas heaved his long frame off the couch—"I'm going to call and cancel my plane reservations to Australia."

"Australia!" Valerie exclaimed, wide-eyed. "Jonas, you were coming after me?" A sensation of pure delight shot through her at his disclosure.

"You're damned right I was coming after you," Jonas growled softly, bending over to take a nip at her lower lip. "And if you ever take off to visit anyone again you'd better keep a sharp lookout over your shoulder, because I'll be right behind you."

The playful nip turned into a lingering kiss. Straightening slowly, he drew Valerie up with him.

"Why don't you get dressed while I make my phone call?" The smile Jonas gave her set her pulses pounding. "Then we'll go home to bed."

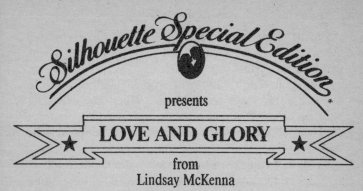

Silhouette Special Edition

presents

★ LOVE AND GLORY ★

from
Lindsay McKenna

Introducing a gripping new series celebrating our men—and
women—in uniform. Meet the Trayherns, a military family as proud
and colorful as the American flag, a family fighting the shadow of
dishonor, a family determined to triumph—with
LOVE AND GLORY!

June: **A QUESTION OF HONOR** (SE #529) leads the fast-paced
excitement. When Coast Guard officer Noah Trayhern offers
Kit Anderson a safe house, he unwittingly endangers his own
guarded emotions.

July: **NO SURRENDER** (SE #535) Navy pilot Alyssa Trayhern's
assignment with arrogant jet jockey Clay Cantrell threatens her
career—and her heart—with a crash landing!

August: **RETURN OF A HERO** (SE #541) Strike up the band to
welcome home a man whose top-secret reappearance will make
headline news . . . with a delicate, daring woman by his side.

Three courageous siblings—
three consecutive months of

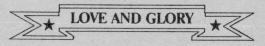

★ LOVE AND GLORY ★

Premiering in **June**, only in
Silhouette Special Edition.

Silhouette Desire®

1989
IS THE YEAR
OF THE MAN!

What makes a romance? A special man, of course, and Silhouette Desire celebrates that fact with *twelve* of them! From Mr. January to Mr. December, every month has a tribute to the Silhouette Desire hero—our **MAN OF THE MONTH!**

Sexy, macho, charming, irritating...irresistible! Nothing can stop these men from sweeping you away. Created by some of your favorite authors, each man is custom-made for pleasure—*reading* pleasure—so don't miss a single one.

Mr. January is Blake Donavan in RELUCTANT FATHER by Diana Palmer
Mr. February is Hank Branson in THE GENTLEMAN INSISTS by Joan Hohl
Mr. March is Carson Tanner in NIGHT OF THE HUNTER by Jennifer Greene
Mr. April is Slater McCall in A DANGEROUS KIND OF MAN by Naomi Horton
Mr. May is Luke Harmon in VENGEANCE IS MINE by Lucy Gordon
Mr. June is Quinn McNamara in IRRESISTIBLE by Annette Broadrick

And that's only the half of it—
so get out there and find your man!

Silhouette Desire's

MAN OF THE MONTH...

MOM-1

Silhouette Intimate Moments®

Let Bestselling Author KATHLEEN EAGLE Sweep You Away to De Colores Once Again

For the third time, Kathleen Eagle has written a book set on the spellbinding isle of De Colores. In PAINTBOX MORNING (Intimate Moments #284), Miguel Hidalgo is all that stands between his island home and destruction—and Ronnie Harper is the only woman who can help Miguel fulfill his destiny and lead his people into a bright tomorrow. But Ronnie has a woman's heart, a woman's needs. In helping Ronnie to live out his dreams, is she destined to see her own dreams of love with this very special man go forever unfulfilled? Read PAINTBOX MORNING, coming this month from Silhouette Intimate Moments, and follow the path of these star-crossed lovers as they build a future filled with hope and a love to last all time.

If you like PAINTBOX MORNING, you might also like Kathleen Eagle's two previous tales of De Colores: CANDLES IN THE NIGHT (Special Edition #437) and MORE THAN A MIRACLE (Intimate Moments #242).

Silhouette Special Edition®

NAVY BLUES
Debbie Macomber

Between the devil and the deep blue sea . . .

At Christmastime, Lieutenant Commander Steve Kyle finds his heart anchored by the past, so he vows to give his ex-wife wide berth. But Carol Kyle is quaffing milk and knitting tiny pastel blankets with a vengeance. She's determined to have a baby, and only one man will do as father-to-be—the only man she's ever loved . . . her own bullheaded ex-husband!

You met Steve and Carol in NAVY WIFE (Special Edition #494)—you'll cheer for them in NAVY BLUES (Special Edition #518). (And as a bonus for NAVY WIFE fans, newlyweds Rush and Lindy Callaghan reveal a surprise of their own. . . .)

Each book stands alone—together they're Debbie Macomber's most delightful duo to date! Don't miss

NAVY BLUES
Available in April,
only in *Silhouette Special Edition*.
Having the "blues" was never
so much fun!